A KISS FOR HER RIVAL RANCHER

ANNA GRACE

ISBN-13: 978-1-335-46046-2

A Kiss for Her Rival Rancher

Harlequin Enterprises ULC
22 Adelaide St. West, 41st Floor
Toronto, Ontario M5H 4E3, Canada
www.Harlequin.com

HarperCollins Publishers
Macken House, 39/40 Mayor Street Upper,
Dublin 1, D01 C9W8, Ireland
www.HarperCollins.com

Printed in U.S.A.

"Mylie, you have a gorgeous—" Cash fished for words as a judge walked by "—trifold display board."

Mylie stifled a laugh, whispering, "How bad are you at this?"

"Flirting?" His deep voice seemed to reverberate inside her. "Very bad. Lower twentieth percentile. Let's see you try."

Mylie waited until Clara neared, then let out a peal of fake laughter. "What an amusing anecdote about Team Oregon Build! You're so funny." Cash closed his eyes, shaking his head.

Clara didn't even deign to look at her clipboard, let alone move a sticky note.

"We're terrible at flirting," Mylie admitted.

"The worst. Guess we'd better stick to arguing." Something about his smile made the proposition sound way more fun. "But seriously, this poster is impressive." Without a single judge nearby, he said, "You do so much for the community. I respect that."

"Thank you." Mylie felt her face heat up. She managed not to point out that this was less than half of the community service projects she was involved in.

Dear Reader,

Welcome back to Holiday Ranch! I'm thrilled to share *A Kiss for Her Rival Rancher* with you.

Cash Holiday and Mylie Saunders never met a topic they couldn't disagree on. But when they're paired up to compete in the Mountain Country Most Eligible Pageant, they find it's a lot more fun to work together. Will sparks take the place of sparring this Fourth of July?

Growing up, I loved spending the Fourth of July on our family's farm. Warm summer nights, playing in the creek and watching fireflies are some of my favorite childhood memories. I particularly loved the Independence Day parade in nearby Pleasant Hill. I've always wanted to re-create that parade in a book, and I finally got my chance with *A Kiss for Her Rival Rancher*!

I'd love to hear what you think of Cash and Mylie's story. Would you dress up alpacas and walk with them in a parade? You can message me on social media (@annagraceauthor) and at my website, anna-grace-author.com.

Happy reading!

Anna

Award-winning author **Anna Grace** writes fun, heartfelt romance novels about complex characters finding their way with humor and heart. Anna's Oregon roots and love of family and community shine through in her Harlequin Heartwarming series.

Whether exploring the West in a remodeled Sprinter van or wandering new city streets in search of an art museum, Anna loves to travel and spend time with friends and family. You can find her on social media, where she's busy stamping likes on images of cappuccinos, books and other people's dogs.

Social Media: @AnnaGraceAuthor
Website: Anna-Grace-Author.com

Books by Anna Grace

Harlequin Heartwarming

A Holiday Ranch Romance

A Firefighter's Ranch Homecoming

The Teacher Project

Lessons from the Rancher
Winning the Sheriff's Heart
Mistletoe at Jameson Ranch
Her Secret Homecoming

Love, Oregon

A Rancher Worth Remembering
The Firefighter's Rescue
The Cowboy and the Coach
Her Hometown Christmas
Reunited with the Rancher

Visit the Author Profile page
at Harlequin.com for more titles.

This one is for my cousins

CHAPTER ONE

TUESDAY AFTERNOON WAS SUBLIME. All Mylie Saunders wanted was to be still and absorb the splendor of a perfect June day. To breathe in the fragrance of creek water splashing over sun-warmed stones, and the particular scent of an oak grove in summer. She wanted to close her eyes as the soft breeze swirled past, a butterfly kiss on her cheek.

But that's not what happened.

Eyes wide open, she doubled down on an argument with the best man minutes before the wedding was about to start. Because, apparently, that was the type of person she'd become?

"I don't want to hear one more word about homegrown arugula," Mylie whispered.

"Then maybe you shouldn't have shown up, Mayor." Cash Holiday was clearly trying to keep his voice down, but the deep rumble had several guests looking their way. "This is my property, my brother's wedding—"

"Which I'm here to celebrate. You started this—"

She was not about to call it a fight. Mylie was *not* a walk-into-a-delightful-outdoor-wedding-venue-

and-start-arguing-about-zoning-laws-and-egress-violations type of person.

"—animated difference of opinion. This is a *you* problem." Mylie splayed her fingers, indicating all six feet, two inches of her irritated-cowboy nemesis.

"Umm?" Cash tilted his head, powering the *umm* with sarcasm. "I'm not the one who's packing a copy of the Deschutes County Health Code."

"But you are the person bragging about violating it with a salad."

"You asked about the menu."

"Because you brought up farm-to-table. Can you even hear yourself?"

"Mylie— You—" Cash couldn't quite get his sentence started until he turned to face her, jacket flaring as he put his hands on his hips. "You just can't stand to see the Holiday family bounce back."

"That is patently untrue."

It was a tiny bit true. Like every thinking person in Ripple Creek, she'd been wary of all things connected to Cash's father, the late Bruce Holiday. But like any thinking person anywhere, she'd allowed herself to be proven wrong. Cash had not returned the courtesy.

He continued grumbling. "And since you seem to have a problem with anyone enjoying a party, or having fun within a thirty-mile radius of Ripple Creek—"

"Pshaw."

Cash's lips twitched in derision at her use of the

old-fashioned expression. Mylie didn't have one iota of self-reproach. Was she the only thirty-two-year-old to ever use the word *pshaw*? Maybe. But *tarnation*, *whoopsies*, all those grandma words were still on the table as far as she was concerned. Mid-century modern wasn't just for furniture.

"I'm not antiparty, or antiwedding."

"Good thing, since one's about to break out here any minute." Cash glanced over his shoulder at the creek, then refocused on the guests rapidly filling up the clearing.

Mylie pulled in a long breath as she attempted to see the situation from his perspective, to step into his cleaned-up cowboy boots for a moment.

This was an important day for the Holiday family. Obviously.

Cash was protective of his siblings, and wanted his brother's wedding to go well. As he should.

A lot of time and love had been poured into the event. The setting for this woodland wedding was stunning. No one could contain their delight as they emerged from the path through an old oak grove and into the magical space. Sparkle lights wound up tree trunks and were woven into branches. Persian rugs were spread out across the clearing, and music from a string quartet blended with birdsong and the rushing creek. Behind Cash stood an arch decorated with June wildflowers and young fern fronds. Everything was gorgeous, including the best man. He wore a dark suit with Western detailing. The Stetson covering his auburn hair made his deep hazel eyes appear even more intelligent. Not that looking good had ever been much trouble for Cash. It was *being* good that had him stumped.

"It's not your new business venture, but your approach to working with the city I take issue with," Mylie said quietly, a smile plastered on her face as she nodded at the fire chief and his family.

"Seems like the city could make itself a little easier to work with."

"Respectfully, that's not my job."

"If it's not the mayor's job, then whose is it?"

"Whilst your question—"

"Whilst?" Cash interrupted her, abandoning any pretense of not arguing as guests gathered for his brother's wedding. "Did you just say *whilst*?"

Mylie narrowed her eyes, the Cheshire cat grin emanating from the center of her heart. When Cash Holiday attacked her word choice, it meant he was running out of logical arguments. She had him on the defensive and he knew it. Which was great, because the wedding really was about to start and she needed to win before the bride came floating down the aisle.

"Cash, I'm here to celebrate your brother's wedding. Beau and Elliana invited me, and I wouldn't miss it for the world."

"You sure you're not just here hoping for a noise violation?"

"Shh!" Mylie admonished him.

"What? I'm whispering."

Why did Cash's voice carry so well? It was like

he'd been gifted with some special, extra-audible frequency. An event could be packed with people and she could still make out his words on the other side of the room.

Or woodland clearing, as the current setting was. Guests continued to filter into the space. A warm breeze tugged at her hair, pulling strands loose from the French knot she'd wrangled it into. Birds twittered over the creek, as excited as everyone else about the wedding of Beau Holiday to Elliana Wright.

The occasion was too joyful to waste locking horns with a cowboy.

She'd just get in one last word.

"What you serve at a family wedding is your business. But you'll be hosting the Mountain Country Most Eligible Pageant. It's a huge event—"

"I know how big it is." A flicker of concern in Cash's expression suggested the family had a lot riding on the pageant. Mylie had a lot riding on the pageant, too, but that was a different story.

"You're going to have some big crowds, and I won't be the only person with an eye out for mistakes," Mylie continued. "My job is to look after the interests of Ripple Creek. If you get in my way, that's gonna be an issue."

Cash turned to face her fully. "My job is to look out for the best interests of my family."

Mylie crossed her arms. Cash widened his stance.

Then he blinked, the flash of a camera startling

them both. They turned toward the seating to see an older woman in the front row holding out her phone as she examined the screen.

"Aren't you two just as cute as pie," she said, then gleefully set about pressing buttons.

"Gramma Birdie." Cash's voice had a note of concern in it. "Whatcha got there?"

"I have the most handsome grandsons."

"Umm? Gramma—"

"And I have to say, you boys have good taste in women."

Cash groaned, and Mylie got the sense this wasn't the first time he'd been through something like this. "Gramma, please put your phone away."

Gramma Birdie gave him a look over her reading classes, then refocused on her device. "Just a minute."

"Excuse me," Cash said, placing a hand on Mylie's arm. "I need to check in with my grandma. She's a little reckless when it comes to social media."

He started to step past her as Mylie began to say *no problem.* Then the reality of the situation hit her.

"Wait. Are you apologizing for stepping away from an argument *you* initiated?" Mylie asked.

Cash's gaze jumped to hers. He seemed to be as surprised by his action as she was. His hand was still on her arm. Honestly, it felt kind of nice there.

Then he scoffed and dropped his hand.

Mylie couldn't keep herself from saying, "You know that's a forfeit."

"Saunders, you are something else."

"You're incorrigible."

He shook his head. "I don't even know what that word means."

"It means someone who can't be corrected," Gramma Birdie said, not looking up from her phone.

Cash gazed at Mylie, a wicked grin spreading across his face. "Good thing I'm always right, then."

She glowered in response. Unfazed, he winked and stepped past her to confiscate his grandmother's phone.

Mylie let out a quick breath.

Okay. Time to grab a seat.

Preferably a seat way in the back, as far from Cash as possible. She might be at a wedding, but that didn't mean she was off duty. As mayor, any public outing was a chance to connect with the citizens of Ripple Creek. Mylie made her way through the crowd, shaking hands, literally kissing a baby. It seemed as if all of Ripple Creek had turned out for Elliana and Beau's wedding. As she made her way through the cheerful hubbub, Mylie relaxed. She loved the citizens of her little town. Some were a little eccentric, others could be cantankerous, but they were all lovable in their own way.

"Mayor Saunders!" A woman in an off-the-shoulder jumpsuit and an oversize collier necklace unfolded herself from a seat and stood, just barely blocking Mylie's way.

Okay, sure, some of the citizens of her town were more difficult to love than others.

"Alice. Hi." Mylie offered a smile and a handshake, as she would to anyone.

"Beautiful day, isn't it?" Alice scanned past Mylie, not giving her a chance to answer the first question before throwing out a second. "You here with anyone?"

Because a date was a necessary prerequisite for a wedding? It wasn't like Mylie had shown up without an invitation, or shoes.

"I'm here with friends."

"That's nice for you." Alice leaned in and nudged her with an elbow. "Never thought I'd be celebrating a wedding on Bruce Holiday's property, am I right?"

Mylie took a step back, her eyes inadvertently running to Cash. He was a pain, but he wasn't his father.

"They've really transformed this place," she said diplomatically, omitting the fact that Cash couldn't file a zoning permit to save his life. "Hard to remember how we got along without an event center so close to town."

"Oh, one-hundred-percent," Alice said. "Elliana's events are tip-top. Great excuse to do a little shopping. Hubs never needs to know."

Alice slipped her hands in her pockets and leaned back, giving Mylie a once-over, as though scanning for fault in her outfit. She wasn't going to find it. Mylie had mayor-appropriate down to a science.

The cyan blue sheath was festive, while still appropriate to her position. Could it double as an outfit for serving on a panel at the Municipal Leadership Conference? Technically. If her ensemble didn't quite match the whimsical vibe of this woodland wedding, it wasn't a crisis. No one was looking at her today.

Except for Cash, and he'd be scowling no matter what she wore.

"Well, it's been nice talking—"

"Hey." Alice bobbled her head, the necklace shifting along her collarbone. "I know this isn't the most opportune time to discuss policy—"

"Oh, I know." Mylie raised her hands, as though she'd love nothing better than to get deep in the weeds about program funding, but what could you do? A string quartet was playing. No one could possibly discuss city policy with a cello nearby.

But Alice wasn't easily deterred, and certainly not by stringed instruments.

"You should know, there are some *real* concerns about this Club 75 idea of yours. We don't want to rush into anything. Let's schedule a work session to discuss it."

Oh, God.

Who did Alice think she was, calling yet another meeting to debate reasonable funding for a program to engage senior citizens? Aside from a city council member and the director of the special committee on community engagement, that is.

"Um. Mm-hm." Mylie moved her head in various directions, not quite able to nod in agreement. "I'd love to meet with folks to hear and alleviate all concerns. Let's enjoy the wedding for now, and we can pick up the conversation later this week. Sound good?"

Alice gave Mylie her biggest fake smile. "Perfect. I'll catch you after the ceremony."

Not perfect, and not what I suggested.

But Alice was already on to the next conversation. Mylie walked away, her vision blurring in frustration. There was more than enough money in the city coffers to fund Club 75, and it would have a huge impact on their often-overlooked population of seniors. Alice was dead-set on blocking it, and wasting Mylie's time in the process.

Mylie found a seat with some of the regulars at the pickleball court. Her equilibrium had nearly returned when she made the mistake of glancing back at Alice, who was now whispering with her husband. Her eyes were still on Mylie, but she'd dropped the smile. It wasn't just Club 75 that Alice and Brick Henderson were trying to block.

Mylie shook off the thought. It was fine. The whispers of a recall were just that, whispers. So she'd stepped on a few toes during her first year as mayor. That had to be pretty normal. And since ten of those toes belonged to Cash Holiday, the Hendersons really shouldn't be complaining.

She glanced toward the arbor. Cash settled his eyes on Mylie. A note of sympathy flickered in his gaze.

Then, he *smirked.*

There was literally nothing worse than a smirker. Mylie had no tolerance. Even in books with swoony heroes she couldn't abide a smirk. Single rudest facial expression, hands down.

Could this day get any worse?

As though in response, a violin player drew her bow across the strings in a long, sweet note. The rest of the quartet joined, the soft strands of music settling in Mylie's heart. It took her a moment to recognize the tune as "Halo," by Beyoncé.

No, the day was not going to get worse. It was getting better. The world was getting better as two wonderful people were about to join their lives here in this special place.

A collective "awww!" rose through the crowd, peppered with joyful laughter. Beau made his entrance floating down Ripple Creek on a raft, a big grin on his face and not a single crease in his sharp black suit. Beau was lankier than his brother, his auburn hair a little longer than Cash's, but the errant smile and brown-green eyes were from one mold. Beau leaped off the raft onto the banks of the creek, where he was met with a big hug from his brother. Mylie could hear the rumble of Cash's voice as he said, "I love you, man."

Well...okay. That was one endearing thing about Cash. The guy loved his siblings. He was constantly talking them up, defending their choices, and outright telling them he cared. It was a far cry from the competitive nest Mylie had flown at seventeen, where trophies were currency, report cards the measure of a life well-lived.

Beau's response to Cash was lost on the breeze, but it sounded reciprocal. Everyone caught the spring in his step as he jogged to the arch and stood next to the officiant.

Guests swiveled toward the path weaving through the woods. Tia Holiday, wearing a tiered floral dress, her wavy auburn hair spilling over her shoulders, came first, leading one of the rescue alpacas. Guests couldn't help but reach out and pet the lovable animal as they passed. Mylie rose as the music shifted to an old Willie Nelson tune. Elliana emerged from the oak grove into the clearing. All shimmering silk organza and wildflowers, she looked like a woodland fairy, radiant on her wedding day.

Elliana was ethereal; Beau was somehow earthy. The look they gave each other was filled with gratitude. What must it feel like, to love like that? To let yourself be loved so completely? It had to be some crossroad of beautiful and terrifying.

Mylie's eyes flittered to Cash as he pressed a thumb and forefinger against his tear ducts. His gaze connected with hers. And there they stood, not glowering at each other, both holding back tears in this beautiful moment. A wild, unexpected warmth settled in her heart, like a dragonfly briefly touching down on her skin, resting for one beat of her wings.

Alice noticed the look, then tapped her husband

to draw attention to it. With that, the sweet feeling was off in a rattling buzz. If Cash wanted to spend his brother's wedding breaking rules and boasting about it, she'd add the newest violations to his file. No one was going to accuse her of not doing her job. With whispers of a recall trickling through town, Mylie needed good press and a drama-free July. She had a plan for just that—more specifically, a pageant for it.

Mylie pulled in a deep breath against the ever-present tension. Everything was going to work out, so long as Cash Holiday didn't stir up any trouble.

"To Beau and Elliana." Cash held his glass aloft. The party lights in the renovated barn reflected off the crystal, bubbles of champagne echoing the joy of the evening. "I love you guys."

Cash took a long drink as both Elliana and Beau responded, "We love you, too!"

While Cash couldn't claim to be quite as happy as his brother, he was thrilled to have the level-headed, creative event planner as his sister-in-law.

He was also thrilled to have his speech over and done with. Cash set down his glass and dusted his hands together. He wouldn't have to stand in front of another microphone until Tia got married, and that didn't seem to be on the horizon. One down, one to go. Then he was scot-free for the rest of his life where public performance was concerned.

Cash sat back down next to Tia and, if he was honest, he expected to be congratulated on his speech. He'd worked hard enough on it. Impromptu public speaking was not his thing. If Cash had to talk into a microphone, he prepared long in advance. It paid off today when the guests, including Mylie Saunders, laughed at all the right places, sighed when they were supposed to and applauded at the end.

But instead of congratulating him, Tia exhaled and pushed a piece of radicchio around on her plate.

"Everything okay?"

"What?" Her wavy auburn hair sprang out as she looked up from her plate, as though it had a guilty conscience all on its own. Her hair was as unruly as it had been when they were kids and he was the one responsible for brushing out the tangles. Over the years she'd grown into her hair, and the responsibility for taking care of it. It suited her.

"I asked if you were okay."

"I'm good." Tia nodded several times, then returned to the issue of where that radicchio was going to wind up. She glanced at him out of the corner of her eye. "I am. This is the best. I'm super-happy today."

She leaned past him to smile at Elliana. Tia had been off for the last week. He'd hoped the wedding would cheer her up.

Cash pulled in a breath and took a guess at what was bothering her. "Are you upset Mom's not here?"

"What? No. I mean, was she supposed to come?"

Cash shrugged. Was the average mom supposed to come to her son's wedding? Yes. Would anyone expect *their* mom to be here for the big day? Not so much.

"I did invite her," Cash said.

Tia waved away his concern. "I know. And I invited her, too. But since this whole thing was last-minute due to Sydney Reece's cancellation, I didn't expect her. Honestly, Mom just brings the drama. It's easier this way."

Mom had brought the drama; Dad had provided a steady stream of accusations, litigation and affairs. Cash had conflicted feelings about both his parents, but there was no question that life was easier without them.

Tia let a sigh slip. Cash swung his focus straight back to her.

"What's *wrong*?" he pressed.

"Nothing."

"You're normally at the center of the action at a party."

"I wouldn't say that."

"Umm?" Cash tilted his head, giving the *umm* the same inflection all the Holiday siblings did. An *umm* said, *I don't buy it, so please don't insult my intelligence by trying to close the sale.*

"What? At all our events I'm just doing my job. Hostessing."

"What about the Mobley anniversary party?"

"Well, sure. The Mobleys." She waved dismissively. "That was one party."

"Yup. One party where you befriended the adult children of the couple, sat at the family table, got invited to the after-party and, if I'm correct, you all still hang out."

"What? They're nice."

"Then there was the Irish Society's Emerald Gala, where you initiated, and won, the limerick competition."

She shrugged. "Someone had to get things rolling. And are you sure we're not Irish? Because Sean O'Callahan really wanted me to look in to that."

"You are not Irish. You *are* the life of the party."

"That's an exaggeration."

Cash shot his sister a look, and said the only words he really needed to. "Ripple Creek High School prom."

Tia furrowed her brow, as though not remembering the prom. Then she nodded slowly. "Ye-e-eah. Okay, fine. I was trying to help everyone have fun."

"You were accepted as an honorary teenager. You spent the entire evening with the kids. You choreographed a flash mob to 'Single Ladies.'"

Finally, a little grin flickered across her face. "Can you believe they didn't know that dance? What's even happening in education these days?"

"They know it now. Elliana says you're the secret weapon at her events, getting everyone into party mode. Which makes me wonder why, on this happiest of days, you're so quiet."

"Everybody's already in party mode." She gestured to the assembled guests, who really were having a great time. Elliana had planned things down to the last detail, then turned the running of the show over to another event coordinator so the Holiday family could enjoy the evening. "And you pestering me isn't exactly celebratory."

"I know. I love you, Tia."

"I love you, too." Tia picked up her fork and scooted the piece of radicchio up to the remains of her baby potatoes. "Life is good," she said, as though convincing herself. "Life is really good."

Cash knew this wasn't the time or place to have the conversation, but something was wrong. He'd never been able to let things rest where the health and happiness of his siblings was concerned. "You've been worried about something."

Tia dropped her fork and stood. "I'm fine! Now that your massively important speech is over, we can start dancing. Good job, by the way." She stepped around Cash, then draped one arm around Elliana and the other around Beau, asking, "Time to fire up the band? We need to start dancing before cousin Jean gets a hold of the microphone."

Cash exhaled. Conversations with Tia could be like this. All three of them carried scars from their upbringing with Ripple Creek's notorious narcissist. They each had bits of Dad's personality in them, and tried to make the best of what they'd inherited. Tia could be secretive, but given space and time, she'd open up. Cash needed to be patient, which wasn't his strong suit. But he'd patiently brushed the tangles out of her hair when he was twelve and she was six, both of them complaining the whole way through. He could wait, then eventually help her untangle whatever mess she was facing now.

He had one purpose in this life: to protect Beau and Tia. He'd accepted the mantle early, and never wavered. That meant long evenings as a teenager, making sure everybody ate and did their homework. He got everyone to bed on time and was the one his siblings woke up if one of them had a nightmare. He kept the cattle operation up and running as Dad chased one get-rich-quick scheme after the next and plunged the family into debt with his outrageous spending. It meant pivoting to this new venture after Dad passed away.

It meant watching his fiancée walk away when she realized Cash was a package deal. She couldn't accept that Beau and Tia would always come first. Their welfare was priority number one.

A drumbeat sounded through the room, drawing everyone's attention. The leader of the band implored the guests to join him in celebrating Beau and Elliana's first dance as husband and wife. Beau joked about the dance floor he'd built as Elliana's sparking laugh rang out. Cash, along with the rest of the guests, came to stand in a ring and watch.

"Oh, my God, how wonderful is this? Literally the most perfect wedding ever." Clara Broughman, cofounder of Love, Oregon, a local matchmaking service, stood next to him. He hadn't gotten to know her as well as his siblings had, but her use of hyperbole was legendary.

"My favorite wedding, without a doubt," Cash said.

"She looks amazing."

Cash nodded. "She looks happy."

"Look good, feel good," Clara said. "And is his suit…custom?"

"It is. We call it the family suit."

"That will be great on you."

Cash nodded, although there was no reason why he would be wearing that suit anytime soon, or ever.

"And just so you know, I am superexcited about the Mountain Country Most Eligible Pageant. I hope you are, too."

"We are." Cash kept his intonation low, but they were all very excited. The weeklong pageant would be their biggest event yet. It wouldn't settle all of Dad's outstanding debts, but would go a long way toward warding off the collectors.

"You're going to have so much fun!" Clara said. "We modeled it on a regular beauty pageant, but with our own spin on things. And, of course, it's not really a competition. Just an opportunity to raise money and celebrate all the contestants."

Cash nodded, eyes tracking Tia as she remained on the outskirts of the fun.

"I'm sure you already know this, but in addition to community service and a trivia night, contestants will model work attire and activewear, and there will be a line-dance competition!"

Cash snorted.

"Right?" Clara said, as though it was natural for

people to snort when they liked something. "Literally so much fun!"

Tia must have sensed his gaze because she glanced up sharply, then faked a smile.

"Well, I won't steal your time." Clara grinned, her dimples and honey-blond hair making her look like an advertisement for a vacation package that was supposed to make you happy. "I just wanted to say how thrilled I am you're taking it on. See you Thursday!"

She waved and stepped away before Cash could ask what was happening Thursday. He thought the first event at the ranch wasn't until Friday afternoon.

Whatever. Elliana would fill him in. She and Beau were postponing a honeymoon until after the Most Eligible Pageant. Cash wished they hadn't needed to, but neither of them seemed to mind. Starting their new life together as soon as possible was worth it to them, as was taking advantage of this fully paid-for event. The couple originally planning to wed this day had made the wise decision to call it off, leaving a very-much-in-love Beau and Elliana with the celebration of their dreams all planned and paid for. Cash would make sure they carved out the time to get away soon.

The first dance ended and the band struck up a popular tune, drawing more people onto the floor. Tia was finally letting loose. Several children had gravitated to her; she was laughing and spinning them around on the floor, two at a time.

A couple of women had the latest Hank O'Brien mystery out on a table, looking for similarities between Holiday Ranch and the one described in the popular series by an anonymous author. A group of Beau's buddies from the fire station were inspecting his handiwork in the renovated loft.

Mylie, untouched glass of champagne in her hand, was trying to be polite to Brick and Alice Henderson. He wouldn't wish the Hendersons on anyone, but he wasn't going to rescue Mylie from what was probably an argument of her own instigation.

But it *was* a little weird that he wanted to.

Cash took a moment to try to figure it out. The feeling had some connection to jealousy. Like if Mylie was gonna be arguing, why'd she choose to tangle with someone other than him? Surely, the two of them had better things to argue about than whatever Alice and Brick had going on.

Her gaze flickered to his, as it had during the wedding, bringing with it that same, unexpected, inexplicable rush.

Then she raised her brow at the salad plates. What, did she think he didn't know how to wash the greens? He didn't need a health inspector to teach him to clean veggies.

"If I could have everyone's attention!" Elliana's voice came through the speakers as she waved from the dance floor. Her face was flushed, eyes bright with some wedding-planner secret.

Cash took his attention off Mylie, and placed it firmly on his newest sister.

"Thank you all for coming," Elliana said into the microphone. "As you may imagine, over the years I've had a few thoughts about what I wanted my wedding to look like." Elliana gave a guilty smile as she tucked a strand of hair behind her ear.

The guests laughed.

"In addition to the wildflowers, strawberries with whipped cream—" she turned to Beau and slipped her hand into his "—and the most amazing man…"

A collective "aww!" rose from the group as Beau pushed aside the microphone and kissed his bride. Again.

Then Beau addressed the crowd. "In case anyone is wondering about my contribution to the party, my job was cake." He pointed to Karen Johnson, the owner of Ripple Creek bakery, who let out a whoop of appreciation for the callout. "Let's hear it for Karen's seven-tiered masterpiece!"

Elliana applauded along with everyone else, then took the microphone back from him.

"So many dreams have come true tonight. And I have one more you all can help me with. I've always imagined that at my wedding everyone, every single guest, would get out on the dance floor—" she widened her eyes, bit her lip and grinned "—for a line dance. The Cupid Shuffle…let's do it!"

Cash chuckled as folks let out good-natured groans and headed to the dance floor. He turned away to go check on…well, whatever he could figure out to go check on.

"Everyone!" This time, Elliana's voice was more serious.

Cash paused. But no. He was a good brother, but he wasn't that good.

The intro to a song Cash recognized filled the room. What party chores needed to happen next? The cake would be cut in about forty-five minutes—

"There are no other party chores!" Elliana's voice seemed to come from all around. Cash glanced back to see her looking straight at him as she bobbed to the music.

He pulled in a deep breath and glowered.

"Let's do it, bro!" Beau called out.

Elliana waved him onto the floor.

This was gonna turn into a scene real quick if he didn't get out there.

"I'm coming," he grumbled, stalking to the floor.

He'd do anything for his siblings, but line dancing felt like a stretch. Stumbling around like a drunk penguin wasn't his idea of a good time. If he was going to do something, he was going to do it right.

The definition of "right" being "better than everyone else."

Cash scanned the crowd as they followed the singer's instructions, stepping to the right, then to the left.

Not all that difficult.

The lyrics suggested a series of kicks. Cash inadvertently followed the directions.

Some guests were really getting into it, adding claps and a few shimmies. It looked…hmm. What was the word he was searching for? *Fun?* No, that couldn't be it.

Cash watched intently for one more rotation. The music was kinda catchy. Beau and Elliana were having the time of their lives, surrounded by family and community as they danced. From the center of the floor, Mylie caught his eye as she executed the dance with precision. Then she added an extra groove of her shoulders as she walked it back.

So that's how it was gonna be. *Fine.* He could turn the move into more of a strut.

Cash jumped in, right up front, between Beau and Tia. Elliana grinned at him. He could do this for his newest sister. He moved as instructed by the song, allowing his body to sway with the music, building on the claps and shimmies of others. He hooked his thumbs in his belt and let loose on a serious cowboy strut as he walked it back.

It was the least he could do for his siblings.

Tomorrow he'd be back at work, running cattle, helping prepare for the pageant where eight unwitting contestants would battle it out for the title of most eligible single in their small town. Tomorrow he would sit down with Tia and get to the bottom of whatever was bothering her. As of right now, he'd checked speeches off his list for the foreseeable future, and he literally wouldn't ever have to line-dance again.

If Mylie looked awfully cute doing the Cupid Shuffle, this dance and his desire to watch her do it would end soon enough. She'd go back to her life, and he'd go back to his.

Mylie's laugh rang out as she bumped hips with his Gramma Birdie, then the two of them shimmied to the left together. She caught him watching her and responded with a wicked grin.

If he'd ever needed a definition of *incorrigible*, she had to be it.

CHAPTER TWO

"MORNING," CASH SAID, even though it was after one o'clock when Beau and Elliana finally rolled into the main house for breakfast. Made sense, given that they'd been on the dance floor with half the population of Ripple Creek not twelve hours ago. "What's on the docket for your first day as a married couple?"

"Coffee?" Elliana asked, sending a hopeful glance toward the espresso machine.

"On it," Cash said. Beau had finally repaired the expensive Nuova Simonelli machine, but it was Cash who turned out to have a knack for making espresso drinks.

Beau pulled a tier of chocolate cake out of the fridge, along with eggs and leftover potatoes and asparagus from the night before.

"Wedding leftovers." Beau nodded at the spread. "Breakfast of champions."

"Or event planners," Elliana quipped. "Cake for breakfast has to be one of my favorite parts of hosting parties."

"Everything about hosting parties is your favorite part," Beau teased her.

"Technically, you're my favorite. That makes you, fixing me breakfast, the second favorite."

Beau grinned as he cracked eggs into a bowl. Elliana pulled up her to-do list on a laptop.

"You can't take one day off?" Cash asked.

Elliana shook her head as she accepted the double shot breve in one of the teacups from the china set Dad purchased and never used. "I have a meeting with the DuBoff family at three o'clock. Their only son is planning a Christmas wedding, and if we can book this one, it's gonna be big."

"You got *married* yesterday," Cash reminded them.

"And we've got a business to run today," Elliana said, grinning up at Beau. "Fortunately, I have a crush on my coworker. It makes the time fly by."

Cash chuckled. "I don't love the fact that you two have to head straight back to work, but I get it."

"I love the fact that we're married," Beau said, wrapping his arms around Elliana. "I love that our wedding was the best function ever, and someone else paid for it."

"Wasn't it fun?" she asked.

Beau signified his agreement with a kiss. Cash stalked over to the window, since it was clear this conversation was gonna be shut down for several smooches. The kitchen overlooked an area Tia had dubbed the town square: a wide yard connecting the big red barn, horse stables, guesthouse, second guesthouse, bunkhouse, greenhouse and main house.

The main house was the most extravagant building in the overpriced collection. A showy mansion of glass and timber. Over time, Dad had alienated one friend or family member after the next, until there was no one left to show off to.

The whole complex was over-the-top, like something built for a Hollywood set where the director's instructions had been "wealthy rancher." As if anyone ever got rich ranching.

But now, they held parties in these extravagant buildings, and rented out the bunkhouses and guesthouses for destination events. It didn't feel so ostentatious. It felt like a really great place for a party. Like the espresso maker, once repaired, it was a real asset.

Speaking of, an afternoon pick-me-up might be nice. Cash flipped the machine back on, the scent of ground coffee filling the kitchen. He scanned the counter to see if Beau had left the cake out. He had.

"The next couple of weeks will be a whirlwind," Elliana said, emerging from Beau's embrace. "What with the Mountain Country Most Eligible Pageant and trying to book the DuBoff wedding. But we can take a few days off after the fifth of July."

"I'm looking forward to it," Beau wrapped an arm around her waist as she took another sip of coffee.

Elliana smiled at Cash over the rim of her cup.

"I'm really excited to see you on stage. I wouldn't miss it for anything."

"What?" Cash pulled his perfect shot of espresso out from under the portafilter and added steamed half-and-half.

When he looked up, he found Elliana and Beau staring at him, as though they were the ones asking the question, not him.

"I'm excited to see you on stage," she said again.

"On stage…where? And why?"

Elliana gave Beau a meaningful look. Beau continued to whisk the eggs as he raised his brow. She blinked twice.

The pair had been married for less than a day and they were already using covert forms of communication?

"On stage," Elliana said to Cash, clearly and slowly, "in the Mountain Country Most Eligible Pageant. Your first meeting is on Thursday."

Cash set down his coffee and tilted his head at his new sister-in-law. "Umm?"

Elliana, who knew the *umm* all too well by now, pushed aside her cup and looked at him directly. "Remember? I signed you up for the pageant. You're competing—"

"You did what, now?" Cash asked, unable to conceal his frustration.

Elliana turned to her new husband, baffled. "I'm confused. What Holiday family communication hole have I stumbled into this time?"

"No, *I'm* confused." Cash was trying to keep

calm in front of the newest family member. They'd let Elliana have her run of the place, trusting her to lead the business. That didn't include putting him in a pageant.

"I'm sorry, man, but how do you not know this?" Beau asked.

Was Beau seriously putting this back on him? Cash was gonna be nice to Elliana, but Beau had been his brother for twenty-nine years. No need to tread lightly there.

"How did you *do* this?" he roared. "I'm not participating in a singles pageant."

"Someone has to." Beau turned to Elliana, a wry grin spreading across his face as he said, "I took the hit last time and agreed to a fake engagement party."

"Stop. No." Cash waved a hand in between the two of them before they could start kissing again and lose the thread of this conversation. "No one has to be in a pageant."

"We all thought a little representation by the Holiday family would be in good form," Elliana said, a blatant appeal to his sense of duty if he'd ever seen one. "Plus, the pageant supports funding for childhood literacy. You're in favor of kids reading, aren't you?"

"Do we have a problem with literacy around these parts? Because it seems like everyone is reading just fine, with the number of Hank O'Brien fans we get around here."

"The winner gets five thousand dollars?" Elliana turned the statement into a question. "So that's good, right?"

This gave Cash the tiniest pause. Not the five thousand dollars, which would be nice but not urgent as their new business continued to flourish. It was the word *winner.*

He really did enjoy winning. It didn't matter the competition: foot race, wrestling match, sushi consumption, a game of cornhole, an argument with Mylie Saunders. Preparing to compete and winning were his two favorite activities.

But a competition for who was the most eligible single in the area? No.

Cash changed his tack. "How is this not a conflict of interest? I can't compete in the pageant and host it."

Elliana was already shaking her head. "I asked about that. Clara and Piper, of Love, Oregon, are the only judges, and they have a holistic scoring system that mitigates any advantage you might gain from hosting. They specifically asked for a member of the family to participate."

"Well, were you gonna tell me?" he asked. "Or just push me out on stage when the time came?"

A flush ran up Elliana's neck. "Tia was supposed to tell you."

"She's in on this, too?"

"I mean, when you put it that way, it sounds like we were plotting…" Elliana's words trailed off as Cash gave the pair a hard look.

They *had* been plotting. A scheme to get him in a pageant? First-class plotting.

"You entrusted Tia to relay this information?" he asked.

"It was her idea," Beau said.

"And you didn't think to loop back and check to see if she actually did it?"

"We got *married*," Beau said, emphasizing the word the same way Cash had earlier in the conversation.

Cash sighed. He really could not be giving them grief the morning after their wedding. Tomorrow, next week? Sure. But not on the first day of their new life together. That would be a classic Dad move.

"I love you guys."

"We love you, too," they both mumbled, eyes downcast, understanding of what they'd done dawning on them.

Dang it. Now, he felt bad. He didn't want to let them down, but there was no way he was going to participate in a pageant. Clara's words from the day before came back to him: a cheery description of modeling activewear, answering trivia questions and line dancing.

Absolutely not.

Cash was fully in favor of increasing funding for childhood literacy. Having taken on the responsibility of helping both his siblings master the concept, he wouldn't have minded a little extra help back in the day. But they were already supporting the cause by hosting the event here. He loved his siblings, and would do anything for them. That included keeping them in line. Signing him up to participate in a pageant and not telling him was so far out of line, it'd be hard to navigate back there.

Beau and Elliana were talking at him, a constant stream of words making about as much sense as the babbling of Ripple Creek. He wasn't going to dampen their first day as a married couple by arguing.

"I'm sorry," he said, cutting them both off. "I can see this was an honest mistake, but you should have checked with me first. I would have said then what I'm gonna say now. No."

"Cash—" Beau began to argue. When was that kid going to learn he never won an argument with his older brother?

"I'm out. Now, I want you two to enjoy your breakfast. You won't find much cleanup left to do before the DuBoff family arrives, I got most of it taken care of this morning. Let me know if I can help when they get here."

Cash scooped up his phone and stalked out of the kitchen. He didn't want to disappoint Beau and Elliana, but there was no way he was doing this pageant. He'd helped both of them along in their relationship, kept the ranch afloat and worked overtime to get the event center up and running. Heck, he'd even line-danced for the two of them the night before.

Surely that was enough.

A few quick swipes and Cash had the contact for Love, Oregon up on his phone. He tried to remember the name of the perky matchmaker he'd spoken to the night before. There were two of them, sisters with identical vocal patterns and a lot of enthusiasm. The phone rang as Cash stalked down the long, wood-paneled hallway into the great room. The vaulted cedar ceiling and expansive parquet flooring framed a wall of windows. The room had a view of the vast front lawn, calling to mind the time he'd dressed up like the Easter Bunny and herded a massive crowd of children in an egg hunt. He'd done plenty for his family recently.

"Cash?" Tia's voice slipped in over the ringing of the phone.

Cash whipped around and pointed at her, mouthing the words *stay right there*. He was angry. Yes, she'd had something going on recently. Yes, she could be absent-minded about anything not related to the welfare of animals. That didn't excuse forgetting, or omitting, to tell him he'd been signed up for some nonsense pageant.

She nodded, keeping her chin up even as her lower lip wobbled.

"Hello! Love, Oregon!" the voice rang out through the speakers on Cash's phone.

"Can I talk to you when you're done on the phone?" Tia asked quietly. She looked as frail and as tired as the two greyhounds at her heels had been when she rescued them. "There's something I need to tell you."

Cash paused, then swore gently under his breath as he tapped the red icon on his phone.

"What's up?"

MYLIE JUGGLED HER breakfast as she exited the café, coffee in her right hand, croissant in the left, and nothing but elbows to open the door. Which was how she came to be face-to-face with the poster, and her immediate future, once again.

The Mountain Country Most Eligible Pageant!!
Get your tickets now to watch eight singles compete for the title in this fun, family-friendly competition!
The drama begins Friday, June 27, at Holiday Ranch!

The poster continued from there. So many promises of fun, so many exclamation points.

So much pressure on Mylie.

Suffice it to say, Mayor Mylie Saunders was not a pageant girl. She was, however, the first citizen of Ripple Creek to sign up for the Mountain Country Most Eligible Pageant. Did she like pageants? No. Was she interested in posing in a gown or taking part in a competition in front of her community? Absolutely not. But the pageant was a chance to raise money for an early childhood literacy initiative, which was one thing her constituents could agree on. It was also a chance to raise awareness for the town's as-of-yet unfunded programs, like Club 75.

No, Mylie was not a pageant person. She was a person who had an immediate need for five thousand dollars.

Because while she could pull out her checkbook and just pay for the senior program on her own, that would make her look petty. Mylie's image as a collaborator mattered. As the mayor, she needed to work with others. Or at least give others the impression she was working with them. But if she won the pageant—no, *when* she won the pageant—she could walk up to the microphone with a crown on her head and donate the money then and there to Club 75. Alice and the rest of the committee would appear foolish if they didn't fund the final three thousand.

Entering the pageant was a win-win-win situation. When she won on stage, she would win this standoff with the special committee on community engagement, and she would win the goodwill of the greater community, ending any real threat of a recall.

And even if she didn't need the money, as mayor of Ripple Creek, it was her duty to participate, and win. She might even buy a new dress. No need to tell Alice's husband.

"I'll get that for you." Myron, an eighty-three-year-old retired librarian, appeared at her side.

"Thank you," she said, then addressed the corgi at his feet. "Good morning, Rocky."

The back half of the long, short dog wagged in response.

"That was some wedding last night, wasn't it?" Myron asked.

"It was." Images of Cash standing up beside his brother, giving what Mylie could admit was a great toast, flashed through her mind. Her brain was under strict orders not to recall any images from the line dance.

"Must be why it's so quiet around here this morning. Who ever heard of having a wedding on a Tuesday?" Myron asked.

"Quiet" at Karen's bakery meant only two thirds of the café tables were full, and the line wasn't out the door. Behind the counter, Karen, who had been one of the last to leave the dance floor, was serving up scones like it was nothing.

"Young folks today." Myron shook his head. "You're all so creative. Weddings on Tuesdays. Lavender in coffee drinks. What will you think of next?"

Mylie laughed as the former librarian flipped expectations of the way the elderly talk about younger generations. Something like Club 75 would be perfect for Myron—a chance to meet new people, possibly even start dating again.

"You'll find out what my next project is soon enough," Mylie said. "But to make it happen, I'd better get to work. Thanks for the help!" She held up her coffee and croissant as she stepped through the door.

"At your service. I'll be seeing you Thursday, then."

"Thursday?" Mylie paused mid-exit. Her calendar had been jam-packed recently. What engagement could possibly involve Myron?

"We've got the first meeting for the pageant," he said, nodding at the sign. "I saw you were signed up."

Mylie stared at the elderly gentleman in his cardigan sweater with elbow patches. "Did *you* sign up?"

"Yup! I was the second person to sign up, right after you. Are you excited? I know I am."

Conflicting thoughts pinballed through Mylie's brain. She liked Myron immensely. But he was participating in something with a fashion show and dance competition? Recommending books on amphibians to seven-year-olds was more his skill set.

"Do you know who else is competing?" she asked.

"Oh, the usual suspects, I imagine." Myron listed a few townsfolk who, while very nice, didn't strike Mylie as serious competition. Then he leaned in and spoke quietly. "I have heard those matchmakers are bringing in a few out-of-towners. You gotta watch out for the ringers."

He nodded seriously, as though they might want to form an alliance of convenience against these unknown out-of-towners.

Maybe his excitement was infectious, but Mylie felt a little flutter in her heart. She'd assumed she was going to have to work to win the title, but—zero shade intended—if this was the competition, she had it in the bag.

"I *am* excited," she said, answering his original question. "This is going to be fun. I will see you Thursday and we can scope out those out-of-towners together."

Myron gave her a firm nod as Mylie stepped into the sunshine.

"Good morning!" Mylie nodded to locals as she headed down Main Street to City Hall. People responded sleepily. Mylie felt great. A decided lack of sleep was nothing new to her. Her best work was done late at night, so the morning routine was essential. Shower, power outfit, brisk walk to the bakery for sustenance, then a slower stroll to her office. Mylie used her morning walk to multitask, covering breakfast, exercise, transportation and connection with her community in one forty-minute interval. The citizens of Ripple Creek felt comfortable approaching her with issues and concerns on these walks. Informal conversations allowed her to keep a pulse on public opinion. She was also able to connect with local business owners, who weren't shy about popping out of their shops to chat when they saw the mayor.

Any community member she met face-to-face and worked with to resolve reasonable concerns was unlikely to be moved by talk of a recall.

Mylie was well aware of her strengths and weaknesses. Her family certainly hadn't been shy about pointing out both as she was growing up. She was a good mayor. Her one significant flaw in public service was an aversion to working in committee. Mylie worked best alone. If you want something done right, do it yourself. Preferably at 10:00 p.m., fueled by a quad shot of espresso on ice with two splashes of caramel syrup.

From the first collaborative project she'd been ordered to do in the third grade, to last Thursday's work group on storm-water runoff, Mylie had to grin and bear it while working with others. As mayor, she got in a lot more hot water when she rewrote someone else's contribution to the assignment. The habit had earned her reputation in some circles as a bad team player, making her daily ask-me-anything stroll all the more important.

But this morning, most folks were still a little foggy from the night before, leaving Mylie alone with her thoughts and a buttery croissant. Thursday's pageant meeting was at the community center, but almost everything else was scheduled for Holiday Ranch. She would do her best to ignore Cash during the events. That meant she needed to not take the bait if he tried to strike up an argument.

And she really, really needed to not strike up any arguments of her own.

Mylie's phone vibrated in her pocket. She popped the last bite of croissant into her mouth and pulled out her phone as several more texts came in. She stopped walking.

The family thread was blowing up, which could

only mean one thing: her brother got another promotion, award, or some other outward sign of status. *Great.*

No, really...great!

Mylie was happy for her sibling. It was awesome that Nate—she glanced at her phone—was the youngest head of surgery ever to be appointed at Mt. Olive Children's Hospital.

Of course, he was.

Totally awesome. Her phone buzzed as images of his picture-perfect wife and kids came through. The whole happy family celebrating Daddy's promotion.

Yay.

Mylie shoved the phone back in her pocket. She could put the requisite likes and hearts on the images when she got to the office.

Being a respected trial lawyer, and now, mayor of Ripple Creek was…fine. Her family was fine with it. She wasn't a disgrace, but she sure wasn't the first one mentioned in the family newsletter. What would they think if they knew she was about to compete in a pageant? Nate would roll his eyes. Her sister-in-law, Sadie, would act supportive, but wouldn't want her kids to attend any events, lest they get ideas about standing in the limelight while wearing a sparkly dress. Her parents would want to have a conversation about how this could affect a future political career.

What she hadn't told her family, and couldn't just drop in the chat, was that she didn't want a future political career past being mayor. She loved Ripple Creek—she always had. Her family had once owned a vacation home at Creekside Resort on the outskirts of town. Throughout Mylie's childhood, they came here for winter skiing, hiking in the spring and fall, and in the summer to play on the banks of Ripple Creek itself. Those were the happiest times of her life, when the family took a break from the endless cycle of achievement to enjoy Oregon. Waking up in Ripple Creek was a dream come true. She wanted to spend the rest of her life supporting this little town.

That was a much bigger conversation than one about a pageant. Sure, she'd find a way to spin her involvement in the Mountain Country Most Eligible Pageant. It was a fundraiser, for heaven's sake. Who didn't love the idea of little kids reading? It was the conversation about the future that had her stymied. The next time her mom asked how many more years she planned on spending in Ripple Creek, the answer was going to be all of her years. And her parents were never, ever going to understand how their precocious daughter could be satisfied with what they considered a small life.

Love in the Saunders family was contingent on a strict definition of success. Mylie walked a tightrope between earning her parents' approval and securing her own happiness. The gaping cavern below. holding neither love nor happiness, was a very real threat. There was no safety net. If this recall materialized, she would plummet.

Unbidden, a series of images slipped into her mind. Cash hugging his brother, the low rumble of "I love you" floating across the clearing. The serious conversation he had with Tia at the head table when she seemed so forlorn. The family lined up together, laughing as they did the Cupid Shuffle.

She shook her head. They had happy sibling relationships, she didn't. If she ever got married and started a family, she would do things differently than her parents. Not that she was in any danger of getting married. It was hard enough to earn her parents' love. Just the thought of the daily grind involved in winning and keeping a partner's love was exhausting.

No, Mylie was very single at present. Eligible. Some might even say *the most eligible*. And she had work to get done here in Ripple Creek.

Mylie grinned and took a long drink of her coffee. Then she pulled up the list of pageant competitions on her phone. She could wait to tell her family until after she won, and drop a few pictures in the thread for Sadie to have to hide from the kids. This was gonna be a slam dunk. It might even be fun.

CASH STARED AT his sister from across the room, phone still in hand. She pressed her lips together, then drew in a deep breath.

"I need to borrow some money from the family business," Tia said quietly.

It was a money problem. Okay. Things could be worse.

"How much?"

She swallowed, then turned her large hazel eyes on him.

"I'm not quite sure yet. Maybe ten thousand dollars?"

"Ten thousand dollars? What—?"

She held out a hand to stop him from speaking, then waved it around as though maybe she meant something else.

"I could take out a bank loan—"

"Absolutely not," Cash said.

Tia nodded. They had spent their lives watching their father apply for one loan on top of the next, paying off a credit card with two new ones, always with an excuse as to why, this time, it made sense. They were still battling their way out of his mess.

"Our finances have stabilized," he reminded her. "We're no longer in danger of losing the ranch."

"We're not exactly in danger of being rich, either."

"No, but we've got a place to live, and if we keep hosting parties like this we can live on the leftovers."

For the first time, an honest smile spread across her face. "Let us eat cake?"

Cash laughed. "Works for me."

"I *will* be able to pay it back." Tia was serious as she looked into his eyes.

Her statement brought up another question, one he had discussed with Beau on more than one occasion. "You'll be earning the money from your veterinary practice?"

She nodded.

Cash held her gaze, searching for honesty.

Tia had returned home from Oregon State University with her doctorate in animal medicine, a degree she put to use rescuing animals, rather than joining a practice and getting paid to take care of other people's critters. Holiday Ranch was home to rescue cats, dogs, peacocks, alpacas and even a turtle. She occasionally brought money in, but there wasn't a lot of evidence of her doing the kind of work that resulted in a paycheck.

"What do you need it for?" he asked.

Tia nodded, like she'd been expecting this question. "Yeah. So. I'm, uh— It's complicated."

Cash waited. Tia studied her hands.

"In what way is it complicated?" he asked.

Tia didn't answer. No surprise there.

Tia was secretive to a fault, a response to growing up under the domineering personality of their father. It wasn't that she had anything to hide; rather, she feared judgment. After a childhood of being ostracized for her father's actions, Tia didn't intentionally open herself up for criticism on any topic. The more something mattered to her, the less willing she was to talk about it.

As a kid, she was constantly scribbling in notebooks. Paper got her innermost concerns and dreams; everyone else got a carefree, quirky girl gliding through life unbothered. He couldn't fault her coping mechanisms without taking a good, hard look at his own.

But she wanted to take out a loan from the family business without sharing the reason? Ten thousand dollars was a chunk of money. How would he even get half that much on short notice?

He glanced up, the thought occurring to him in bold, capital letters; *five thousand dollars for the winner of the Mountain Country Most Eligible Pageant*. It was almost too easy.

He narrowed his eyes. "Is this how I got entered in the pageant? Because if so, you should be the one—"

Tia's mouth flew open. "Oh. Dang." Then she squeezed her eyes shut and wrinkled her nose. "I forgot to tell you, didn't I?"

"You did."

She shook her head, eyes still closed. "My bad?"

Cash exhaled. "Look, Tia. I don't know what's going on with you. I'm worried."

"I know."

"I can't help you if you won't tell me what's going on."

Tia was silent for a long moment, hands clasping and reclasping in front of her. Then she pulled in a deep breath.

"Can you give me some time? I want to…talk, to you, about all this. It's just complicated and I don't know where to start." She looked up at him. "Just let me get it taken care of first."

"Can you give me an assurance that you're okay?"

"I'm okay. I'm not in debt, or mortal danger. Beau is okay. And the money is not for an animal. When I explain it all, you're going to be surprised, but not in a bad way."

Cash contemplated his sister. This was all he was going to get for now, but he knew Tia. If she said she'd tell him eventually, she would. Dad would have dealt with this differently: withhold the money so long as she withheld the information. But that's not how Cash chose to operate. He gave one sharp nod.

"Thank you," she whispered. "For trusting me."

"I appreciate you checking with me before borrowing the money."

"I wasn't going to take a massive amount of money without asking anyone. I mean, hello? Classic Dad."

Cash gave a weak laugh. "Let's do it. And when you're ready to talk about whatever's going on, I'm here."

She nodded, relief flooding her face. She held out her arms for a hug.

"I'm really sorry I forgot to tell you about the pageant."

"I'm furious, but we're gonna talk about that another time."

Tia tightened her arms around him and said, "I know you're mad, but we really had to have someone in the family participate, and it couldn't be me because of the thing."

"The thing you need ten thousand dollars for?"

"Yeah. It's, I don't know—a thing." She stepped back. "Thank you."

He nodded, then glanced out the window. One of the rescue peacocks strutted across the lawn, tail feathers fanned out to protect the ranch from a squirrel going about its business. Cash felt about as useful as that bird right now. How was he going to solve the problem for Tia if he didn't know what it was?

Tia's footsteps receded, followed by the *tap-tap* of the dogs' paws on the parquet flooring. They all paused at the door. "I love you, Cash."

"I love you, too. We'll get this taken care of."

"I know." Tia nodded, then slipped out of the room.

And just like that, Cash was stuck in a beauty pageant.

CHAPTER THREE

MYLIE STRODE ACROSS the activity hall at the community center. She could feel the other contestants' eyes on her as she pushed her sunglasses up on her head and took a chair on the far side of the circle.

It was 4:56 p.m. on Thursday, June 26th. *Let the Mountain Country Most Eligible Pageant begin.*

"How's everyone doing?" she asked.

A nervous, cheerful energy filled the room as people responded. Mylie steered the conversation with an easy smile, inwardly sizing up the competition.

Rafael, a newly single teacher in his early forties. Moderate threat. No serious worries, but his hip clothing and easy smile made him one to keep on her radar.

Caleb, a young man who worked as a chef in Outcrop. Quiet, with an air of mystery. Or as much mystery as any twentysomething could muster.

Nesa and Daisy, a grandma and granddaughter who signed up for the pageant on a mutual dare. Both were completely charming; neither was remotely interested in winning.

Bobbie, a stylish loan broker in her mid-fifties with a quick wit. One to watch. Gen Xers could get scrappy when they needed to.

And, of course, Myron, Ripple Creek's favorite former librarian, wearing yet another cardigan sweater with elbow patches.

Mylie crossed her legs and leaned back in her chair, the brilliant feeling of confidence swirling through her. It was like the glorious moment of sitting down to take an exam she'd overprepared for. The joy of flipping over the paper and realizing all you had to do was name every country on the map of Oceania.

She was going to slay this competition.

"Yay!" Clara Broughman clapped her hands and beamed at everyone, the dimple in her cheek flexing. "Welcome, everyone! We're so glad you're here. We're just waiting on one more single and we'll get started!"

Piper Wallace-Benton, Clara's twin and co-owner of Love, Oregon, joined the circle. "This is literally going to be the most fun you've had in your lives."

Caleb gave her a dry look.

Ooh! Did he not want to be here? Even better.

"And while we hope every one of you finds love as a result of competing in this pageant—"

At this, Myron sat up expectantly. Rafael gave a solemn nod. Mylie scanned the room, realizing that these people were here, in part, to meet someone. They were honestly looking for love.

OMG! There was no way she was going to lose.

"—our stated aim is to raise money for childhood literacy initiatives in Deschutes County," Piper continued. "I know this is an issue dear to many of our hearts."

Bobbie leaned back in her chair and gave a sympathetic smile. Okay, she was here for the kids. Not necessarily for the title, or the money.

Mylie hadn't felt this good in ages. Sure, the pageant might be a little cheesy. And, yes, she would be modeling a pickleball outfit while her brother bossed people around about the proper way to remove a spleen.

But in the end, she would have five thousand dollars with which to start Club 75 and some really good local press as she participated in a lighthearted community event. Piper was right. This *was* going to be fun!

The door to the community center opened, light spilling across the linoleum floor, silhouetting the man entering. Tall, broad-shouldered, boots—

Oh, no.

"Cash! Yay!" Clara clapped her hands.

"You're late," Piper said cheerfully, but with an undertone suggesting he'd wasted three minutes of everyone's time, which added up to twenty-seven minutes he'd be expected to make up at some point.

Cash Holiday did not respond. He stood just outside the circle, staring in horror at Mylie.

She returned the greeting in kind.

The matchmakers were chirping away as Mylie,

and she had to assume Cash, wrestled with the implications of his arrival. They were in the same room, ready to participate in the same pageant, and there was only one empty chair left.

"Have a seat!" Clara told Cash, pointing to the seat right next to Mylie.

He didn't even try to hide his distaste, but stalked over and dropped himself in the chair next to her, leaning forward, elbows on his knees.

She imitated his posture, her face locked in a smile as she said, "Nice to see you, too."

"Are you really doing this?" he muttered, eyes forward.

"Winning this competition? Yes."

He straightened, shoulders settling as they always did when he was ready to argue. "You think you're gonna win?"

"I know I'm gonna win."

Or she had known, five minutes ago. Cash was serious competition for this title. Not that he was some fabulous catch, but she knew how he operated. When Cash wanted to win, he prepared for every eventuality.

He was dressed sharply today. Over time, she'd come to recognize his battle wear. On the ranch he was almost always in jeans and some old work shirt, provided there wasn't an event in progress. When he came into town to argue about a permit or dispute a noise ordinance, he looked good; slacks, a fitted oxford, polished-up cowboy boots, his auburn hair freshly cut. He wasn't messing around today. He was here to win.

Unless...?

An odd, indefinable feeling shifted through her. They didn't have the sort of relationship where her question was in any way appropriate, but she couldn't stop herself from asking… "Are you here to meet someone?"

He turned fully toward her, confusion spreading across his handsome face. Then he scoffed. A scoff so loud, and ill-timed to a moment when conversation had dimmed, that the entire group turned to stare at him. Cash quickly morphed the scoff into a cough, covering his mouth with a fist and waving apologetically with the other hand as he faked a few more coughs. Genial conversation resumed.

Cash leaned toward her, close enough that she could smell the beeswax soap he used. "I'm here to win five thousand dollars."

Mylie's heart dipped slightly, as though realizing she had to include the capitals of Oceanic states along with the names of the countries. Not insurmountable, just more of a challenge.

"That's too bad," she said. "Because I'm gonna win the title, and the money."

He turned his dark hazel eyes on her. "Not this time."

"No, this *is* the time I'll win. In fact, this will be the only time I ever compete in a pageant. Since I won't be back, it makes sense to win while I'm here."

A sly, almost appealing grin appeared on his lips. "You don't know what you're up against."

"You have a whole history of pageant competition you've been keeping a secret?" she asked.

"I'm just saying, when I compete, I win. The Mountain Country Most Eligible title is no exception."

"I wouldn't count on it. Although, I'm sure you're very good at being single," she quipped.

The smile dropped from his face, followed by a sharp crease in his brow. The comment didn't land as she expected. Rather than ratcheting up the argument, as was their pattern, he deflated. It was uncomfortable. She didn't like Cash. She didn't want to care about his feelings, but she didn't intend to hurt them, either.

"Cash, Mylie, let's go!"

They both looked up to see an exceedingly well-groomed matchmaker hovering over them. It was Piper. Mylie wracked her brain for everything she could remember about her: married to the Deschutes County commissioner, split her time between Portland and Tumalo, active legislative lobbyist for environmentally sustainable ranching practices, dachshund owner.

Piper gestured impatiently for the two of them to get on their feet. They stood.

"We're going to do a few icebreakers," Clara said.

Mylie glanced at Cash, her eyes rolling before she could stop them. He seemed to feel similarly about games where full-grown adults had to do silly things in the name of getting comfortable. Like how did that make sense?

"I'm going to ask you all to find a partner," Clara said.

Mylie and Cash immediately turned away from one another, making eye contact with anyone and everyone else.

"Look for someone with the same color top you're wearing."

Mylie had opted for a sky-blue poplin oxford, in a tonal outfit that said, *This mayor can be fun! But also, she's still the mayor.*

She wove through the group, skipping over folks with flowered tops, white tops, green University of Oregon sweatshirts, tan cardigans sweaters with elbow patches—

Until she was standing face-to-face with a man in a fitted blue oxford.

Cash muttered several expletives under his breath, then gave Mylie a fake smile. "Nice shirt."

"Thanks."

Clara clapped to get their attention. "If you could only eat one food for the rest of your life, what would it be?"

"What kind of question is that?" Cash asked.

"Seriously," she said quietly. "If a person only ate one food, the rest of their life would be pretty short, given a lack of nutrients."

"And lack of joy," he added.

Mylie managed to keep from giggling, turning her attention to the ice-breaking question at hand. "Hmm? I guess, tacos. There's lots of different things you could put in a taco, so I'd never get bored. And they can be healthy."

He nodded, like she'd been waiting for his approval of her answer, then said, "Party leftovers."

"Party leftovers?"

"Yeah. Charcuterie boards, salads, cake, dinner rolls."

"That's not *a* food. That's all foods."

"You were the one talking about the variety of tacos."

"A taco is a recognizable type of food—"

"So are leftovers."

"No, they're not!"

"Let's google it," Cash pulled out his phone.

"Okay! Switch partners!" Clara clapped again. "Find someone with the same, or the closest, birth month to yours."

Mylie gave Cash a final glare, then stepped away. She wound through the group, hopefully suggesting, "May?" but everyone responded with the pumpkin-spice and peppermint-mocha months.

Bringing her, once again, to Cash.

"May?" he asked.

"The seventh."

He swallowed and nodded. "May tenth."

"Of course." Mylie drew in a breath and turned to Clara for whatever inane question she was going to ask next.

"If you could be any animal for the day, what would you be and how would you spend the day?"

A lively argument about the relative intelligence and life satisfaction of dolphins versus octopi ensued, while all around them people spoke genially of cats, dogs and river otters.

And on it went. It didn't seem to matter what the prompt, Mylie and Cash nearly always wound up in conversation together, disagreeing on everything from sunrise versus sunset, to what one should do if they won the lottery. All the while, the matchmakers bopped around the room, listening to conversations, moving sticky notes around on a clipboard, communicating with one another in a series of hand gestures and facial expressions.

"Are they already judging us?" Mylie asked.

"Feels like it," Cash responded.

"Then you'd better stop scoffing if you want to win."

"You'd better stop getting that look on your face."

"What look?"

"That one." He pointed to her face.

"What's wrong with my face?"

"Nothing. But your blatant contempt for this activity might be shaving off a few points."

As though on cue, Clara looked straight at Mylie, then moved a sticky note on her clipboard.

"I'd want the superpower of flying," Mylie said, as enthusiastically as she could manage. "With the power of flight, I could better serve my community."

Clara moved the sticky note back to where it had been originally.

A battery of random questions later, Piper finally commanded everyone back to their seats. "We'd like to go over the schedule and give you a few pointers for the pageant, then we highly suggest you review the interview questions you'll find in your pink folders."

Mylie spun on her heel and marched for a chair as far from Cash as it was possible to get in a circle set up for ten people. She sat in between Clara and Myron, accepting her pink file folder of information. Abruptly, Clara stood and took a chair next to her sister, leaving one space open.

Cash pulled in a deep breath and sat next to Mylie, again.

"As I said, this is going to be so fun!" Clara enthused.

Mylie smiled and nodded, making sure her face looked fascinated. Clara moved another sticky note on her clipboard.

"It's also extremely important," Piper said, more seriously. "Children's reading abilities are in your hands. If you don't step up, who will?"

"Teachers?" Cash mused.

"Hush, you," Mylie whispered.

"No one uses the word *hush* anymore," he grumbled back.

"Would your preference be for me to ask you to put a sock in it?"

"It's going to be a busy week," Clara continued.

"We have three on-stage events. Modeling activewear and the interview—"

Cash raised his hand, then spoke without being called on. "Activewear?"

"Right. You'll wear whatever you exercise in. So running clothes, tennis whites, a golf ensemble."

"Can I wear my lucky birding sweater?" Myron asked.

"That's perfect."

Cash leaned back in his chair, baffled. Mylie guessed his lean, fit frame was a result of actual work rather than working out.

"Are your tennis whites at the dry cleaners?" she asked.

"Must be." He closed his eyes briefly, then sat up in his chair as though this was all very interesting.

Piper continued. "If you'll all look at the schedules we provided in your packets, you'll see the events ramp up as we near the Fourth of July. On the Fourth, we have the parade, then fireworks will be at Holiday Ranch that evening."

Mylie read over the schedule as Piper discussed each event and impressed upon them how earth-shatteringly important they all were.

This was going to suck up a *lot* of time. Mylie's heart sped up, fluttering uncomfortably in her chest as she thought about everything else she had to do. But this was good press for Ripple Creek, and good press for her.

As her sister spoke, Clara studied her clipboard,

brow furrowed, smiling dimple nowhere in sight. She moved sticky notes from one place to the next.

"So that's what your next ten days will look like!" Piper said, as though a schedule jam-packed with pageant activities was everyone's dream staycation.

Wordlessly, Clara handed her sister the clipboard she'd been working on. Piper's eyes widened, an identical smile to Clara's spreading across her face.

"This is literally so perfect!" She looked up at the group. "We've got your partners assigned."

"Partners?" Cash asked.

"Yep! Partners, buddies, coconspirators, however you want to put it. For the next ten days you're going to be spending every free moment with—" She checked the list again, but Mylie was already stifling a groan as Piper said, "Mylie Saunders."

"OKAY! 'BYE! See you all Friday at four o'clock—"

Clara's cheerful end to the meeting was cut off by her sister. "Four o'clock sharp. Don't be late."

Cash launched out of his chair, the way he might have on the last day of school as a kid. Other contestants moved toward the door more slowly, chatting and laughing, exchanging numbers and getting ready for the next day.

Except for Mylie.

Cash paused at the exit and looked back. She was rearranging chairs, dismantling the circle, setting up for something else.

Outside, sunlight washed over Main Street on

this perfect June day. His truck was parked right across the street. A fifteen-minute drive and he'd be home.

Mylie sighed as she pulled two chairs from a stack in the corner and added them to her new configuration.

"You need help?" he asked.

She startled, dropping a chair. "Thanks. No. I'm good."

Cash didn't leave, or respond. He just stood in the doorway like one of Tia's cats, weighing a universe of relative merits between inside and out.

"We have a listening session about the new housing development tonight," Mylie continued. "I'm getting set up now, so Becky doesn't have to."

Cash didn't know who Becky was, or why she needed to be rescued from chair duty, but it seemed real important to Mylie. He took one last look at his truck gleaming in the sunshine, then walked back into the room.

"Let me help. I've gotten pretty good at arranging chairs over the last few months."

Mylie straightened, staring at him as though he'd offered to pay off her mortgage. "Okay? Uh, I'm going for a *V* shape, with chairs facing the podium."

"Got it." Cash walked over to the stack of chairs and picked up several. Neither spoke. Just two people who didn't like each other, making a little less work for Becky. Each scrape of a chair leg on linoleum amplified the lack of conversation.

Finally she asked, "You want to talk about Friday?"

"I don't even want to *think* about Friday," he said.

She gave a light laugh. Not the humorless chuckle he was used to from her, but something softer, nicer.

"I take it volunteering for the pageant wasn't your idea," she said.

"It was not. But I'm here. And if I'm competing, I'm gonna win."

"You're going to *try* to win," she amended.

He grinned at her. "Same thing. What about you? What brought you to this pageant? Besides the chance to engage in awkward icebreakers, obviously."

"Myriad reasons," she said. "The big one is I need the money to fund a program that's in danger of being written off."

Cash glanced at her from over the chairs he was carrying. It hadn't occurred to him that anyone else might have a need for the prize money. "Which is?"

"It's a program to connect seniors with service opportunities for wildlife conservation. We have a lot of community programs for families and teenagers, which is great. But our elderly population is underserved, and vulnerable to depression."

"I like it. My Gramma Birdie could use something like that. Can I help?"

"You're being serious?"

"Sure." Was he really offering to help? It sounded

like a nice idea. Maybe the seniors could meet at the ranch, or he could offer to drive or something.

"Okay, great! Don't win this pageant. Judging from today, you're my biggest competition."

He gave a dry laugh. "Sorry. I gotta win."

"Why?" she asked.

"It's a family thing."

"Ah." She nodded. "The all-important Holiday-family things."

"They are important," he said. "What are the rest of your, what was it you called them? Myriad reasons?"

"Beyond the money, and the winning?"

He dipped his head. "Besides that."

She looked thoughtful for a moment. "Being a young, single woman in a position of power can be tricky. Sometimes I just lean in, let people think I'd love to meet a great guy and plan a big, beautiful wedding at Holiday Ranch."

An uneasy feeling slipped through Cash's midsection. "So you're looking for someone? To date?"

"If by *looking* you mean I'd be totally happy if the perfect man landed in my life with absolutely no effort on my part, sure. But I'm in the pageant to win. You should probably just accept that I'll take the first round modeling activewear and focus your efforts elsewhere. I have a super cute pickleball outfit."

Ooh. Dang it. He'd seen her on the courts, playing the improbable game with a posse of work-from-home moms, including his cousin Liz. Mylie was adorable in an athletic skirt.

He nodded in acknowledgment. "That's fair. I'll gain the points back with work wear."

Her head bobbed up from where she was positioning a chair, brow flexed. Then she groaned. "You're really gonna do the whole cowboy getup?"

"It's not a getup. It's practical work wear for wrangling cattle. And, yes, I do know how to spin a lasso."

She made a face. He grinned.

"Whatever. Now, I'm prepared." She widened her eyes. "Speaking of, want to go over the pageant tips and tricks together?"

Cash picked up the pink folder, then flipped through various pages of instructions and timetables until he found the tips-and-tricks page.

"'Be yourself,'" he read out loud. "'Lean into your own character and quirks, don't try to be someone you're not for the sake of the pageant. Authenticity is engaging, confidence is key.'" He looked up from the page.

"I guess that means you're free to be hardheaded and stubborn," she quipped.

"And you can be relentless while trying to make a point."

"Relentless. Ooh. I like that." She grinned at him. "Thank you."

"I feel the same way about *incorrigible*." Cash smiled back at her, holding her gaze for a moment before glancing back at the piece of paper.

He cleared his throat. "'Tip number two, practice your poise. You'll be surprised by how nervous you are once you hit the stage lights, so spend time practicing a few stances that feel natural and confident. Move with good posture, eyes forward, shoulders back and a walk that suggests you own the place.'" He looked up. "That should be easy. I do own the place."

Mylie crossed her arms, but she was still smiling as she cried, "Unfair advantage!"

"Yes!" He clenched a fist. "Maybe I'll get kicked out of the pageant?"

"You'd forfeit?"

So tempting. But no.

"Naw. I gotta step up for the fam. Apparently Clara and Piper have a 'holistic scoring system' that mitigates any advantage I might have by being part of the family that's hosting the event."

"*Holistic scoring system?*" Mylie snorted.

"My thoughts exactly."

She met his gaze, her grin telling him she had similar feelings on competition. Something along the lines of *let me know where the finish line is and I'll do what it takes to get there first.*

Cash cleared his throat and returned to the list. "'Demonstrate emotional intelligence—self-awareness, kindness, maturity and the ability to relate to others are all positive qualities in a potential dating partner, and can make or break your pageant experience.'"

Uh-oh.

"That's actually a good piece of advice," she said.

"It is." He gazed at her, then admitted, "I guess I haven't been great about emotional intelligence over the last few months."

She furrowed her brow, questioning the statement.

"With you," he amended.

She was quiet for a moment, then flagged a hand between the two of them as she said, "We might not bring out the best in each other, but I've seen you with your siblings. You've got plenty of emotional intelligence."

He glanced into her pretty blue eyes, caught off guard by the compliment. She didn't seem to be as affected by the moment as he was. She didn't seem to be affected at all, and was just standing there waiting for more pageant advice.

Cash reexamined the sheet, but all the words swam together. Advice about "knowing your why," "looking good and feeling good" and "having fun" all jumbled together in a mess he wasn't emotionally, or otherwise, intelligent enough to untangle.

He stretched his triceps, then tossed aside the paper. "This is mostly just…stuff. And things. You wanna go over the list of possible interview questions?"

"Sure. But just so you know I have every intention of memorizing the list of tips so don't think you're gaining any kind of advantage right now."

"I don't need to gain an advantage I already

have," he responded, bluffing, then rifled through the folder for the list of questions.

The interview questions were even worse than the pageant tips. Were those matchmakers *trying* to get him to bare his soul?

If you could give a twenty-minute TED Talk, what would the topic be?

A twenty-minute—or even one-minute—TED Talk was the last thing he wanted to do. What did he even have to talk about?

How to battle your way out of generational debt?

Five signs your sister has adopted a herd of hoofed mammals?

"Question?" Mylie asked.

Cash scanned the sheet of paper, looking for an easy one. "'If you could be a character from a book, who would you be and why?'" He looked up. "That's easy. The police chief in the Hank O'Brien books. I love that grumpy old guy."

She laughed, another cheerful, honest laugh. Cash had to get his eyes back on the paper before he could appreciate how color rose up her neck when she found something funny.

"You've read the books?" he asked.

"Of course. I love a good mystery."

"Me, too." He was looking at her again. More specifically, he was staring into her pretty blue eyes. Trouble. This friendly, easygoing Mylie was trickier to deal with than her normal, hardheaded self.

"It really is wild how similar Lost Song Ranch in those books is to your place."

Cash shrugged. "Kind of. But when you consider my dad built up Holiday Ranch to look like something out of a Netflix series about wealthy ranchers, it's not that remarkable."

"I guess you're right." She frowned. "But you've heard all the theories people have about who wrote the books?"

"Oh, yeah. Someone Dad cheated out of money, a former employee, one of the women he had an affair with—"

"Some folks say they're written by the son of your old foreman. What was his name? Macintosh?"

Cash sobered. "Heath. Heath Macintosh."

Heath had grown up at Holiday Ranch. All the kids were close, but he'd been a best friend and second brother to Beau. When Dad inevitably tried to cheat Heath's father out of his share of the land, the family packed up and left, never looking back. Dad had done a lot of damage in his day, but creating a rift between Heath and the Holiday siblings had to be one of the hardest to bear.

"Naw." Cash shook his head. "It's not Heath."

"Are you sure? I hear he's a police detective, same job Hank O'Brien has."

"I'm sure." Cash faked a big smile. "What about you? What character from a book would you be?"

"Easy. While you're a grumpy police chief, I'd be Nancy Drew."

"I can see that," Cash said. "Smart, inquisitive, in everybody's business."

"Relentless," she added to his list.

Cash dropped his eyes to the list of questions, lest she use any of the detective skills she'd picked up to read his thoughts. All this sharing made him feel…what? Emotionally squishy? Warm in an uncomfortable way? Definitely not in control. They were similar to feelings his ex-fiancée, Luna, had once inspired, and that hadn't turned out well. Luna had bailed when the family became too much to handle, just like Mom. He couldn't say he blamed either of them.

He scanned the interview questions, each one worse than the last. These weren't topics he wanted to get into on stage, and much less with Mylie.

Who is someone you consider your role model and why?

Dad, who was a daily example of everything I never want to be in this world.

Complete this sentence: I want to win this pageant because—

I'm incredibly worried about my sister. I want to throw money at whatever trouble she's gotten into until it goes away. But if I learned one thing from my antihero role model of a father, it's that throwing money around has dire consequences.

If you were to pick someone other than you to win this pageant, who would it be?

Mylie, obviously. But I have to win, re: my answers to previous questions.

"Oh, here's a good one," he said, finally landing on something that didn't touch on familial dysfunction. "'How would you describe Ripple Creek to someone who has never been here?'"

Mylie was thoughtful for a moment. Then she said, "Ripple Creek is the perfect community."

"Really?"

"Yes." She gave him a quizzical look. "Don't you think it's perfect?"

"No."

"What do you mean *no*? This place is incredible. We're close to some of the best skiing and rock climbing in the world, the town is thriving economically, the citizens are involved—"

"Like Alice and Brick Henderson?" he asked.

"Okay, they're not the easiest to work with. But I'm not real stoked on group work to begin with, so that's just me. You want something done right, do it yourself."

Cash tilted his head to one side. "I disagree. I don't always love working with my siblings, but we accomplish more when we work together."

Something shifted in her eyes, as though the words landed deeper than he intended.

"That's nice. Good for you. I prefer to work on my own." She turned and started straightening the chairs he'd put out, as though to prove her point, muttering some grandpa expletive under her breath.

"Did I say something?" he asked.

"Other than criticizing Ripple Creek and my preferred mode of working?"

"I wasn't criticizing. There are some difficult people in this town—"

"Oh, I know. There's this one guy? Cannot file a zoning permit."

"Hey now, I got that turned in."

Mylie spoke over him. "This town is great, *most of* the people are fantastic. I can't think of a better place, and we're lucky to live here."

"I'm just saying the people here aren't always fantastic. My siblings and I have faced a lot of prejudice for the actions of our father."

"Your father hurt a lot of people."

"My siblings being two of those people," he reminded her.

Maybe his voice was a little harsher than he intended it to be, but Mylie turned on him, a look of hurt in her eyes. "Why are you picking an argument with me right now?"

Was he picking an argument? That was like suggesting he got into it with the weather and the clouds dumped rain in response. Arguments with Mylie, like rainstorms, just happened. He didn't start them, although he was prepared.

"I'm not picking an argument. I'm clarifying your position."

"Well, maybe you can clarify on your own time. I've got work to do."

Cash opened his mouth to remind her he also had work to do. His family was hosting this whole circus. He needed to get back so he could help Beau build the stage they'd be strutting down the next day.

He crossed his arms and stared at her. She raised her chin. It might not be very emotionally intelligent of him, but he wasn't going to apologize for speaking his mind.

"Look, we're stuck together." She gave him a sad smile. Five minutes ago he wasn't feeling stuck at all; he was starting to look forward to Friday afternoon. "I don't like it any more than you do, but there's no getting out of it. You don't need to be nice to me. If I could count on you to stay out of the way and maybe not sabotage me—"

"Who's talking about sabotage?"

"It's what your father would have done."

Wow. Really?

Cash dropped his arms. "That was uncalled for."

"Don't say you haven't thought about it."

"I have not thought about it. I've been thinking a lot of things since this session started, but sabotaging someone in a pageant? That's what you think of me?"

"I just meant—"

"No, I get it. You're like everyone else in this town. You all are perfect, and I'm Bruce Holiday, two-point-oh."

"I didn't say that."

"You did. Thirty seconds ago."

She exhaled, like he was just one of a long line of people she had to deal with today. "Here's what I know about you. You play to win. You put your family first. I'm guessing your willingness to participate in the pageant and urgency to win have something to do with one of your siblings—"

"I'm gonna ask you to leave my family out of this."

"—so I'm sorry if my comment offended you, but how would I know you're not going to try to sabotage me?"

Cash started to defend himself, then stopped. He'd been through this before. People in Ripple Creek made assumptions about his family. Mylie was no different.

"Here's what I know about *you*," he said. "You think you have some kind of moral superiority over me and my siblings because our dad was a problem. We forgot to cross a couple of *t*'s and dot an *i* when we were forced to embrace a new business plan. We turned our way of life upside down in a matter of months to keep our land, and—this may come as a shock—paperwork wasn't our first priority. My siblings asked me to step up and represent the family in this pageant and that's what I'm gonna do."

Cash turned abruptly and headed for the door, but not before he caught a glimpse of vulnerability in her eyes.

But that was the problem with Mayor Mylie Saunders. One minute she was a perfectly nice person, and an attractive person, too. Championing senior citizens, setting up chairs for someone named Becky, all good things. Then she would turn on him in an instant.

He would never sabotage someone in a competition. He didn't have to; he planned to win fair and square. But a lack of sabotage was as far as he was going with Mylie. Not that she wanted his help, or any real partnership in this competition.

She liked to work on her own? Fine by him.

CHAPTER FOUR

THE HAMMER CAME down squarely on the head of the nail. Three solid swings and Cash was onto the next one.

He'd forgotten how much he enjoyed building projects. In recent years Cash had been so focused on keeping the ranch economically viable, he hadn't had time to fix things, let alone build something new. Everything changed when they expanded their business plan to include an events center. When Elliana arrived on the scene, everything on the ranch got a makeover.

He could still remember Tia's glee when she'd earned enough money from her spotty veterinary practice to buy lumber and supplies to repair the split-rail fence that ran around the central yard. The two of them had worked together, joking and laughing as they made their first major repair.

But building the stage he was supposed to walk down modeling activewear while Mylie won round one in her cute pickleball outfit? That felt a little more like building his own plank to walk off a ship.

"Hello?" a voice called out from the open slider door.

"Hi, there!" another voice exclaimed.

"Oh, my God, this looks amazing!"

Cash pulled in a deep breath. The matchmakers had arrived. He pounded in one last nail, then straightened and turned toward the barn door.

"You have outdone yourselves, and literally everyone else on earth. This is perfect!"

Cash couldn't help but smile at Clara and Piper. Enthusiastic hyperbole was not a problem in their world.

"Glad you like it. We haven't hosted any events that required a stage, so I hope this does the trick."

Beau had designed a wide, curved stage at the far end of the barn, plenty of space for contestants to step forward while modeling, but no serious catwalk.

Small blessings.

Elliana had decorated the rest of the rustic barn with a festive, Americana feel: red, white and blue bunting, large bouquets of daisies and black-eyed Susans, fun rows of Broadway lights lining the stage. For a normal event, Cash would look forward to helping out on the sidelines, making sure everything ran smoothly. This time, he was the center of attention. He'd be up on the just-now-finished stage, attempting to be authentically excited about standing next to Mylie and answering interview questions.

Just a normal day in the life: wake up at 5:00 a.m., move the cattle to the west pasture, arrange five bouquets of flowers, finish building a stage and participate in a singles pageant. The next person to refer to ranching as "the simple life" was gonna get an earful.

Cash dropped his hammer back in the toolbox and jogged over to Piper and Clara. Their arms were full of clipboards, scorecards and other pageant paraphernalia, including a pale blue sash with Round One Winner written across it. That sparked his interest.

Cash's childhood bedroom had been brimming with trophies, banners, carefully constructed, first-place-winning Pinewood Derby cars and flyers acknowledging his achievements. He wasn't much of a sash guy, but he intended to claim this one.

"Is that what you're wearing?" Piper asked.

Cash looked down at his jeans and tool belt. "Umm?"

"No," Tia called out as she slipped into the barn, two greyhounds at her heels. "Cash, I've got your outfit right here."

Tia, and the rest of the family, had been incredibly helpful with all things pageant—a blatant attempt to assuage their guilt over signing him up for it in the first place. It was all very nice, but it robbed him of the opportunity to be annoyed. That said, when Elliana had offered to help with his wardrobe, he gratefully accepted, no questions asked or grumbles given.

"Well, go get changed!" Piper flagged him toward the main house. "Run-through is in ten minutes and the show starts in an hour."

“Also, Mylie’s going to be arriving at the last minute because she has a meeting at the senior center,” Clara said. “You’ll have to fill her in on everything.”

Cash started to make a comment about Mylie being late but held his tongue, emotional intelligence and all.

Tia tugged his arm and he followed her, and her greyhounds, into the sunshine.

“How are you doing?” he asked as they crossed the central yard toward the main house.

“You know…great!”

“Do I know that?”

Tia pressed her lips together. Cash wondered if this was the moment she was finally going to tell him what was up. She inhaled, then glanced at him out of the side of her eye.

“Well, the matchmakers were all like ‘maybe don’t let the donkey roam free while everyone arrives.’ That’s not optimum. Kevin has been a little depressed recently and—”

Cash groaned.

“What? He has been sad. Guests always cheer him up.”

“Tia, I love you.”

“I love you, too.”

“But we can’t assume all visitors to Holiday Ranch feel as comfortable around animals as you do.”

“That’s what Elliana said about peacocks at a

dance party and you remember how that turned out."

"Tia!" he snapped. "I'm worried about *you.* Not Kevin the donkey, not that herd of self-important peacocks."

"It's called a muster," she said quietly, as though she was compelled to keep bickering, but her heart wasn't in it. "That's what you call a group of peafowl, a muster. Or an ostentation." She was full-on mumbling now. "But that's more of like an internet thing."

Cash forced himself to drop the conversation and smile at other contestants as they arrived, all looking sporty in their chosen outfits. He scanned the drive for Mylie. They'd had one quick text exchange. She'd written This is Mylie Saunders. He'd stamped a like on her text. That was the only communication since the meeting. So far, this partner thing wasn't going real well.

Cash settled an arm around his sister's shoulder and said the same phrase he'd been using with her since she was twelve. "I'm here to talk whenever you're ready."

Tia nodded. "Same. I know you're upset about the pageant and if you want to talk about it, I'm here for you."

He scoffed. Like talking out his feelings was gonna help. He could talk all day long and he'd still be stuck doing it, so why dwell on it?

He'd tried to prepare for the interview questions and still had no idea how to respond to any of them.

It was hard to be authentic when you didn't want to relive a painful past. He closed his eyes briefly, drawing up an image of the blue winner's sash. Mylie would do well, no question. He needed to rally and make the most of the opportunity. Tia needed money, and he intended to win it for her.

Tia changed the subject, chattering on about a meeting with the DuBoff family. Apparently, the wealthy couple wanted to come back a second time before they decided if Holiday Ranch was the right place for their only son's wedding. Cash had faith in Elliana's ability to get them to book the ranch, but they'd all be relieved when she nailed down a deposit.

As they neared the main house, Cash held out his hand to accept the outfit Elliana had prepared for him. For the first time, he registered the garments: plaid shorts, a polo shirt and boat shoes.

What the what?

"Can you please explain what I'm wearing?" he asked Tia.

"Not really, Elliana picked it out."

"Picked it out of where? A yacht club from 1987?"

She shrugged. "Maybe?"

"Okay, I love you, Tia."

"I love you, too. And those shorts aren't too bad."

"These shorts should be banned by international law. Or *Vogue*. Whoever makes those decisions." Tia started to interrupt him but Cash spoke over her. "You realize that if you all had come together and picked the *one* thing I would never want to do, it would be a pageant?"

Tia tilted her head to one side, an *umm* ready to roll, but Cash cut her off. "This is the worst! *This?*" He held up the outfit. "I have to talk in front of an audience, and Mylie's going to be here—"

"Oh, do you not want Mylie to see you in that outfit?"

"I don't want anyone to see me in this outfit. I don't want to *be* in this outfit."

"Because Mylie did just see you all dressed up for Beau's wedding, and she noticed. I think the sharp suit and this—whatever this is—evens out. She'll still think you're attractive."

"This has nothing to do with the mayor finding me attractive. Which she doesn't."

"Umm?"

"Enough. Why am I arguing with you?"

"Great question."

"I'm gonna get this over with."

Tia came back with some chipper response, but Cash couldn't hear her over his own grumbling. He stalked into the house, muttering in a manner exhibiting neither poise nor emotional maturity. Minutes later, having squeezed into the polo shirt and shorts, he returned to the barn. Other participants bopped around in hiking gear, cycling shorts, even a full-on retro Jazzercise outfit. Cash just tried to ignore the uncomfortable feeling of his bare feet in leather shoes. What even was he supposed to be representing?

"Can I have everyone's attention?" Piper asked. "We're gonna do a quick run-through. Remember, authenticity is the name of the game here. You don't have to be perfect, you just have to be you."

Cash's authentic self never would have agreed to this outfit.

The matchmakers led them through the opening sequence. They would all came out on stage and pose as an announcer read off their names and professions. Then everyone would reassemble behind a set of large black curtains Elliana had rented for the occasion, and wait for their turn. The announcer would call up each pair, they'd model their outfits, then be asked an interview question at random.

"Up first, we have Mylie and Cash."

"We're first?" Cash asked. That was good. Not only would they get it over with, but he'd also have the opportunity to make a good impression right off the bat.

Or as good an impression as anyone could make in plaid shorts.

"Yep!" Clara said. "Then Rafael and Bobbie."

Cash glanced at the open slider door at the far end of the barn. Mylie still wasn't here. If she ran in late, she might not be in top form. That would allow him to establish a firm lead in the first event, making it easier to maintain the lead for the entire pageant.

Except…

Was that fair to Mylie?

Sure, she was the one running in late. That was on her. Where had Piper said the meeting was?

Cash thought back to the conversation. She was at the…?

At the senior center.

Right, she was most likely helping seniors get more involved in Ripple Creek while he was plotting her pageant demise. Classic Bruce Holiday move, just like she expected.

Music blasted out the speakers, an upbeat, joyful song about having high hopes. Seating in the barn was filling up quickly. Were all these people really here to watch eight unmarried people walk across the stage?

"Ten minutes!" Clara called to the contestants.

Finally, Cash broke down and pulled out his phone to text Mylie.

Where you at?

Little bubbles popped up, then disappeared. Finally a message came through.

Don't end a sentence with a preposition.

Cash resisted the urge to hurl the phone out the barn door.

Bubbles popped up again, then: You don't need the 'at.' It's implied.

He texted back.

Are you okay!

Then he sent an additional text with the intended question mark.

?

Or was that *implied*?

OMW was her response.

What did she mean? Was it a mistake? Had she gotten into a car accident texting and driving, and all that came through was this nonsense pile of letters, *OMW*?

"Line up, everybody!" Clara called.

Cash ran over to Clara, holding out his phone. "Mylie's not here."

"She'll get here," Clara said cheerfully, like she had a drone out keeping an eye on the highway and had just received an update on Mylie's location.

"Yeah. But she's not *here*."

The music faded. Piper's voice came rolling out over the speakers. "Let's hear it for this year's Most Eligible contestants!"

And suddenly, Cash was being shepherded through the black curtains. He was not prepared for the massive audience, cheering as they walked on stage. His competitors were, though. They took up poses highlighting their outfits. Bobbie wore a bright, sporty dress and brought a golf club with her. Daisy jogged in place in her Nikes. Myron wore a floppy-brimmed hat and posed with a pair of birding binoculars.

Since Cash had no idea what his outfit was, he just crossed his arms and struck a pose, trying to look like he knew what he was repping in his ridiculous shorts.

The music was loud and the lights blinding as Piper introduced everyone and stated their profession. Cash was gratified to hear a cheer go up when he was referred to as Head Cattle Wrangler and Chief Florist at Holiday Ranch. He couldn't say what possessed him, but he stepped forward as the crowd cheered. In a cocky move with a serious expression on his face, he pointed to the bouquets of flowers he had grown and arranged, thank you very much. The cheer grew louder. Cash grinned at the crowd and pumped a fist over his head. Myron turned his binoculars on a large arrangement and pretended to see a bird in it. The crowd laughed as Myron and Cash exchanged a high five.

Huh.

This was unexpectedly enjoyable. The first five minutes of the pageant were turning out to be a lot more fun than he'd anticipated.

The music changed and everyone exited the stage. Piper took the microphone and spoke seriously about childhood literacy while Clara checked her clipboard backstage. "Cash and Mylie are up first!"

Mylie still wasn't here. She couldn't win the first round if she wasn't here for it.

If I could count on you to stay out of the way and maybe not sabotage me.

Was it sabotage to follow the rules, and reap the benefits of being here on time? Maybe not, but inasmuch as he lived here, it wasn't like being on time was any big achievement for him. Plus, it felt like the type of letter-of-the-law technicality Mylie was always drilling down on. If he was going to win the pageant, he needed to embrace the spirit of it. In spirit, he needed to help his partner out.

Cash drew in a deep breath, and approached Clara again. "Hey, Mylie's still not here. Are you okay if we change up the order?"

"Oh, wait, she's *still* not here?" Clara looked over his shoulder to scan the group.

Cash shook his head.

"She had a meeting at the senior center, and I bet it went long," Clara said. "Okay, Caleb and Daisy, you're up!"

As Caleb and Daisy ran on stage, Clara smiled at Cash. He had the feeling he'd just passed some kind of a test.

He'd studied the scoring rubric pretty carefully. Some of the terms were a little vague. Poise? What even was poise? But maybe his move had gained him a few congeniality points. He didn't kid himself into thinking he'd gain any points with Mylie for delaying their entrance. That was a sum-zero game.

MUSIC BLASTED OUT of the barn as Mylie sprinted across the yard. She took a detour around the Holiday peacocks, tail feathers spread in annoyance like a menacing 1970s glam-rock band.

If she missed the first event, it would be hard—nearly impossible—to make up the points. Then she would be stuck competing in this pageant, forced to watch Cash win. There would be no source of funding for Club 75. She'd look foolish in front of the community, which could fuel the recall. The whole thing would be a waste of time, a blow to her ego and fodder for her opponents.

Not at all what she hoped to get out of the experience.

It was her own fault. She'd slid in the meeting at the senior center because she wanted to get ahead of the game with Club 75. And anyone who thought a meeting with a group of underserved citizens excited about an idea aimed to support them wasn't going to go overtime deserved to be late. That said, it had been a productive meeting, and fun. Some of those ladies had a wicked sense of humor.

Mylie ran in through the open sliding door at the end of the barn. Her first impression was, "Wow!"

Which she said out loud, to no one in particular.

The Holiday siblings had gone all out. Not four days ago, the barn was all wildflowers and whimsical wedding decorations. Today, it was Americana chic. The decor was rustic, but cool and fresh at the same time.

"Mylie! Over here!" Cash's deep rumble met her ear through the music.

Making her second impression, "Whoa!"

Because, *plaid shorts*?

Mylie slipped backstage with Cash as she asked, "What are you wearing?"

"Where have you been?"

"Did I miss our catwalk?" she asked. Myron and Nesa were already out on stage, so the answer was yes. *Dad burn it!*

"No, you didn't miss it. I asked Clara to move us to the end, but we're up there in minutes. Where were you at? I was worried you got in an accident."

He—he asked Clara to change the order? He absolutely did not have to do that. He gazed at her, something like actual concern in his eyes. Sure, he was human. He wouldn't want anyone to get in a car accident. Presumably. But all the same.

Mylie looked at him, unsure of how to react. She swallowed, then said. "Can you hear how the *at* is unnecessary? You could just write 'where are you?'"

He shook his head, but didn't break eye contact as a smile emerged on his lips. "I cannot remember why I even try with you."

"I was at the senior center, and the meeting ran late. It was completely my fault. I lost track of time, and when I realized how late I was, it was still hard to get out. I'm sorry. And thank you." She gestured to the stage. "You didn't have to wait."

He crossed his arms, his eyes running down her pickleball outfit, then to the stage. "I don't wanna be accused of sabotage."

"I never should have said that. I'm sorry."

He pulled his head back, like he didn't know what to do with her apology. They stood there, Mylie grappling with his kindness, Cash unsure of how to react to a sincere apology.

Good thing no one was judging them on emotional maturity at the moment.

"Cash and Mylie, you're up!"

Mylie glanced at Clara where she was swinging her arm, urging them to walk on stage. In her other hand she held a pale blue sash.

"Oh, wait, the winner gets a sash?" Mylie asked.

"It's gonna go perfectly with my outfit," Cash muttered.

For the first time Mylie took a good look at his clothing. "What…are you? Lawn games?"

"That's what it is!" Cash said. "I couldn't figure it out but you must be right. Wait, I need a croquet mallet or something."

The music shifted, and an upbeat song came blasting through the speakers. No time for him to grab a prop, and she already had her pickleball paddle in hand. Cash sighed, then gestured for Mylie to enter ahead of him.

Mylie was not fully prepared for the lights, or the energy of the crowd. She walked on stage, smile set in place, giving a few perfunctory swings of her pickleball paddle to polite applause. But then, an even bigger cheer rose.

She looked behind her to find Cash completely hamming it up. Somehow he'd gotten ahold of a stack of cornhole beanbags and was tossing them into the audience. He bounded across the stage, making the simple lawn game look like an Olympic event.

She never should have told him he looked like he was dressed for lawn games. He'd have just been standing around awkwardly in boat shoes.

Not one to admit defeat, much less be upstaged by a man in plaid shorts, Mylie swung into action, literally. She morphed her walk into a net rush and mimed an overhead smash. The crowd, which had never seen, or expected to see, their mayor acting goofy on stage, went wild. Energized by the competition, Cash pretended to "catch" her imaginary ball and keep it away from her.

By this point the audience was laughing and cheering. Someone threw one of the beanbags back on stage and Mylie grabbed it, offering it for the imaginary pickleball. They made the exchange and the crowd applauded joyfully.

Cash caught her eye. She grinned back.

Maybe there were times when a little teamwork paid off?

Piper's voice came over the loudspeakers. "It's time to meet Cash and Mylie!" Mylie peered into the audience to see Piper sitting at a table, microphone in front of her. Clara slipped out from backstage and took a seat next to her sister. They were not the judge lineup from *The Voice*, but somehow Mylie felt just as intimidated.

She stood next to Cash, then remembered her signature pose: one hand casually on her hip, one foot forward, big smile. Cash noticed her pose, then attempted one of his own. First he crossed his arms, then he dropped them, then he imitated her pose before apparently realizing that wasn't gonna work at all, and recrossed his arms. All his shuffling around had to shake a few points off him, didn't it?

"It's time for our couples' interview, with a twist!" Piper said.

"So fun!" Clara chimed in.

Why was there always a twist when Piper or Clara were involved?

"Do you remember what the twist is?" Mylie asked Cash through a smile.

"No, am I supposed to?"

"What's been happening on stage?"

"I don't know. I've been distracted, thinking my partner had been in a car accident."

"Why would you think I was in a car accident?"

"Because you were late and texting nonsense."

"What nonsense?"

Piper looked at the two of them expectantly, patience stretched but not quite ready to snap. She spoke slowly. "To recap, contestants were given a list of possible interview questions. For our show today, Cash will answer a question for Mylie, then Mylie will answer for Cash! So fun!"

There's no way that the front row, at least, couldn't hear Cash groan.

"Question number one, for Cash, about Mylie. Who is someone Mylie admires as a role model, and why?"

He stared at her, fear clouding his eyes. They'd had no conversations about people she admired. He didn't even know who her close friends were. She could almost see his brain churning through possibilities, trying to work it out.

She also knew it had to be seriously difficult for him not to make some smart comment about her admiring Boss Hogg or some other ineffectual fictional politician.

Mylie thought hard, hoping the names in her head could somehow float into his.

Jane Goodall, Angela Merkel, Oprah Winfrey.

Then a smile spread across his face, something seeming to come into his mind. All Mylie could do was pray for the best.

"Nancy Drew," Cash said with a satisfied nod. "Nancy is smart, proactive and highly capable. I mean, she solved over five hundred mysteries before she was even old enough to vote."

The audience laughed.

"Beyond that, Nancy has a sense of service to her community. Say what you will about her, Mylie's priority is Ripple Creek. In her own words, this town is perfect. She'll do whatever it takes to keep it that way. Mylie, and Nancy, are relentless when something important is at stake. They'll get the job done. And when they finish one project they're not sitting back waiting for applause, they're on to the next."

Mylie felt oddly warm. Possibly happy. Cash, whom she'd had as many arguments with as Nancy had mysteries to solve, was smiling at her. She was grinning straight back.

He hadn't said anything untrue, but the way he said it felt sweet. Often, her work as mayor was thankless. And Cash had one of the loudest "no thank yous" around. But without lying, or padding the truth, he'd illuminated her best. That wasn't something most folks, or anyone recently, had taken the time to do.

Of course, he did it so he could beat her in the pageant, but whatever.

"Thank you, Cash." Clara looked from one of them, to the other. "That's lovely."

"Mylie, you're up next," Piper said. "If Cash could give a twenty-minute TED Talk, what would it be about?"

Okay, now that just wasn't fair. Cash could talk for twenty minutes about a whole mess of topics. Why he shouldn't have to abide by business zoning laws. Why it was okay, in their case, to serve alcohol without a permit because their signature cocktails were intentionally low-alcohol. That the two rescue greyhounds snoozing in the kitchen they used to prepare food for guests shouldn't count because no one could actually consider them dogs.

She bit down on her bottom lip, searching for a good answer. What did she even know about Cash? He liked herding cattle, he grew the flowers they used at events. He gazed into her eyes, as though reminding her he had some important reason for wanting to win. What was it again?

Right. It was his reason for wanting to win this pageant and for engaging in every single argument with her.

"Cash would talk about the importance of family."

Mylie could hear the gasp from the crowd. The memory of Bruce Holiday and his unethical, harmful actions were fresh in Ripple Creek's collective memory. So was the prejudice against the Holiday family. The siblings had made huge strides to overcome the stigma. That didn't mean there weren't still people, even here in the audience assembled on their ranch, who still cringed when they heard the words *Holiday* and *family* in the same sentence.

"More than most of us, Cash understands families can be complicated. But he is steadfast in his support of his siblings. Spend five minutes around him and you'll hear him tell Beau or Tia that he loves them. You'll find him putting out a saucer of milk for one of Tia's cats, or texting Beau to remind him of weather conditions as he drives over Santiam Pass. All this—" she gestured to the renovated barn and the land beyond "—was done to hold on to their property so Tia and Beau could have a place to call home. Cash, as the oldest, has always supported his brother and sister."

She had the audience now; citizens who had gleefully misjudged the family were misty-eyed as she praised Cash.

"Don't get me wrong, during his TED Talk, Cash will take a little time to brag. We'll hear all about how Beau is a firefighter and a hero, about his work in fire prevention. We'll be regaled with stories about how truly incredible Tia is with animals, and how he's proud of her rescue efforts. Even if he pretends to be annoyed by her alpacas." The audience chuckled. "He'll boast about his new sister-in-law, Elliana. Speaking of, isn't this event fantastic?"

The crowd gave a huge cheer. Mylie could see Elliana standing at the back of the crowd, tucked up under Beau's arm, wrapped up in Mylie's kind words about the family.

"The message coming through in Cash's TED Talk, which, by the way, he'd never agree to in the first place, is that being part of a strong family is a choice. It's about telling your family members you love them. It's about working together to solve problems. It's about taking one for the team, whether that means dressing up in a bunny suit, or entering a singles' pageant."

Warm, heavy applause broke out, like a summer rainstorm on a tin roof.

Cash was staring at her as though he'd never seen her before. And after giving her little speech, it felt like maybe she'd never exactly seen *him* before, either. Sure, all those words came out of her mouth, but when she put them together she realized something that hadn't occurred to her before. Cash Holiday was actually a pretty good guy.

Why did that realization make her nervous?

"Love it!" Clara's voice came through the speakers after they'd been staring at each other in silence for who knew how long. "Let's hear it for Cash and Mylie!"

A second round of applause and loud music were a welcome distraction. Mylie slipped past Cash and headed offstage.

She intentionally greeted others backstage, chatting with Myron, then Rafael, getting herself farther away from the man she'd just praised up one side and down the other in front of their community.

On stage, Piper was talking. "Before we announce the winner of round one, we'd like to remind you all about the community service meet and greet. Sunday afternoon, each of the contestants will be on hand at the community center to tell you about how they serve Ripple Creek and offer ideas on how you can get involved!"

"Uh-oh," Cash mumbled, and even though there were a solid four people between them, Mylie could hear him clearly. She excused herself from a conversation with Nesa and looped back to Cash.

"What's wrong?" Mylie whispered.

He shrugged dismissively, but his face told another story.

"What?"

"I don't exactly have a robust résumé of community service."

Mylie felt a zing of excitement at his words. She had a very robust résumé of service. If one had no respect for the English language, they might even say the robust-est.

"My family was ostracized from Ripple Creek for years," he continued. "Kinda hard to volunteer at the library when your dad cheated the head of the library board out of her water rights, then tried to seduce her."

Mylie deflated. She intended to win the community service category, but could she leave Cash out on a limb? He'd orchestrated this afternoon so she could participate. It would be petty of her not to return the favor.

"What about the whole Easter celebration your family hosted?"

"That's just once a year, and we've only had one year. Plus, there's no way I'm dressing up like a bunny again."

Cash's jaw was set; he looked legitimately nervous. Then he glanced over his shoulder. Mylie followed his gaze and saw Tia, who wore the same worried expression she'd had at the wedding. Cash had told her he had to participate in the pageant to help out his family. Did it have something to do with Tia?

"I'll help you come up with a community service platform," she said.

He pulled back his head, shocked. "Umm?"

"It's only fair. You asked them to reorder our entrance so I could get a chance to participate today. I'll help you come up with a service idea."

He held her eye for a moment. "Do you have time tomorrow?"

"We'll have to make time. The meet and greet is on Sunday."

He dropped eye connect, then gave one solid nod. "Thank you."

Music blasted through the speakers again. This time, the theme to the Miss America Pageant. Cash inhaled and Mylie gave the slightest eye roll as they walked back on stage with the rest of the contestants. The audience applauded, and some let out whistles. A group of teenagers yelled out, "Let's go, Mayor Mylie!"

"Your fan club?" Cash asked under his breath.

"Future Leaders of America," Mylie whispered back. "A club I advise at the high school."

"I didn't realize our future leaders were gonna be so loud."

While it felt nice to hear the kids cheering, Mylie's gaze caught on a couple in the third row. Not everyone in town appreciated her doing well in this competition, or on any occasion. For Brick and Alice Henderson, the more popularity Mylie gained, the more threatened they felt.

"What a phenomenal showing for our first event!" Piper cried.

"Can you believe how amazing everyone was?" Clara asked the crowd.

The applause grew louder as Piper asked, "Who's ready to meet our winners?"

Clara took the microphone from her sister, her dimpled smile flashing. "First, I want to say all the numbers were very close. It's basically an eight-way tie at this point, but a few contestants edged ahead."

Mylie locked eyes with Cash. Were the numbers really close? Because even though she'd only seen one other couple, she and Cash had delivered a significantly more exciting performance.

"Contestants gain points with each competition, and the winner is the contestant with the most points at the end," Clara said.

"So a person could not place in a single competition, but still accumulate the overall highest score and win," Piper explained.

"But it's a pageant, so we have to have sashes," Clara added. "We're excited to announce our third-place contestant—"

Piper took the microphone and said, "Look out for our bird watcher, Myron Banks!"

Myron put his hands on his cheeks, thrilled with the third-place victory, and stepped forward to claim his sash.

"This is so perfect," Piper said. "The green totally coordinates with his outfit."

"You look amazing!" Clara concurred.

Myron puffed out his chest and straightened the sash.

"And second place goes to—"

Cash tensed. His jaw twitched, like it did when he was pretending to be calm in a meeting.

"Cash Holiday, rocking the lawn games!"

Mylie could feel his exhalation of annoyance.

But he kept a smile locked on his face and didn't swear out loud.

"Congratulations on second place," Mylie said. Cash glowered at her, but managed to act excited and grateful as he walked forward to accept his pink sash, which did *not* go with his outfit.

"The winner tonight, of the activewear and interview portion of the contest, is—"

Clara paused dramatically, scanning the group on stage before she spoke, but Mylie already knew. The cool feeling of satisfaction and relief. She'd done her best, and her best was better than anyone else's.

"Our pickleball-playing mayor, Mylie Saunders!"

Mylie grinned wickedly at Cash, then stepped forward to claim her sash. As Clara slipped the satin over her head, Piper lifted the microphone to speak.

Mylie tensed briefly, wondering what they would say. Growing up in a family that valued public validation of success, praise mattered. Her parents had certainly written more than one strongly worded email dressing down a presenter for not celebrating one of their children to their standards.

"We are all impressed by our mayor's energy and elegance, but what really tipped the scales was how well she represented her partner. Mylie, your understanding of Cash and his connection to family is admirable. Your poise and consideration in describing his TED Talk earned you big points tonight. Interpersonal skills are part of what makes someone a contender for most eligible, and you certainly have them. Congratulations, Mayor Mylie!"

Music came pouring through the speakers, and applause made it impossible to hear the congratulations from the other candidates. But the look Cash gave her spoke volumes. She'd won this round, but in doing so she realized she wasn't the only one with something to lose.

CHAPTER FIVE

*W**as this a* *good idea?*

It didn't feel like a good idea as Mylie stood at the split-rail fence, scanning Holiday Ranch. The property was quiet this summer afternoon. Peacocks pecked the ground outside the barn. A turtle had its head stretched up to catch the sun as a cat crept by at a leisurely pace. That was about all the action going down in the normally busy central yard.

Mylie had been to Holiday Ranch countless times, attending parties, informing Cash about basic business violations. But she'd never come out to do anyone a favor. Unless you counted enforcing a noise ordinance as a favor.

But Cash was expecting her. Right? It had been a pretty quick conversation after the show. Her offer to help Cash choose a community service platform had been made in an honest attempt to repay his thoughtfulness in reordering their appearance in the pageant. He'd thanked her for the offer. She said something about it being no trouble. Somehow they'd wound up at the idea that she'd come back here. Did he invite her, or did she suggest coming out? She couldn't remember. And at this point did he even remember she was coming at all?

No, this had been a bad idea from the start. Now that she was here, it felt like an intrusion.

"Hello there!" Elliana called, stepping out of the main house. As always, she looked perfectly put-together in a cotton floral dress and cute sneakers. "I love your top!"

Mylie glanced down at her shirt, a simple, white sleeveless blouse she'd kept a jacket over for a quick meeting with the interfaith council. "Thank you."

"White is great on you."

"Is it?" Mylie asked.

Elliana widened her eyes and nodded.

"I never really know what works, you know? I feel like I have a good business wardrobe, but I'm not really sure what to wear in my off time."

Or even what to *do* in her off time, but that was a different story.

"I'm always up for a shopping trip if you want to go," Elliana said with a warm smile.

"That would be great." Mylie was taken aback by the unexpected offer. "I could use some help, and you have fantastic style."

"And now that we're finally making some money, I can go shopping again." Elliana smiled. "What brings you to Holiday Ranch today?"

She asked the question with no malice, as though Mylie hadn't shown up here with complaints for months on end as the event center got up and running. Mylie drew in a breath. Why was she here? Something about helping her nemesis make a decent showing in the community service meet and greet.

Before she could answer, Tia came streaming out a side door, her head cocked in true confusion.

"Really? Is this where we are? You like Holiday Ranch now?"

"I— Well…"

"Nope. Stop." Elliana held out a palm to Tia. "No arguing. Mylie was just doing her job. We made a few mistakes when we got this business running. All is *good*." Elliana emphasized the word, making it clear she would brook no argument. Everyone was required to be good.

"I wasn't arguing, I was checking. I heard all the nice things she said yesterday." Tia turned to Mylie. "Are you here to practice with Cash?"

"I'm here to help—"

"He's in the house," Tia said. "I'll take you. Do you want to say hello to the donkey first?"

"Sure?" Mylie looked at Elliana to see if this was the right response, but Elliana was already slipping a cross-body bag over her shoulder and heading toward the circular drive.

"Have fun practicing with Cash!" Elliana waved to Mylie, then turned to Tia. "You all should go ahead with dinner whenever. Beau is heading into town to work with some kids at the high school this evening. I'm meeting with the DuBoffs to discuss the viability of transporting cream puffs."

"Have they still not booked the site?" Tia asked.

"They have booked three sites, and will be canceling all but one of them by Friday. Holiday Ranch is in the lead, but they want to make sure there's not going to be a freshness issue with the cream puffs."

"And we're bending over backward for these people, why?" Tia asked.

Elliana placed her fingertips together in front of her heart and spoke seriously. "So much money. Imagine a lake full of cash."

"Would the cash not get wet?"

Elliana rolled her eyes.

"Joking! It's a great image, though. Go have fun with the DuBoffs," Tia said, then she turned to Mylie. "Let's go say hi to Kevin."

Presumably Kevin was a donkey, but who really knew at this point? Maybe they had another sibling stashed away on the premises somewhere. Tia took long strides across the central yard. Mylie hurried to keep up.

"I'm glad we don't have to dislike you anymore," Tia said, two physical steps and any number of conversational steps ahead of Mylie. "Because I have this whole thing I wanted to talk to you about."

Mylie paused in their walk across the central yard. Her gut told her Cash's determination to win the pageant was somehow tied to Tia. Was it something Mylie could help with?

"What's up?"

Tia paused with her, and crossed her arms. She

looked over her shoulder at the turtle, then back at Mylie.

"How do you feel about alpacas?"

Okay, so maybe this wasn't the big family issue.

"Love 'em." Mylie said. "There's the one you brought to Pam's bridal shower, what was his name?"

"Alfonzo. He's such a glamor guy."

"He was very sweet."

"So I was thinking. Cash mentioned you were trying to start a club for older people—"

"He did?"

"Was it a secret?"

"No, but—"

But Cash was talking about her to his siblings? In a presumably good way, if he'd mentioned the club. Unless he, too, thought helping Ripple Creek's seniors "wasn't a good use of city funding."

"I mean, honestly, a secret club for elderly folks sounds awesome. You could call it a gang and have a special handshake."

"No. It's not a secret. As the mayor, I do almost nothing in secret."

Tia threw up her hands and let out a dejected sigh. "Well, there goes that theory."

"What theory?" Mylie was really trying to keep up here.

"That all politicians are funded by, and accountable to, secret societies started by Leonardo da Vinci."

"Is that a widely acknowledged theory?" Mylie

asked, before catching the sly smile on Tia's face. "You're joking."

"I am. About the funding of politicians. I do think a secret club for senior citizens would be lit." Mylie started to interrupt but Tia kept talking. "But since it's not a secret, I was thinking maybe Alfonzo could come visit sometime?"

And finally, like a flight touching down after a turbulent ride, the conversation landed on solid ground.

"Yes! I love the idea of Alfonzo coming to visit Club 75. If the club gets approved." And funded, which was contingent on Cash *not* winning this pageant. But if Cash didn't win, he couldn't help his family with whatever it was they so desperately needed.

"Why wouldn't a gang for elders get approved?" Tia asked.

"I really think we need to not call it a gang," Mylie said.

"Then the *only* option we have left is a secret society."

Mylie laughed. Tia's eyes shone for a moment, then clouded over. She turned to study one of the buildings across the central yard, something that looked like a fancy, two-story guesthouse. Her head drooped, the action accentuated by the movement of her wavy, auburn hair.

Mylie's instinct was to keep talking, to start in on the plans and logistics of visiting alpacas. But she forced herself to remain silent, hoping to encourage Tia to speak more freely.

"You're a lawyer, aren't you?" Tia asked.

"I am. Mayor of Ripple Creek is a full-time job, but I still take the occasional case."

Tia gazed at her, like she wanted to ask something more. Then she gestured toward the main house. "Cash is expecting you?"

"I think so."

By this point she actually couldn't remember. They'd parted awkwardly the day before. Mylie had messaged him a time window in which she could come out to the ranch, and he'd responded by liking the text.

This whole encounter with Cash was getting more awkward by the moment, and it hadn't even started. Fortunately, there was a donkey to meet. Alfonzo the alpaca, not to be left out of a social gathering, joined the conversation. Tia's cheerful suggestions for renaming Club 75 something out of a Dan Brown novel were a welcome distraction. Together they'd burned a good twenty minutes before arriving at the large double doors and formal entry into the main house.

"Okay, have fun! I'm sure Cash is wondering where you are by now," Tia said as she opened a door for Mylie.

"Thank you." Mylie held Tia's gaze for a moment, then said, "If you ever want to talk about practicing law or legal issues, just let me know."

Tia froze, ever so briefly, like a kid with one

hand in a cookie jar and the other clutching four snickerdoodles. Like if she moved ve-e-ery slowly no one would notice she'd even been there.

"Or the nonexistent role of secret societies in local government," Mylie added.

"Yes. The last thing." Tia grinned, but the smile didn't reach her eyes. Mylie had clearly said the wrong thing. Tia waved, head drooping as she and the greyhounds took off, moving back across the central yard, in the direction of the guesthouse.

Mylie stepped over the threshold into the cool quiet of the Holiday family home. She'd only entered through these doors once, attending a bridal shower for her dear friend Pam. At the time, she'd experienced trepidation at walking into what she thought of as Bruce Holiday's home. There was a lot more trepidation now that she fully understood it was Cash who lived here.

"Hello?" Mylie called out.

She was standing in what was arguably the world's most beautiful entryway. Or at least the prettiest in central Oregon. Solid wood floors and wainscoting gleamed in the natural light. Large bouquets of flowers stood on either side of the doors, and a long, antique sideboard held brochures for Holiday Ranch. An open, double staircase curved around either side of the foyer, creating a visual portal into the main room. Mylie drifted down two steps, into the larger space. The last time she was here a cheerful group of women were accepting cocktails from Beau as Elliana directed guests to settle in on the rich, leather sofas. A stone fireplace and thoughtful groupings of furniture lent a coziness to the big space, while sky-high vaulted ceilings ensured grandeur. A wall of windows faced west, with a view of the rolling front lawn, the lake and a little stone bridge crossing a tributary to Ripple Creek. In the distance, Mylie could see the Cascade Mountains.

But she didn't see any people.

"Hello?" she called out again.

What if Cash hadn't really wanted her help and was just being polite when she offered? What if she'd driven all this way and he wasn't expecting her to show up? So awkward.

Hello there, gorgeous, frustrating man! I'm just stopping by to give you, my biggest competition, tips on how to win.

Whatever. She said she'd come out to help, and she was coming out to help. She had five proposals of community service he could get involved in. If he didn't want to talk, she'd just leave. No problem. It wasn't like this would be the first time Cash had insulted her.

Mylie turned in place, calling out another greeting. When she'd been here for Pam's shower, she'd desperately wanted to snoop around. She loved exploring homes, and had a guilty pleasure of scrolling through real-estate sites. There was something oddly relaxing about looking at houses she would never want to be responsible for maintaining, in places she would never want to live.

Was it snooping if she was trying to find the person she was here to meet?

Mylie moved across the main room, coming to a hallway with wainscoting, and large, framed oil paintings at eye level, that led into a massive dining room. The furniture was huge and heavy, like it had been purchased by a really fancy giant. But at one end of the carved, wooden table there were four placemats set out, a notepad, several pens and a pile of mail next to a water glass someone had left. The room might be overkill, but that didn't stop the Holiday family from cozying up at one end of it.

From there she poked her head into the kitchen: tall wooden cabinets, expensive appliances and… was that the Nuova Simonelli espresso maker? Mylie laughed out loud, alone in the kitchen as she faced the machine that launched her law career in Ripple Creek.

One of her first cases had been defending the man who used to service the machine. He was the only brand-certified service tech in a hundred miles, and the finicky, many-thousand-dollar machine needed to be cleaned and tuned up regularly. Bruce Holiday had insulted the technician, and the guy, rightfully, refused to come back to the house. Bruce then sued the service tech, trying to force him to return and care for the espresso machine. Where a case like this might ordinarily just get thrown out, Bruce Holiday had done his research. He came armed with case studies, precedent and civil-rights concerns.

He was a force. But so was Mylie.

She'd won the case, much to Bruce's shock. He'd bad-mouthed her all over town. Bruce's smear campaign backfired, resulting in several requests for Mylie to run for city council.

Mylie examined the machine. Judging from the hopper full of espresso beans, it looked like the Holiday siblings had the machine up and running. Good on them.

Mylie backtracked out of the kitchen, all trepidation replaced by the fluttering excitement of exploring a big, beautiful house. She passed through the great room and down a hall. She peeked into a stately home office that looked like it hadn't been used in years, possibly abandoned for the dining-room table. She looked in on a craft room, poked her head into a library with a *rolling ladder*.

This mansion was no joke.

She stepped into the library and scanned the shelves. The Dan Brown that Tia had referenced was in attendance, along with what looked like the entire cannon of Agatha Christie, including her Mary Westmacott romances.

And in the center of a shelf, on prime, eye-level real estate, were every one of the Hank O'Brien mysteries. Mylie pulled the first one off the shelf and opened it to the title page. Like all the mysteries, the author was listed as Noma DePlume. The cheeky pen name was apt for an author who peppered jokes and puns throughout her books. There was no dedication, with the only acknowledgment to a patient editor. But this copy had a written inscription.

For my brother Cash,

I hope you like this book. I think you might like it, but I don't actually know.

Happy birthday!

Tia

P.S. If you don't like this book, just don't read it.

Mylie examined the book, then ran her finger across the broken spine of the next book in the series.

A short blast of steel guitar drifted in through the open door, followed by stomping feet, then the same few notes of country music again. Mylie fumbled the book, then put it back on the shelf and hurried into the hallway.

"Hello!" she called out, then added, "Tia let me in."

Still no response. Mylie followed the music, which seemed to be coming from upstairs. She passed bedrooms but forced her eyes straight ahead.

Except for one quick peek into an elegant room with all-white bedding and a view of the lake.

But then it was back on track, right down the hall, until she came to an open door. Sunlight, along with country music, spilled into the wide hallway.

The music stopped abruptly, replaced by Cash's

low rumble of annoyance. Then it started up again. Mylie slipped into the large room.

A Ping-Pong table stood at one end. Foosball, air hockey and other selections were scattered around the space. One wall held shelves of board games and puzzles. Glossy tables and chairs had been pushed out of the way to make space for…well, whatever it was Cash was doing.

He had his back to her, his phone resting on the edge of a sideboard. He pressed a button and the song started over. He tapped his left heel in front of him, then the right in time with the music. He turned, executing a grapevine to the right, then clapped. He moved fluidly, as though a lifetime of roping cattle and caring for the land was some kind of *Karate Kid* dance training. He repeated the sequence, adding movement as he became more comfortable with the steps.

Cash Holiday was line dancing, by himself, in the game room. A secret society of one.

And as much as Mylie didn't want Cash to practice this dance, or get any better at it than he already was, she couldn't bring herself to interrupt him.

He ran the sequence again, his movements becoming more relaxed as he made the dance his own. Then he turned with the song, coming into a clear view of the door. He took one look at Mylie and froze in his boots.

"Hi," Mylie finally said, adding an unnecessary wave. "How's it going?"

"How long have you been here?"

"Not… Minutes."

How long *had* she been here? Long enough for the stars to realign as she watched a gorgeous man scoot his boots across the floor. She shook her head.

Cash dropped his gaze and stalked over to his phone to stop the music. If she'd been worried about this meeting being a little awkward, it was ten out of ten now. Was he mad? Embarrassed? Should she just boot-scoot it out of there before any more damage was done?

"Was I supposed to come out this afternoon? I thought we said…um." Mylie pulled her sunglasses from their perch on her head and examined them. "Tia let me into the house. It's nice. The house. So is Tia."

Cash exhaled, then finally turned around. He gave Mylie a long look and she could not read one single thought raging behind his earthy hazel eyes.

"Tia was supposed to let me know when you were here. I'd have been there to greet you. I'm sorry to keep you waiting."

"It's okay. I gave a pretty broad range of when I'd get here."

Which you were supposed to respond to with a specific time, but whatever.

Cash cracked a smile. There was at least one thought in his head she could read.

"And you assumed I'd be late?" she asked.

He pressed his lips together, but his eyes held on to the smile. "I assumed you'd be busy. And since you crushed the competition yesterday, and you're gonna do it again at the community service meet and greet, I figured I'd better nail the line dance."

Mylie laughed. She really wasn't sure where any of this was going. Conversations with Cash could feel a little like bungee jumping: exhilarating with a fear of systems failure.

Mylie reached into her back pocket, then pulled in a breath to start talking about Work for Warriors, a volunteer operation Cash might be interested in, but he spoke first.

"Do you want to dance with me?"

DID THAT REALLY *just come out of your mouth, dude?*

It had been a restless twenty-four hours. At the last event, Cash had come to realize Mylie was even more serious competition than he'd expected her to be. She was charming and elegant. Heck, she was the *mayor*. Of course, everyone loved her.

Mylie had completely knocked it out of the park yesterday. Then she said all those nice things about him, recognizing the way he supported his family.

Cash had taken on the mantle of responsibility for his siblings when he was seven years old. For nearly three decades, he was the only person looking out for Beau and Tia. And while he did it willingly and took pride in what great people they turned out to be, he'd never gotten a lot of credit for the sacrifice. Teachers would talk to him when Beau fell behind in class, but none of them ever stopped to give him credit for the fact that Beau showed up every day, showered, fed and dressed. Everyone was impressed by Tia's extraordinary skills as a veterinarian. Cash was brimming with pride at her white-coat ceremony, but no one called him out for handling her FAFSA, tracking down scholarships and working nights at a lumber mill to help pay for her degree.

Cash didn't support his family to achieve recognition. He'd been doing it for so long, and with so little thanks, he'd forgotten there might be recognition involved. But wow, had it felt good to know someone noticed. Someone who was smart, and funny, and not prone to giving false praise.

Then again, saying nice things about him helped her win round one in the pageant. She was, as Clara put it, emotionally intelligent. She could probably read every thought passing through his mind right now. He needed to get it together.

"I mean, we could practice this dance, or just get started with community service stuff. Thank you, by the way, if I didn't already say that."

"It's no problem."

"Do you already know this dance?"

Man, why are you stuck on the dancing?

"Kind of?" She wrinkled her nose, then shook her head. "Actually, no. Line dancing is not a skill I ever thought I'd need. Then at Beau and Elliana's wedding—"

"We all got dragged on the floor. Now, we've got the competition." He shook his head, mock serious.

"I thought we left line dancing behind in the nineties, along with dial-up internet."

Mylie laughed, color rising to her face. Cash felt warm, and unexpectedly pleased, when he made her laugh.

"You want to run through it with me? I know we're here to get me something to talk about at the community service meet and greet, but we may as well multitask."

Her face lit up. "I love multitasking! It's my favorite."

"Even more than you like working in committees?"

She shuddered dramatically, then strode across the game room to stand next to him. Her posture was the same, as though she was showing up to argue, shoulders back, confident tilt to her chin.

"You don't think helping me practice is going to give me an unfair advantage?" she asked.

He shook his head. "Naw. I'm gonna take the line dancing."

"That's a lot of confidence."

"I need it. You'll crush everyone with community service."

"I hope so."

"What do you mean you 'hope so'? You do more for this town than anyone else."

"Technically, yes. That's probably a fair assessment. We have great volunteers and city employees, but if we were to pull out our calendars, it's likely I do more than anyone else."

After this completely fair and reasonable statement, Mylie sighed.

"What?"

"What are you asking 'what' about?"

"That sigh."

"What sigh?"

"The…sigh." He pointed, as though the mournful exhale was still in the room. "You said you do a lot for the community, and then you sighed."

She sighed again. "Sometimes, when you do your job well, it attracts a certain kind of criticism."

"How so?" Cash asked, then caught himself. He'd been giving Mylie grief for trying to do her job from the first day they'd met. He hitched a thumb at his chest. "Except for the obvious."

She gave a quiet laugh. "You were a different situation."

Cash lowered his head to look into Mylie's eyes. "What's this situation?"

She shrugged, but there was nothing casual about the tension around her eyes. "I think some people might feel threatened. My MO is to try to do whatever I do to the best of my ability. But there are people who don't want to see me succeed. Does that make sense? They're more comfortable if the mayor doesn't have all her bases covered. A weak mayor gives them someone to blame, or someone to save. The more competent I am, the more uncomfortable they become."

Cash shifted, surprised. Mylie's competence was something he'd always admired about her. While they were often on opposite sides of an issue, he never suspected she hadn't done her due diligence.

Wait, did she lump him in with the people who didn't want to see her succeed?

"Hey, I'm sorry if I ever came off that way." He placed a hand on her arm, trying to convey his sincerity. It had nothing to do with the fact that she was wearing a pretty, sleeveless blouse and had very attractive arms.

She laughed. "You? Never. I'm not saying I loved all our arguments, but you respected me enough to hash things out head-on."

Cash studied his boots, an uncomfortable realization hitting him. He *had* loved all their arguments. Going head-to-head with Mylie had been an exhilarating challenge.

"When people feel threatened by my competence, they don't come right out and argue. They work around me, talk behind my back, belittle the work I've done. The better I am at my job, the more insecure they get of their own position."

Cash gestured to an empty chair, then pulled another up to face it. Mylie looked suspicious for a moment, then sat. Cash sat facing her. He gazed at her for a moment.

"Why do I feel like this wouldn't be a problem if you were a man in his sixties?"

And not such a beautiful and brilliant woman.

"There really is a lot of energy directed at my age. And also, just who I am, you know? People are always commenting on what I wear, how my hair looks, how nice I am, like it's some kind of surprise when I respond to others with basic politeness."

Cash interrupted her, "For the record, I have never commented on how nice you are."

Mylie laughed. "I know! I've always appreciated that about you. You get what you see."

Cash felt heat rising up his neck. Most folks might not consider it a huge compliment, but he did. Dad had constantly schemed, plotted, laid on the charm on his way to ripping someone off. Cash very much valued being thought of as a book one could easily judge by the cover and back blurb.

"Part of the problem is my lack of collaboration," Mylie continued. "I own that. I'm able to see the pros and cons of proposals pretty clearly, so I'm not interested in wasting time on something that won't work. I don't like sitting around and going over something ad nauseam in a committee. I'd rather just get things done."

"This is gonna sound like a dumb question—" He raised his brow, waiting for her response.

"What?"

"Is this the point where you tell me there are no dumb questions?"

"Oh, there are definitely dumb questions," she said. Cash laughed. "Not that I'd say anything, but go ahead."

"Why do other people like going over things, and hashing them out in committee forever?"

Mylie gave him a wry smile. "That's not a dumb question at all. It's one of the first things I tried to figure out when I was elected to city council. People are pretty good at coming up with grand plans, right? Head down to Public House right now and you'll find three guys at the bar solving the world's problems. It's fun. But implementing a plan takes work, it carries a risk of failure. Identifying problems? Complaining? So easy. It makes people feel smart and powerful to point out a problem. Attempting to solve a problem can be frustrating, and you open yourself up to criticism if your ideas don't work."

"I never thought of it that way."

"Most people never think about it at all. But I'm just not that person, you know? I do not have the patience to sit around and listen to a committee masticate over an issue, then come up with a solution they're never going to implement."

"I take it these are the same people who don't want your Club 75 to succeed?"

She nodded. "I've been going round and round, trying to figure out what the issue is. I know it's a lot flashier to help kids and families. But Club 75 is inexpensive, and could be a powerful way to reconnect seniors with the community. I mean, some seniors are already pretty well connected—" She waved a hand in the direction of the barn, indicating Myron.

"That guy was hamming it up!" Cash said. "My gramma was posting pictures of him all over social media."

"But not everyone has his confidence. Many

older citizens have lost a spouse, along with lifelong friends. People who are no longer employed need a reason to leave their homes. And also, why would we *not* do whatever we can to support people who have contributed so much to our town?"

She was making a lot of sense here. But there had to be other ways Club 75 could, and should, get funded than by her winnings.

"Well, my offer of help still stands," he said. "We'd be happy to host folks out here, or anything else."

She gave him a hopeful grin.

"Except throw the pageant," he said. "That's a no-go."

She groaned and stood up. "I guess we'd better get dancing then. If I'm gonna beat you in the line dance, I need to see your moves."

"You can see them, then admit I'll win. You're gonna take community service, and I'm assuming you'll win at Ripple Creek trivia night, too, although Myron might give you a run there."

"He's a wild card," she admitted.

"That means I have to win everything else. Line dancing and work attire on Tuesday, then the formal event."

"How are you going to win formal…?" Mylie paused, a look of comprehension spread across her face. "Please tell me the black suit Beau wore at the wedding doesn't fit you."

"The hand-tailored Armani suit my dad had

made for himself? Like a glove. I don't love getting stuffed into it, but I wear it well."

"Not fair."

"Says the woman I have to compete against for community service."

"There's no way I have time to find a new formal dress before Saturday."

"But don't you have those dresses?" he asked.

"What dresses?"

Cash shrugged, like he couldn't remember what dresses he was referencing. Definitely not the jewel-toned, knee-length dresses she wore to various events, looking adorable. Not those.

"I don't actually have a formal gown. I just assumed…" She trailed off, gesturing to the stage.

"You assumed you won't have any real competition and every activity would be a slam dunk?"

"Actually, yes. That was the plan."

He grinned. She was, undoubtedly, the most eligible single in Ripple Creek. In fact, the more he got to know her, the harder it was to understand why she was single at all.

Cash cleared his throat, then scratched the back of his head. "Either way, this pageant paints us both in a good light. You look relatable as the mayor. My family takes a step further toward the good graces of Ripple Creek."

"You're right," she acknowledged. "Shall we dance?"

"Yeah. Let's do it."

Cash trotted over to his phone and backed up to the beginning of "Boot Scootin' Boogie."

The movement, like any line dance, was pretty simple. A grapevine, some claps, grooving forward and back. Once she'd mastered the basics, Cash turned to her and winked.

"How are we gonna make this look good?"

She grinned back, reminding him of how cute she'd been dancing at Beau and Elliana's wedding. "I'm thinking we add in a little rodeo?"

Cash followed her lead, slipping in a lasso move as they stepped forward, then strutted back. On impulse, he grabbed her hand at the turn and spun her under his arm. Mylie laughed and they moved into the next sequence. He kept his hand at her waist, holding her close as they tapped their heels, then toes, and he spun her again.

All in the name of making the dance look good and winning the competition.

Obviously.

Cash reset the music and they practiced the dance again, laughing together as they executed what had to be some of the best boot scooting on record.

The song ended, slipping into the next tune on the Brooks and Dunn playlist. Cash didn't pause to replay the song, but responded to the music, twirling Mylie. The mournful regret of "Neon Moon" filled the room. Cash took her other hand and pulled her into a simple promenade, then released one hand to spin her under his arm.

Neither of them said a word as they danced. It felt like the moment they'd locked eyes at Beau's wedding. This dance took place out of time—a sweet, something extra that would last until it was acknowledged.

"Hey, have you seen my Makita drill?"

Cash jumped at the sound of Beau's voice. Then he froze. He was holding Mylie's hand, her face flushed from laughter. They were dancing to a romantic song that was definitely not part of the pageant.

"Uh. Yeah, isn't it in the workshop?" he asked.

"I couldn't find it," Beau said, his eyes running from Cash to Mylie and back again.

Should he drop her hand? Technically, yes. They weren't dancing, so no need to keep her fingers in his. But would that look suspicious, if he suddenly dropped her hand?

Very suspicious. So he just stood there, casually holding the hand of a woman he professed to dislike and was determined to beat in a pageant.

As one does.

"I'll come help you look," he finally said.

Any excuse to get out of the game room and away from whatever this feeling was. Mylie was turning out to be a good person, but she was still the person he had to beat in order to help Tia. He shouldn't be here cozying up to her.

Of course, that meant he was gonna have to let go of her hand now. Reluctantly, he released her fingers.

"What do you need the drill for?" he asked.

"I'm heading into the high school to meet with the woodshop teacher and a few kids. They're piloting a construction class through Team Oregon Build next year."

"Team what?" Cash asked.

"Team Oregon Build. It's this new program where kids learn construction skills by building temporary dwellings for victims of wildfires. We're working on portable tiny homes. It's a blast."

"That's a program?" Cash asked. "That exists?"

"At our high school?" Mylie added.

"They're just getting started," Beau said. "The actual class will start next year, but enough kids are interested we're getting a jump on things now. We're gonna train some students as class leaders so they can develop foreman experience. You wouldn't believe how excited the kids are about getting to work with power tools."

Cash stared at his brother, then finally asked, "What genius thought of that program?"

Beau shrugged.

Cash and Mylie exchanged another look. She'd been real nice in coming out to suggest ways he could volunteer, but—

"I got nothing on that," Mylie said, reading his thoughts. "That's your platform."

"You're good if I…?" He gestured toward the door.

"Yes," she said. "Go get it." Then she grinned. "I might just practice 'Boot Scootin' Boogie' a little longer."

"Don't you dare get better than me!" he said.

She laughed, brushing a strand of hair from her face. "It's not my fault you're racing off to take part in an excellent community service opportunity."

"You're welcome to stay…" Cash trailed off. Where was he going here? Mylie was welcome to stay and dance in his game room, and hopefully would still be there when he got back? She was welcome to stay for dinner so he could impress her with his cooking?

No. Mylie was still Mylie. It was one thing to work together if it served his ultimate goal, to win the money to help Tia. But he couldn't afford to get any more wound up in her than he already was. It hadn't gone well the last time he fell in love. It took him years to bounce back from Luna, and he had a feeling Mylie would be significantly harder to get over.

She smiled, fortunately not privy to the freeway pileup of thoughts in his head. "I should get back. I have a poster board to make for tomorrow."

"A poster board?"

"Of course. A nice trifold poster board illustrating my many and varied service activities."

"Am I supposed to make…?" Cash stopped when he realized Mylie was laughing at him. He shook his head. "If you show up with a poster board, you and I are gonna have words."

"Oh, then I am definitely showing up with a poster board."

Cash crossed his arms over his chest and shook

his head. He'd just ensured Mylie would show up with the biggest, fanciest poster board in tow.

"Are you going to help me find my drill or what?" Beau asked.

"Yep. Right now, let's go."

Cash gestured for Mylie to walk ahead of him as they exited the game room. At the door, Mylie stopped and looked back.

"This is a really cool house, by the way."

"It's too much," Cash said. "And mortgaged six ways to Sunday."

"But still cool."

Cash glanced into the extravagant bedrooms of the second floor, then over the balcony of the double staircase. He'd never really allowed himself to like the house, because it was a reminder of all his father's excesses and indulgences. But as they settled into the new business venture, the place was growing on him.

"It's a great house for a party," he admitted.

Mylie nodded. "A great setting for a mystery series, too."

CHAPTER SIX

CASH ARRIVED AT the Mountain Country Most Eligible meet and greet with two goals.

One: Appear completely committed to, and knowledgeable about, Team Oregon Build.

Two: Keep himself as far away from Mylie Saunders as possible.

The first goal was attainable. The night before, he and Beau had spent three hours at the high school. There he'd met teachers, industry professionals and kids who were as excited about construction as he was. It was Cash's first opportunity to volunteer in Ripple Creek, and he was hooked. He wanted to stop people on the street and tell them about it.

Have you heard about volunteerism? You can hang out with interesting people, do something fun and *help folks at the same time. Check it out!*

But most people probably already knew that.

His second goal—keep away from Mylie—was trickier.

He had been completely inappropriate the day

before, dancing with her, taking any opportunity to slip his fingers into hers, spin her close to him.

They'd had so much fun. It could *not* happen again. His purpose in this life was to care for his siblings, and right now, Tia had something major going on. Mom had split early on in their lives, Luna left when she realized Beau and Tia were part of the package; the pattern was clear. Mylie had more than enough going on in her life. Any type of romance between them would end with her high-tailing it out of the Holiday family carnival. This was his circus. Beau and Tia were not her monkeys.

So today, there wasn't going to be anything but an appropriate greeting and a wide berth. This time he was armed against his feelings, so they couldn't become dangerous.

The community center was alive with the cheerful hum of chitchat. The place was packed. All the contestants were there, in the same room they'd met in originally, but this time lined up in front of a long table. Community members milled around, asking questions and learning about the programs. Mylie wasn't the only one with a poster board, but most folks just came with a few brochures.

Mylie was set up at one end of the long table, so Cash headed to the other.

Several paces into the room, he came to an abrupt stop. Myron was wearing a suit jacket. Nesa had on a stylish blouse with a jaunty bow at the neck. All of the contestants were dressed in what he had to assume was business-casual, making his worn-in jeans and T-shirt feel farmer-casual, which wasn't a look anyone ever requested. Had he not gotten a memo? His gaze flickered to Mylie. She was in blue jeans and a T-shirt with Ripple Creek, Oregon, est. 1893, scrawled across the front. Around her neck, she wore a silver chain with a little pendant dangling from it, and tiny pearl earrings.

Okay, no memo. And no more looking at Mylie. Cash nodded to Piper and Clara, then took his place at the far end of the table.

Team Oregon Build, let's go.

The moment he took up his spot with the other contestants, Cash was approached by people interested in the program. As he'd hoped, everyone was as impressed with the idea as he was. He kept his eyes on the people he spoke with, even as Mylie's voice floated across the hall. How did her voice carry like that? There was a roomful of people in between them, yet her words were perfectly clear as she described a trail-building effort the city and a local mountain-biking group were working on together. Her pitch was so convincing he had to fight the urge to sprint out of the building and start spreading bark-o-mulch on a hillside.

After several long minutes of engaged willpower, Cash gave in to the urge, eyes sliding to the side as he checked out Mylie.

Was it just him, or did the oversize, trifold display of her community service feel like an invitation to argue? Fortunately, she was surrounded by people. Cash couldn't have gotten in a word even if he wanted to. Folks rightfully identified Mylie as the person with the most up-to-date ideas on how to give back to the community. If someone wanted a taste of volunteerism, he wouldn't be the go-to in this hall.

The other contestants had interesting platforms, too. Rafael volunteered with a local music program, finding and renovating old band instruments for kids who wanted to play but didn't necessarily have an oboe lying around the house. Bobbie taught a financial literacy class for women moving forward out of divorce.

They were all good ideas. Still, his was the only program that involved kids grinning from ear to ear as they fired up power tools. That had to count for something.

"The students actually build tiny homes in class?" a woman asked him.

Cash nodded. "Yep. With a lot of guidance, of course. But they'll come out the other side with new skills and confidence in their abilities."

"That's so great for kids wanting to go into construction."

"It's good for all kids. You live in a house, you're gonna need to know how to fix things."

"Yes!" Her eyes shone. "So true. Are you handy around the house?"

"I have to be. Nothing much would be left standing if I didn't have basic building skills."

The woman looked at him like she was waiting

for him to explain. Cash tilted his head, and if he'd been home he would have let out an *umm*.

Maybe she wasn't from Ripple Creek. She wasn't familiar-looking, but that didn't mean much. There were lots of people he'd never met who knew all about his father. Dad had financed one massive building after the next on the ranch, managing to nickel and dime contractors down to almost nothing. When he did pay full price, he could almost always find something wrong enough with the work to bring a lawsuit. It wasn't long before any tradesman within a hundred-mile radius knew all about Bruce Holiday, and refused to come out to the house.

Cash and Beau had learned to fix almost anything, and had a deep, abiding appreciation for all the kind people on YouTube willing to teach them how.

But this woman didn't appear to know the backstory. She just grinned at him as she said, "Team Oregon Build certainly sounds like a great program."

"It is." He nodded.

Seemed like they were on the same page here. He liked Team Oregon Build, she liked Team Oregon Build. Did he need to do something else?

Or, wait, was this one of the times that his poise was being judged?

Cash kept an eye on Clara, who was weaving between contestants with her clipboard again.

"It's great to meet you. I'm excited about your

platform." The woman reached into her bag, pulled out a card and offered it to him. "I wouldn't be any help at all with this program, but I'd love to chat sometime."

Cash took the card. Why would she want to chat if she wasn't going to be helpful?

He glanced from the card to the woman. She bit her lower lip in a hopeful smile.

Wait. Was this like a date thing?

He looked into her eyes, feeling exactly like he had at the bridal shower they'd hosted a few months back. The one where he got hit on by a multitude of guests out of the blue.

It was the feeling that he was going to be a big disappointment, no matter what he did.

Cash knew he was a reasonably handsome man. They were a good-looking family, and he had work that kept him fit. Women were interested in him when they heard "family ranch." This was generally because they hadn't yet learned that a "rancher" was someone who gets up at 5:00 a.m., is covered in mud or dust by noon and may or may not make it in to fix supper. And when a whole day had run its messy course, the rancher was tossing and turning in his sleep, because agriculture was a gamble against the weather, the environment and the markets that rarely came up aces.

But while any woman Cash would consider could handle those quirks easily, it was the family part no one was fully prepared for. A single dad was a sympathetic character. A brother still looking out for his adult siblings didn't have the same appeal.

Cash didn't want to give this woman, or any other, the impression he'd be calling, because he wouldn't. Until they'd paid off his father's debts, dealt with whatever Tia's problem was and he could be assured both his siblings were going to thrive, Cash's priority was his family. By that time, Beau and Elliana might start a family, then he'd have nieces and nephews to worry about.

He needed to kindly reject this woman's invitation. How did a person even negotiate dating, or not dating, these days?

He glanced over at Mylie. There were two men talking to her. Both wearing suits, like they'd come over on their lunch breaks from office jobs, both vying for her attention. She looked as confused as Cash felt.

He scanned the crowd. Was it his imagination, or were most of the participants having flirty conversations? Another woman in the crowd caught his eye and smiled.

"Great talking to you," Cash said to the woman. "Please excuse me for a second."

Cash looped back behind the long table, heading straight for Mylie. She must have seen him coming because she directed both the men to her poster board, then came around to meet him.

"Did you just get hit on?" she asked.

"You saw that?"

"Yeah, I saw that. Hard to miss. It was like Pam's bridal shower all over."

"That's exactly what I was thinking—" Cash paused, then pulled back his head. Mylie had noticed women hitting on him at the bridal shower?

Hmm.

"What about those guys?" Cash gestured to the two bros in suits who were not at all interested in the poster board they were pretending to study.

"I think they might be hitting on me? I mean, it's hard to tell who's flirting and who just wants to get their proposal in front of the city council."

Cash shook his head. "I don't think the city council handles the type of proposal those guys have in mind."

Voices rose cheerfully around them. Rafael was talking with the deputy sheriff, while Daisy was having an animated conversation with a firefighter.

Mylie caught his eye as the truth dawned on both of them. Piper and Clara gleefully shuffled Post-its around on clipboards.

"The matchmakers—" Cash began.

"They set this whole thing up," Mylie said.

"They want us to meet people. It's like an in-person dating app."

"It's like a dating mosh pit."

"Whoa, wait." Cash looked into Mylie eyes, horrified.

"What if we lose points because we're not…you know…"

"Body surfing in the dating mosh pit?"

Mylie shook her head. "Horrifying image. But, yeah. They can't dock us points for not wanting to go out with these people."

"You have to be right. But why would they think we wanted dates in the first place?"

"Because we entered the Mountain Country Most Eligible Pageant?" she guessed. "We are literally in a contest that draws attention to what a good catch we are."

"Good point." Cash sighed, placing his hands on his hips as he surveyed the room. "So all the other contestants? Do you think they're just here to meet someone?"

"That really does seem to be the motivating factor. Love and raising money for childhood literacy."

Cash shook his head. "Weird."

"Right? I've been wondering why other people aren't as competitive. It's like you and I are the only ones who want to win."

"Maybe..." Cash tried to wrap his brain around the idea before the words left his mouth. "Maybe their idea of winning is meeting someone and being in a relationship."

"Huh." Mylie nodded, as though the thought had never occurred to her. "I mean, don't get me wrong. I'd love to meet the right guy."

"If he fell into your life with absolutely no effort on your part," Cash said, repeating her earlier words.

"Yes. And for the record, I totally intend to put in effort someday. But right now, I'm the mayor."

He nodded, then glanced at the two men who were still studying her trifold poster board, waiting for her to return. He had the sense that either of them would love to fall into her life and be willing to do most of the heavy lifting in the relationship.

She turned her intelligent blue eyes on him. "What about you?"

Was she asking if he was interested in falling into her life? Hypothetically? Because obviously there was no way they were a match, but were he to fall into someone's life...

Mylie continued. "What would happen if the right woman came along? Would you...?" She gestured broadly, indicating the great unknown of a lifetime of happiness with the right partner.

"Well, sure." Cash nodded. "If the right woman came along I'd—" He imitated her gesture. Clearly, neither of them had any idea of what Cash would do in a relationship.

The right woman wasn't going to come along. Someone willing to put up with him, his family history and all his responsibilities? Not likely.

Piper noticed the two of them talking. She kept her eyes on them as she moved a sticky note on her clipboard, then reached over to move one on Clara's clipboard.

"We'd better get back out there," Cash said.

"Yeah but—" Mylie gestured to the bros. "I don't want to pretend like I'm going to go out with people I'm not interested in."

"No, me, neither. That can't be what Clara and

Piper want. Still, I feel like I'm misrepresenting myself just by being here."

"Me, too. I should have thought about it before I signed up," she said.

"I didn't sign myself up, so at least I have that excuse. Unless—" A horrifying thought struck him. "Do you think my siblings were trying to get me a date?"

Mylie turned on him, eyes wide. "Would they do that?"

Would they? Beau might. Elliana and Tia could definitely plot something.

"No, no. Elliana said we needed a family member to represent. And Tia couldn't do it because—"

"Is it Tia?" Mylie asked.

Cash's system went on alert. "What do you mean?"

"Is it Tia you've been so worried about? That's why you're here. You need money to help out your family, and I'm guessing it has to do with Tia."

Cash swallowed hard, then gave a slight nod. This was more than he was comfortable sharing, but it wouldn't hurt for Mylie to understand how much he needed to win. He couldn't back out, not even for the sake of Club 75.

She spoke quietly. "If I can be of service, I'd love to help."

Cash was moved by her offer, but he'd take care of the issue on his own. No need to let the family drama spread outside of the family.

He lowered his voice. "You want to lose this pageant for me?"

She laughed. The sound had both the men at her poster board looking expectantly toward her.

"I appreciate your offer of help. But right now, we have more immediate problems." He gestured to the crowd. "How are we gonna deal with this, and still keep ahead of the competition?"

The woman who had been waiting for him had tucked her card back in her bag, and was now talking to Rafael.

"I can think of one solution," Mylie said.

He looked down into her pretty blue eyes, which was exactly the sort of thing he wasn't planning on letting himself do today. The only solution he could think of would lead to so many more problems.

MYLIE GAZED UP at Cash, wishing he would make the suggestion so she didn't have to. Because there was one, really simple answer.

But heaven forbid Cash Holiday suggested a practical solution. Mylie pulled in a breath. "I guess we could, you know. Team up."

"How so?"

"Stand next to each other, interact with each other. Then maybe the matchmakers will think we're, you know—" she flagged a hand between the two of them "—*interacting*."

Cash's brow furrowed as though he didn't get her meaning. Then he went stock-still at the words.

Had she just…?

She had. She suggested she and Cash collaborate. That they stand next to each other—something she'd promised herself she wouldn't do today—and flirt. It was like she had these…what would you even call them? Bad ideas? Big feelings? They overtook all rational sense.

This was starting to get messy.

And Cash was still staring, obviously disgusted with the idea.

But if that was his reaction, maybe this wasn't a problem. Cash wasn't interested in her. She didn't know what his type was, but definitely not an overworked city employee. He might respond to these waves of attraction that unexpectedly flowed between them. Their dance to "Neon Moon" had already made itself comfy wherever favorite lifetime memories set up camp in her brain. That didn't mean he wanted to date her. She could pretend she didn't find him handsome, intelligent and increasingly sympathetic as she got to know him better. It was fine.

It all begged the question, though: Why was he still single in the first place? His father had been a difficult man, and his mom left when they were kids. Was Cash afraid of commitment? Or just really picky?

"Let's do it," he said. "Can't hurt, and we can at least run interference for each other."

Okay, it *could* hurt. The fascination she'd been developing for this complex man could hurt a great deal if she let it. She needed to contain her heart in something like the deep firepits Beau had on their property. If anything sparked, those sparks had to fizzle out before hitting the open air.

She had to keep it under control, like the entire life she'd built for herself in Ripple Creek.

Cash moved around to the other side of the table. He greeted both men, who took off in a hurry. Clara drifted past with her clipboard, like a cheerful shark using electroreception to seek out flirtation.

"Mylie, you have a gorgeous—" Cash fished for words as Piper swam by "—trifold display board. Community service is attractive."

Mylie stifled a laugh, and whispered, "How bad are you at this?"

"Flirting?" His deep voice was technically quiet, but seemed to reverberate deep inside her. "Very bad. Lower twentieth percentile. Let's see you try."

Mylie waited until Clara neared again, then let out a peal of fake laughter. "What an amusing anecdote about Team Oregon Build! You're so funny." Cash closed his eyes, shaking his head as Mylie added, "And you're helpful to area teens looking to gain employment skills."

Clara didn't even deign to look at her clipboard, let alone move a sticky note.

"We're terrible at flirting," Mylie admitted.

"The worst. Guess we'd better stick to arguing." Something about his smile made the proposition sound way more fun. "But seriously, this poster is impressive." Without a single judge nearby, he said, "You do so much for the community. I respect that."

"Thank you." Mylie felt her face heat up. She

managed not to point out that the poster showcased fewer than half of the community service projects she was involved in. She hadn't wanted it to look too cluttered.

He crouched down, examining the display more closely, and honed in on an image of a woman in camo giving the camera a thumbs-up. "What's the Work for Warriors initiative?"

"That's something I'm really thrilled to have brought to Ripple Creek." Mylie's face lit up. "Work for Warriors is a nonprofit funded by federal grants and private donations. It does salary matching for veterans entering the workforce. So, say you needed to hire someone at Holiday Ranch, but could only pay fifteen dollars an hour."

"We're desperate to hire someone," Cash said. "But we can't afford it and we can't find anyone even if we could."

"That's great!"

"Is it?"

Mylie shook her head. "No, obviously. But, that's what the program is about—matching people who want jobs with small businesses who need employees. Work for Warriors can supplement the salary, making an entry-level wage into a living wage. This helps a veteran learn job skills, get started in the workforce and build up valuable references. Every veteran is eligible for five years, so you could hire someone at Holiday Ranch, train them in hospitality—"

"Or running cattle. I could use a lot of help on the ranching side of our business."

"That, too. They'd be paid well while they're learning a new skill. Employers win by gaining a long-term employee at a salary they can afford, and veterans can make enough money and industry connections for a smooth transition into civilian life. The results have been impressive. Soldiers who have been through the program report more life satisfaction, have lower incidence of divorce and are able to purchase homes at higher rates than those not in the program."

"That is quite the sell." Cash flexed his brow, seemingly impressed. "I'm gonna need you to hook us up."

"I'm happy to."

Mylie grinned at Cash. Piper drifted by, eyeing the two of them, so Mylie smiled even brighter. Cash held her gaze the way he had when they were dancing together. Like she'd done something to surprise him and he wasn't quite sure what to make of it.

Then he gave his head a sharp shake and returned his attention to the poster board.

Or, maybe he'd just been thinking about how nice it would be to have extra help around the ranch.

Then he surprised her by saying, "You have a vision for Ripple Creek, don't you?"

"Of course. That's why I ran for mayor in the first place. Not that much of my work feels visionary at the moment."

"Look at all this." He pointed to the board. "It's like you want everyone to feel like Ripple Creek has all the comforts of home, but is also a place with opportunity and adventure."

"That's exactly what I want. I'm glad you can see it. A lot of people can't."

He lowered his voice. "Is this about the fact that you're young and—" He gestured to her, indicating something.

Young and what? Single? A female? Still rocking a side part?

"Like we talked about the other day?" he continued. "Being a young woman in a position of power."

"To some extent, yes. But let's just say it—I'm competitive."

Cash drew back his head. "Is that a problem? Because if it's a problem, I'm doomed."

She kind of loved his competitiveness. It made her feel…what? Not quite so alone? Like there was someone else who understood the pleasure of an honest win?

"It's just different in my world. City government is a potluck, not Hell's Kitchen, you know?"

He laughed.

"I need to relax, and not expect everything to be perfect all the time. Just make the most of what's on offer."

"Sitting back isn't really your style," he noted.

"No."

That was the conundrum. Mylie had grown up

dreaming of living in Ripple Creek because it was a respite from the grinding work of her youth. Now, she was the mayor, and working harder than ever. Her Ripple Creek didn't have much comfort, opportunity or adventure.

Yesterday, dancing with Cash was the first time she'd allowed herself to relax and have fun in a long, long time. It was a bright reminder of how bleak life had become. But a frightening one, too. She couldn't rely on Cash to be there for her. She needed to solve that problem on her own.

"Well, hello there!" Alice Henderson stepped in between them, both physically and metaphorically in the way. "What fun ideas do we have here?"

Alice looked over Mylie's shoulder and scanned the board for evidence of Club 75.

Ugh. There was working with others in theory, then there was actually working with others.

"Oh, look! You put my program on here!" Alice pointed to a picture of three kids in tutus. "Well, that's a surprise. The mayor noticing my little contribution to Ripple Creek."

Mylie kept her expression neutral. Not only had she "noticed" the program on her poster board, but she'd also put countless volunteer hours into the pet project that served maybe five kids on a good day, two of whom were Alice's daughters.

But Dance 'n' Do was also featured prominently on the brochure for Banks Run, a new housing development Brick and Alice had invested heavily in. There was no question—their interest in programs aimed at families was directly linked to a desire to lure new residents to Ripple Creek.

Cash's eyes flickered from Mylie to Alice, a sly grin growing across his face. "Have you heard of Team Oregon Build?"

Alice's brow furrowed as she pointed back to the poster. "My program is called Dance 'n' Do. It's an after-school program for—"

"Girls with spirit and sass, with a passion for razzle, dazzle and bedazzling," Cash said, rattling off the program description. "You've got those craft-oriented dance girls set up. Team Oregon Build is for high school students. Did you know student engagement, along with career and technical skills are two of the most important initiatives in our school district?"

Alice nodded along as the gorgeous cowboy focused all his attention on her, overloading her with information on Team Oregon Build, describing each and every kid involved in the program. Alice tried to interrupt him a few times but Cash was having none of it.

Mylie kept her eyes forward and tried not to laugh as he rescued her, however briefly, from Alice. She stared out the front windows, letting the action on Main Street distract her so she didn't burst out laughing. That's when she caught a glimpse of wild auburn hair and two greyhounds.

It was Tia, moving quickly across the street. She looked over her shoulder, then opened the door to the law offices of Jordan Ritter. There seemed to be a bit of a debate with an office manager as to whether or not the greyhounds would be allowed in, but eventually all three crossed the threshold. Mylie glanced at Cash to see if he'd noticed. He was still spraying Alice down with information about marketable skills for teens.

So Tia's troubles *were* legal. What could it be? Something having to do with her animal rescue? An issue leftover from the days of Bruce Holiday? Not likely.

Okay, sure, *likely.* But how could something involving their dad only affect Tia? It also didn't make sense that it could be a secret if it was a Bruce Holiday concern. And why was she at his office on a Sunday afternoon? Was Jordan taking this case under the table?

What did Mylie know about Cash's sister? She loved animals, she was the life of any party, she was wildly creative.

What kind of legal trouble did a charming, wildly creative animal lover get into?

This was an area in which she could really help out Cash. If the problem had something to do with law, she was in a good position to be of use. And, if she solved Cash's problem, he'd no longer need the five-thousand-dollar prize, and he'd be willing to cede the competition.

Who was she kidding? Cash didn't exactly have "bow out gracefully" written all over him.

But still. She could be helpful.

"So then I said to the kid, you're gonna want a

framing hammer here, and she agreed. I showed her how to set the nail…" Cash continued, clearly pleased with his ability to make Alice's eyes glaze over.

Mylie grinned to herself. She was going to do what she could for Tia. She might even help without mentioning it to Cash, a legitimate Good Samaritan. That felt right. She didn't have to blabber on to Cash about her growing respect for him, she could just execute a simple favor for the cause most dear to his heart: his family.

The warm, satisfied feeling evaporated as Mylie felt eyes on her. Across the room, Brick Henderson was staring at her. Without taking his eyes off her, he handed a man Mylie didn't recognize a flyer. The man looked at the flyer, then at Mylie.

The moment felt ominous. Mylie repressed a shudder and turned away.

Tia Holiday might not be the only one in Ripple Creek who needed help right now.

CHAPTER SEVEN

CASH PULLED THE heavy leather chaps over his work jeans, then grabbed his Stetson as he walked out of the old tack room into the renovated barn. He paused at one of the large bouquets to adjust a few of the Shasta daisies.

He'd barely gotten the hay bales loaded out of the south pasture in time to get back to the house, shower and change into a clean rancher's getup. Audience members were already arriving. By the look of things, there were going to be twice as many people at this performance than the last.

He forced himself to step back from the flowers. The bouquet was just gonna have to be what it was gonna be. No amount of flower rearranging was going to lift his apprehension, anyway. He could full-on admit he had a crush on his competition, and that was a problem.

So today, Cash layered on the defenses as he layered on his work wear. He had "Boot Scootin' Boogie" down cold. The newness of dancing with Mylie had passed. He could execute the moves with precision, rather than the emotion that had caused him to take her hand, or slip an arm around her waist.

Today's competition was in the bag, his emotions were in a box.

This was going to be fine.

Cash moved through the barn, greeting audience members as they found their seats, then joined the knot of contestants next to the stage. Mylie was late again. Bobbie, the mortgage broker, looked sharp in a bright scarf and standout jewelry, and she knew it. Rafael, who taught middle school, was in a T-shirt his students had decorated. Middle-school slang phrases covered the shirt, presumably suggesting what a good guy he was. He wore the T-shirt with jeans, a pair of wild, trendy sneakers and a blazer with a tiger embroidered across the back. Somehow, he managed to make it all look not only normal, but also good.

Still, Cash was the only one backstage with a lasso.

A burst of laughter drew his attention to the barn entrance. A group of Beau's friends from the firehouse moved away from the sliding door. Then, there she was.

Mylie strode into the barn, adorable in a deep red power suit. Her hair was twisted into a knot at the nape of her neck. She looked polished, put together, like the one person you would trust to oversee a finance committee, or make a decision regarding a traffic light.

She glanced up and saw Cash. A smile lit her face.

Or the one person you could trust with your heart?

No. He couldn't trust anyone with his heart, not again. He had to get his feelings under control. But how do you control something you can't even understand?

"Hey there! Have a sec?" Someone behind Cash was speaking, possibly to him, but he didn't have the ability to divide his focus at the moment.

"Hi." Mylie walked up to him, then cast a pointed look to the rope he was holding. "The Stetson and chaps aren't enough?"

He grinned. "Not nearly enough."

"Just to be clear, I'm okay with you winning today, but not with you taking a surge in points and leaving me in the dust."

"You think that's gonna keep me from bringing my horse in?"

The color drained from her face.

"Excuse me?" The voice that may or may not have been talking to Cash got louder. He should probably turn around and respond.

Instead, he winked at Mylie and all the color flooded right back to her face.

"You're joking," she said.

"Maybe."

"I wouldn't put it past you to bring a horse on stage, or a cow."

"I'd do it in a second if Beau wasn't so protective of the flooring in here."

He expected Mylie to laugh, but her face grew

serious as she focused on something behind him. He looked over his shoulder to see what was bothering her.

"Oh, hi, Cash!"

Alice Henderson stood at his elbow. Owner of the voice he'd been ignoring.

Could she possibly want to hear more about Team Oregon Build?

"Hi, Alice," he said, then waited. Did she want something, or had she just shown up by his side and stood there while he stared at Mylie so she could say hi?

"Great outfit!" She gestured to indicate everything he had on.

"Thank you," he said, then made the same mistake he made every time someone wished him a happy birthday. "You, too."

She pulled back her head, like she was flattered, but Cash should know better than to flirt with a married woman.

This hole was getting deeper by the minute.

"I'm going to check in with Piper and Clara." Mylie gave Alice a polite nod, then touched Cash's arm as she walked past him. "Catch you in a bit."

Alice watched Mylie walk away, then leaned in close to Cash. "So how is it, working with Mylie? I know you two haven't always gotten along."

"We're doing great." Cash looked around, trying to locate a judge. Maybe this was another test? How long could he be polite to Alice when Mylie was looking gorgeous and being brilliant just a few feet away?

No judges. Just Alice's husband chatting up some guy in a shirt with little lobsters embroidered on it.

"I'm just asking because I know how difficult she can be." Alice put a hand on his arm.

"She's fine." Cash stepped back. "We're fine."

He hadn't had any trouble working with Mylie recently. Or rather, the trouble was they weren't having any.

"That's so sweet of you, not to speak ill of your partner." Alice lowered her voice. "But believe me, I get it. A lot of people do."

Cash scanned his surroundings again. Not a judge in sight. Was Alice serious?

He put his hands on his hips and widened his stance, allowing an edge in his voice as he asked, "Get what, exactly?"

Brick turned from the man he'd been speaking with and answered for his wife. "That Mylie can't be trusted to work with others." He turned his cool gaze on Mylie, his eyes running down her figure as he said, "She's not fit for the position of mayor."

Alice pretended not to notice her husband checking out their nemesis. "There's growing support for putting an end to her reign of terror."

Cash tilted his head and barely held in an *umm*. Reign of terror? She was a small-town mayor, not a player in the French Revolution.

Mylie's comments from earlier came rushing back to him. Her concern over funding for Club

75, her fear that she wasn't good enough at working with others, the pressure of being a young single woman in small-town politics. Were the Hendersons the instigators in all this?

He crossed his arms. "Wait, are you talking about a—?"

Alice widened her eyes and nodded. Inasmuch as Cash hadn't finished his sentence, he could have said "ice-cream sandwich" and she would have nodded all seriously.

He leaned in, hoping she wouldn't say what he thought she was going to. She leaned in, too. Brick followed suit.

"Recall?" Cash asked.

Just then, Piper's voice came over the speakers. "Calling all candidates! Can we get all our most eligible competitors backstage?"

Brick and Alice made various "uh-huhs" and "mmm-hmms," of agreement, as though they, too, were major players in the French Revolution, but the good ones. Whoever that was.

"No." Cash said the only word that came to mind as he backed away. Then he pointed at Alice and Brick. "No, that's not an option."

"It's absolutely an option," Alice said, mistaking Cash's reaction for a lack of optimism.

"Time to go!" Clara was at his side, tugging on his sleeve.

"For our mayor," Brick said ominously.

Before he could respond, Cash was hustled backstage.

What was that?

They couldn't possibly be serious, but it was a heck of a cruel joke if they weren't.

Unsuspecting, Mylie grinned as Cash came near. "You giving out a little more beta on Team Oregon Build?"

He stared at her. She had to negotiate so much, deal with so many people, and still she kept her head up, kept smiling. In high heels and a power suit.

She was perfect.

Why had he been so confrontational with her when they'd started up the events center?

He'd been awful, as bad as Brick and Alice. Fighting with her about city code, suggesting his rights as a business owner were more important than the general interests of the community. Why had he, for one second, thought to take out his frustration on Mylie?

Aside from the all-encompassing fear of losing his family's land.

"Everything okay?" Mylie asked.

No, everything was not okay. She was in danger of getting recalled. A recall would be devastating, and that would be nothing compared to the hurt of being publicly humiliated for trying to serve a community she loved.

"Yeah, I mean—" He stared at her. Did she know what Alice was planning? Was that part of her desire to win the pageant?

Mylie's expression changed. Now, she was starting to look as concerned as he felt.

"Is everything okay with Tia?" she whispered.

He gazed at Mylie, shaking his head. First Tia was in trouble, now Mylie. He wasn't sure how much more of this he could stomach. "I don't know. Mylie—"

"Gather up!" Piper called, gesturing everyone into a circle.

Mylie leaned in close. Her perfume was subtle, but that didn't make it any less dangerous. "You've got this competition. Personally, I'm just hoping our practice of 'Boot Scootin' Boogie' allows me to place in the top three. You'll win this round. I'm not saying you're gonna win the crown. But today, you can relax and enjoy the glory."

Cash tried to chuckle at her words. He would help Tia out of her legal troubles, but it was definitely time for his sister to fess up and tell him what the problem was. Mylie needed a win around here, and he wasn't going to take it from her without a good reason.

He joined the backstage circle with the rest of the contestants.

Clara held her thumb and forefinger a quarter inch apart and said, "We have a teeny, little, tiny last-minute change."

"Are you suggesting the change is small?" Myron asked.

"Beyond minuscule," Clara said with a grin.

"Almost imperceptible," Piper said.

It took Cash a second to realize they were all joking, so his laugh came out just as Clara said, "We're gonna line dance to 'Shivers,' rather than 'Boot Scootin' Boogie.'"

"What?!" Cash and Mylie both yelled.

The rest of the contestants had significantly calmer reactions.

"Ooh, I love Ed Sheeran," Nesa said, as her granddaughter, Daisy, began to not only sing the song, but also execute the dance.

Cash cleared his throat. Mylie's attempted smile looked more like a grimace as she asked, "Why?"

"Just for funsies," Piper said.

Cash and Mylie stared at one another. *Funsies?*

"It's also a little easier," Clara explained.

"Is it?" Cash asked.

"I think so." Piper narrowed one eye at Cash. "Are you a connoisseur of line dancing?"

Cash held up both hands. "You said 'Boot Scootin' Boogie,' so I was just planning on a little Brooks and Dunn."

He wasn't going to admit he'd been boot scootin' around the property for the last few days in an attempt to nail this part of the contest.

"Well, this is a pivot," Piper said.

Things had been pivoting nonstop around here: rules, expectations, feelings. Why hadn't Mylie told him about Alice and Brick? Did she know? Did she not trust him enough to tell him?

He had to accept that his past actions had to be partially responsible for any animosity toward

Mylie. Which meant it was on him to help her out of this situation, no matter what it took.

"WHAT'S WRONG WITH you today?" Mylie asked Cash. They stood shoulder-to-shoulder backstage, Cash still muttering through clenched teeth.

A stormy look of concern passed over his face. After a moment, his lips twitched. "You tell me. You have a long enough list of my flaws."

"Oh, hogwash. We're beyond that."

"Hogwash?" That finally got a smile out of him. "Seriously?"

"The word has the exact meaning I was going for."

He scoffed. She held up a hand. "Scoffers gonna scoff. I'll use the vocabulary I want."

A real laugh escaped. Then he shook his head, gazing at her. "Sorry. I'm just trying to figure out how things work around here. Things are one way, I get prepared to handle a situation, then someone throws a curveball."

"You're going to do fine with the dance."

He gave her a long look, then nodded. Something about his expression suggested it wasn't the dance he was worried about.

They turned their attention back to the stage. Caleb, in a chef's apron, and Daisy, an ultrasound tech wearing pink scrubs, had choreographed a modeling routine. They were very cute and just the right amount of awkward to ensure they wouldn't win.

"How well can anyone dance to 'Shivers,' anyway? We'll be fine."

Cash pointed to the stage. "Daisy might give us a run for our money."

"Maybe, but she's completely uninterested in winning. She could dance circles around us and it wouldn't be a problem."

"No. Dancing circles around someone in a line dance would be a big problem."

Mylie giggled. Cash's smile disappeared as he glanced into the audience.

Should she tell him she could help with Tia's legal problems? She didn't want to overstep. She really didn't want to get more invested in his life. On the other hand, if Tia needed legal help, who better to step up?

"Let's welcome to the stage, Nesa and Myron!"

Nesa glided onto stage like Vanna White, followed by Myron hamming it up on stage, pretending to reach up and grab a book, then kneeling down to show pictures to an imaginary child.

They were charming and fun, but not a threat for the sash.

No, the threat came from the front row, and it wasn't the sash at stake. Alice and Brick were alternating between being overly enthusiastic for whomever was on stage, then glaring into the wings, shooting Mylie a warning. Mylie had seen Alice try to cozy up to Cash. She'd also caught Cash folding his arms and leveling a glare at her, so that was sweet.

Mylie's heart quickened as Myron and Nesa came offstage. She'd initially thought this pageant would be a fun chance to get in front of the community. As Alice and Brick mounted their campaign against her, stepping into the limelight felt vulnerable.

"Up next, we have Ripple Creek's own Mayor Mylie!"

Mylie braced herself. She didn't expect boos, but boos could happen all the same. As she stepped on stage, Brick's arrogant sneer captured her focus. Alice yawned loudly.

Then from behind her, a loud voice bellowed, "Let's go, Mylie!"

She looked back to see Cash pumping a fist over his head as he cheered her on. From the audience, Tia leaped out of her seat, clapping and whooping. Beau and Elliana joined in. The Holiday family's enthusiasm was catching, and the rest of the audience followed suit. If Alice and Brick didn't quite catch the energy, they also weren't able to temper it with their frowns.

Buoyed by the applause, Mylie strutted onto the stage. As she and Cash had planned, she waved as she entered, then walked to the edge of the stage to shake hands with audience members. In a moment, he would come swaggering out, swinging his lasso, and she would direct him to wrangle up a bouquet of flowers.

It was a cute little scenario. Nothing mind-bending, but what else are you gonna do with a mayor and a rancher/event planner?

Except maybe argue.

Mylie kept her eyes on the audience as planned, chatting and smiling. The music blasted through the speakers. A gasp rose from the audience and Mylie could only assume Cash was spinning the lasso, cinching his win for this segment of the pageant.

But no one was looking at the stage; rather, they were murmuring as they twisted in their seats toward one side of the barn. Even Alice and Brick redirected their attention. Mylie finally glanced over her shoulder toward the open barn door.

A curious fur-covered, four-legged creature pranced into the barn.

Mylie immediately turned to Cash. His shocked expression and falling lariat suggested this was not planned.

Alfonzo strutted into the barn, attracted first by a bouquet of flowers, at which he politely nibbled. Then he realized there was an audience and a stage: his happy place.

The alpaca trotted straight down the center aisle and started up the stairs. Mylie took a step back—not afraid, just really surprised. Tia, who could, and should, have scooted up the steps to oust her alpaca, just gazed at him. She was like a proud momma who finds her child's inappropriate behavior adorable.

Cash recovered first, and yelled, "Whoa there!"

Alfonzo didn't *whoa* in the slightest, but continued his trot onto the stage. Cash raised his rope and circled it over his head.

"Step back," he yelled at Mylie.

Surprised by the sharpness in his voice, Mylie yipped, which startled Alfonzo. The animal was now fully on stage, but confused by the lights and Mylie's apparent unwillingness to hang out.

Meanwhile, the crowd was going nuts. Cheering and laughing at what they thought was a choreographed skit. Mylie regained her composure and stepped back so Cash could land the lariat over Alfonzo's fluffy head. The moment the rope came down around him, Alfonzo let out a huff of indignation.

How dare you? he seemed to say. *A rope? Do you know who I am?*

The alpaca turned to Mylie, appealing to her for backup. By this time, the silliness of the situation had caught up with her and Mylie started laughing. She walked up to Alfonzo and scratched his ears, placing a kiss on his topknot. He leaned into her affections, giving her a nuzzle as the whole crowd let out an "aww!"

Cash tried to join her, but Alfonzo was having none of it, placing himself in between them and clearly preferring the one who hadn't tied him up.

"Let's hear it for the rancher and the mayor!" Piper called. "And maybe we could get a handler on stage?"

Tia finally snapped back into the reality of her alpaca on stage and came up to suggest they go elsewhere. As Cash saluted the audience, Mylie made the mistake of looking into the front row.

"At least the mayor has one supporter," Alice said, loud enough that several people heard.

A frisson of fear shot down Mylie's spine. Cash dropped a protective hand on her shoulder as he whispered, "Keep smiling. Don't let her get to you."

Mylie took his advice, giving the audience a big wave. Piper, on the other hand, turned to glare at Alice, narrowing her left eye.

"What was that?" Mylie whispered as they walked offstage.

"Alice was way out of line." He glanced back at the crowd. "I think that's grounds to ask the Hendersons to leave."

"No, I mean Alfonzo." Sure, Alice's comment was rattling. But they'd been stage-bombed by an alpaca. It seemed a touch more pressing. "Did you plan that?"

"Did it look planned?"

"Does anything involving Tia's rescues ever really come off as planned?"

Cash turned to face her, placing a second hand on her arm. He dipped his head to look into her eyes, unexpectedly serious as he said, "It's not okay for the Hendersons to bully you like that."

Mylie pressed her lips together and nodded. He was right, but somehow the longer it went on, the more she started to feel like it was her fault.

"Now, you need to get dressed for the line

dance," Cash said, gesturing to the enclosed stall that had been set aside as a changing area. "We'll unpack the alpaca incident later."

Mylie made a break for the change room, leaving Cash to loop up his rope and ditch the chaps before the dance. Everyone else was already in their jeans, white T-shirts and whatever passed as boots in their wardrobe. Bobbie's were red with fun Western detailing. Daisy wore pointy-toed, high-heeled booties. Mylie had brought her pair of Frye boots that she'd owned since high school. The classic riding boot worked for a trail ride, a long walk on a muddy day and even just times when she needed an extra kick in her step, like right now.

These boots were gonna scoot so hard. Or shiver, or whatever they were doing now.

Minutes later, Alfonzo was safely back in the stables, and Mylie was in a T-shirt and jeans. Cash focused on the audience through a gap in the curtains.

"We'd like all our contestants back out for the line-dance competition!" Piper cried.

Cash gestured for Mylie to walk ahead of him. "You've got this," he said, his voice low.

She turned around. "I just survived an alpaca invasion. I think I can dance to an Ed Sheeran song."

"I'm talking about Brick and Alice."

A few strides onto the stage, Mylie turned to smile into the audience. At that moment, Alice rolled her eyes, and muttered something to her husband. Brick folded his arms and glared.

Mylie stumbled into Bobbie. Cash caught her

arm, steadying her as he leaned down and whispered, "I've got you."

She felt, as well as heard, the words, settling them into her heart.

I've got you.

He meant physically. He wasn't going to let her stumble and fall off the stage. But her heart took the words literally, a gentle rain of cool compassion to protect her from the anger emanating from the front row.

Ed Sheeran's catchy hit came blasting through the speakers. The line of contestants swayed on their feet, then at Piper's signal, launched into the dance. It was immediately apparent that others did not approach line dancing with the same intensity she and Cash did.

Cash winked at her. "Follow my lead."

He crossed left, and she followed, then moved into a few easy steps forward. His hand ran down her arm, his palm slipping against hers. He raised his brow, asking if they were going to do this.

She nodded. They were. Clara and Piper could switch up the dance. The Hendersons could glower all they wanted and make biting comments. She and her partner would line dance like they were born to do it.

At the first shift in direction, Cash kicked it into gear. He twirled her, then kept an arm around her waist as they moved through the next rotation. Mylie added a shimmy, Cash threw in a strut. One of them let out a whoop somewhere along the way.

Mylie couldn't help but laugh as they worked together, turning the simple movement into their own fabulous, impromptu choreography.

Ed Sheeran had no idea what he'd unleashed.

The music, the lights and Cash's warm scent coupled with beeswax soap all spun around her. When she had clicked on the registration form online, all those weeks ago, Mylie had no intention of finding a match. But on stage, shivering for all she was worth, it was pretty clear she'd met hers.

Could she handle another tightrope, another love she had to earn and keep? He might like her now, as they worked together to secure the top two places in the pageant, but would he feel the same way when she ultimately won?

"What. A. Show!" Piper cried as the music faded.

Clara joined her at the microphone. "Let's hear it one more time for our contestants!"

"The numbers are very close," Piper said.

"So close."

"Literally the closest."

"In some cases, the same."

"But we do have your winners for the afternoon. Coming in third place, it's our adorable mayor, Mylie Saunders!"

Mylie gave Cash a grateful smile, then stepped forward to receive the green sash. As Bobbie won second place, Mylie didn't feel a speck of annoyance knowing Cash would win first. He deserved it, fair and square.

"And our first-place winner, prepared for anything, ready for everything, the dapper librarian, Myron!"

Mylie's mouth dropped open, but she was so indignant nothing came out. She stepped forward as Cash's hands landed solidly on her shoulders. He was shushing her at the same moment she finally found her voice, pointed at Cash and yelled, "What about him?!"

CHAPTER EIGHT

"JUST DROP IT," Cash whispered.

"You were robbed," she whispered back through a smile. Cash's hands were still on her shoulders, ostensibly to keep her from launching herself at two matchmakers.

But also because that just felt like a good place for his hands.

"We'll see you all for trivia at Ripple Creek Public House tomorrow night!" Clara said to the crowd, waving.

"I would really like to see the score sheet," Mylie muttered.

Cash kept one hand on Mylie's arm as he reached out with the other to offer Myron a handshake. The sweater-vest over a plaid shirt and slacks with reinforced knees was a very practical outfit for a librarian.

"Congratulations," Cash said.

"Why, thank you! I thought you had me when you roped that alpaca. You and Mylie are my biggest competition, you know."

"Are we now?" Cash asked.

Mylie took a decisive step toward Piper, but Cash tightened his grip on her shoulder.

"Let's take a walk," he said.

"Why aren't you mad?" she whispered.

The audience started to pack up and leave. Alice looked pointedly at Cash, then at his hand on Mylie's shoulder. He was mad alright, but not about the scoring.

That said, how exactly had he not won that round?

It didn't matter. There were bigger problems to deal with.

"Let's walk it out," Cash said.

He kept a smile in place, congratulated Bobbie, waved to the matchmakers and managed to get Mylie out of the barn before she was able to yell *dadgummit* or whatever other old-timey phrase that came to her mind.

Although she was muttering a mile a minute. Who knew what had already come out of her mouth?

They walked out of the barn into a wash of afternoon heat. At four o'clock, the sun had thoroughly warmed the land, releasing the scent of pine needles. A breeze drifting across the lake brought a hint of loam. He could see Mylie's shoulders relax as she breathed in the scent of summer.

"Can you take a walk with me? Talk for a second?" he asked.

"You wouldn't rather argue with Piper and Clara? Because you were robbed."

He kept his eyes forward as they moved through

the central yard, toward a copse of aspen trees. "Okay, yep, I thought I was gonna win that."

"It's highway robbery—"

"Mylie—" He cut her off. "You didn't tell me about Alice and Brick."

Mylie stilled. Dappled light played across her face, obscuring her expression. Her voice dropped to nearly a whisper. "Is that what we're talking about right now?"

"Why didn't you tell me they're trying to get you kicked out of office?"

The remaining color drained from Mylie's face. "She said that?"

"Not exactly. She kept making references to the French Revolution." The noise and activity of the pageant receded behind them as they approached the trees.

"Yeah. She was really into the Netflix series on Marie Antoinette."

"Mylie, this is serious."

She pressed her lips together and turned her head away. "You think I'm not taking this seriously?" she asked quietly. "Cash, I have given this job nothing but my best. I have two people who live for the drama breathing down my neck and threatening a recall. Yes, I'm taking it seriously."

As though summoned by her distress, Alice and Brick emerged from the barn. Cash reacted, taking a step toward them. Mylie pulled him back.

"Don't poke the bear."

"They're not the bear." Cash shot the Hendersons a glare. "More like a couple of trash-eating, chicken-poaching raccoons."

Mylie breathed in deeply, as if she was breathing for both of them. "Okay, funny image. Apt. But if you and I are gonna pick a fight right now, it should be with a pair of matchmakers."

Brick caught Cash glowering at him and responded with a warning look. Cash widened his stance.

"The Hendersons are on my property, threatening my—"

My what?

Was Mylie his friend? His pageant partner? His secret crush that kept life interesting even in the darkest moments?

"Threatening *my mayor.* They are not the bear. *I'm* the bear."

Cash stalked toward Alice and Brick. Not to be outstalked, Mylie lengthened her strides to catch up with him. He stalked faster.

"What are you doing?"

"Setting these two straight on who's in charge in this town."

"This is a democracy," she reminded him. "By the people, for the people."

Cash came to an abrupt halt in front of the Hendersons and crossed his arms. No one said anything, the silence emphasized by a chorus of summer insects and the chatter of audience members as they made their way out of the barn.

"What a great show!" Alice declared, like they

were all the tightest group of friends. She inclined her head regally toward Mylie. "Congratulations on third place."

Cash scoffed, but that was about all he had. He hadn't thought this out, hadn't prepared for his next move. His instinct was to solve this for Mylie. Hard to do when he didn't fully understand the problem. And he knew good and well that Mylie didn't want someone to save her. Her vibe was definitely more DIY in that department.

All in all, a dramatic march across the central yard might not have been the most strategic course of action. He should have gathered more information before launching himself at his guests. He was like the peacocks when someone or something didn't immediately respond to a threatening sweep of tail feathers. What came next? A low hiss?

"Thank you," Mylie said. "We're grateful you're here to support literacy efforts."

"We're grateful you singles have a chance to put yourselves out there," Alice said. "It's important to put down roots, particularly if you want to be taken seriously in local government."

Cash tilted his head to one side. "Umm? Are you suggesting a person has to be married to be in politics?"

Mylie placed a warning hand on Cash's arm. Her voice was steady as she said, "I'm glad we caught you before you left. Cash is concerned." She turned to him, giving him a chance to voice his thoughts reasonably. "He's under the impression that you two—"

"Don't appreciate Mylie." He gave a firm nod as he finished the sentence. Not appreciating Mylie should be punishable by fine, or better yet, community service. "She's smart, she cares, she has vision and the work ethic to make her great ideas happen. You're entitled to your own opinions, but I'm gonna ask that when you're on my property, you don't plot against my guests."

"What?" Alice's innocence was so fake there was no way it wasn't intentional.

"Is there a plot?" Brick asked.

Cash shifted, putting his hands on his hips. "Ending a reign of terror?"

Alice and Brick stilled. Blood drained from Alice's face as it rushed to Brick's, as though the two of them shared a circulatory system and took turns with fight-or-flight.

Then Alice let out a long laugh. "Oh, Cash. We appreciate our Mylie." She placed an arm around Mylie's shoulder, in an action similar to hugging a cactus. "We just want to help."

Mylie swallowed like she knew what was coming next.

"But she's not very good at accepting our help."

Mylie stiffened, which was impressive because she was already pretty stiff. Cash was tempted to put *his* arm around Mylie, but that wasn't what the situation called for, either.

Why hadn't he thought this through? When he

was prepared for an argument, he couldn't lose. But he'd just barged into something he had no background in, and was potentially making things worse for Mylie.

Mylie stepped out from under Alice's arm. "I've heard your concerns about my committee work, and I'm incorporating your suggestions."

"You are trying." Alice nodded, her chin-length bob bobbing with the motion. Brick also got in on the action.

"You're just so young," Brick said. "In time, you'll make a great leader."

Anger flooded through Cash. "She's a great leader now. Did you even see her poster board? And Mylie's not that young. She's plenty old."

Mylie gave him a wry smile. "Thank you, Cash."

"I mean, not 'old' old. Old enough."

"I'm thirty-two," she said.

"Thirty-two." Cash pointed at Brick and Alice. "That's a great age. For mayors. And other people."

Okay, dude. Clearly time to stop talking.

His gaze connected with Mylie's, trying to offer an apology. Why had he launched himself across the yard and lost his temper?

The answer was simple. This situation felt unfair. For his entire childhood and early adult life, the Holiday family had been subject to rumors. Word got out of control fast in a place like Ripple Creek, and it could be an uphill battle to change the narrative.

Brick's expression shifted to something colder.

He looked at his wife, and some communication took place there. Cash wasn't sure what was going on, but Mylie picked up on it quickly, and said, "Let's all—"

Brick leaned toward Mylie. Cash didn't like the way he was getting into her space. "Not everyone wants Club 75. But you keep pushing it. You need to step back."

It was Brick who needed to step back, in Cash's opinion.

"Our seniors need more support," Mylie said.

"No family is going to move to town because we have some club for seniors."

"No, but the people who already live here will benefit from it. I appreciate that you and Alice have an interest in selling homes in the new development. But that has no bearing on program funding." Mylie's voice was patient, but firm as she said, "At all."

"Your job is to respond to what the community wants," Brick said.

"Who really wants some program for razzling and dazzling?" Cash barked, firm but not at all patient.

Everyone turned to stare at him.

"Dance 'n' Do?" he asked. "For girls with a passion for razzling, dazzling and bedazzling? How is that any different than your average after-school playdate?"

Alice sucked in a breath, a prelude to spitting out fire.

"How dare you talk about my wife's program that way!" Brick roared.

"How dare you talk about my…mayor, in any way."

Brick had moved from Mylie's personal space into his. "You run for public office, you gotta learn to roll with the punches. She knows that."

"This isn't the best time for this conversation," Mylie said.

"I don't think this warrants a conversation at all." Brick took his wife's hand, glaring at Cash. "This calls for action."

"Umm? Now, you don't want to have a meeting?"

Brick looked utterly confused. Cash was beginning to understand that a big part of the issue here was that the guy just wasn't that smart.

"I thought that was your whole problem. Mylie doesn't like meetings. She doesn't like to sit around listening to you two inflate your own egos and come up with programs to help you sell houses." Cash nodded to Alice. "You think you've got good ideas, but when Mylie shuts you down in three quick arguments, it pokes a hole in your self-image. That hurts. Believe me, I know how it feels. I've been there."

Mylie dropped a hand on his arm, as though to stop him before realizing he'd already gone way, way too far. She morphed the action of holding him back into a resigned pat on the forearm. "Let's table this discussion for now."

Brick pointed a finger at Mylie. "You'll be hearing from your constituents at the next town-hall meeting."

Mylie started to respond but Brick pulled Alice away, blowing past Myron and Gramma Birdie, who were chatting it up. Peacocks hustled out of the way, then spread their tail feathers in a late display of aggression. It wasn't until they'd slammed their car doors that Cash let out a groan.

"I'm so sorry."

Mylie had to be furious. If they weren't plotting a recall before, they certainly were now.

"That was a terrible idea—" Mylie said.

"I know."

"—and *so* awesome." Her blue eyes lit up. "Did you see her face? When you said 'razzling'?"

Cash risked a glance at Mylie. Was she really not mad?

"This is so bad." Her shoulders shook as she laughed. "But honestly worth it to finally have someone call out Dance 'n' Do."

"I never should have started with them," Cash said. "Mylie, I'm sorry. It's just that they were threatening you, and I couldn't stand by and let them insult you."

"No, I get it. You reacted. I know how you get when people threaten—" she broke off, her blue eyes connecting with his.

Cash finished the sentence. "When people threaten someone I care about."

Like you.

How had he come to care about her so deeply in

such a short period of time? It wasn't that he'd never noticed how cute she was, or been impressed by her intelligence. He'd never have engaged in all those arguments if she wasn't smart. What he hadn't seen, or perhaps been shown, was how sweet she was. That touch of sweetness, like the honey in a spicy BBQ sauce, changed everything. He couldn't get enough of her.

And, man, it was going to hurt when she no longer wanted to stick around.

In the silence, birdsong and the summertime hum of insects filled the central yard. Mylie cocked her head, listening. "I love this sound. Early July on Ripple Creek."

"Me, too."

There was a lot to discuss here, but all he could think to say was, "Do you still want to take that walk?"

Mylie nodded. "That's exactly what I want. Thank you."

Cash glanced around the yard. The quickest way to the creek was through the oak grove, past Beau's favorite spot. But Cash knew another deer trail through the aspen trees he thought Mylie might like.

He placed a hand on her arm and pointed past the guesthouse, toward the path. "This way."

They headed down the trail, into the cool, shady woods. Being in the trees settled her breathing. Light filtered through the shimmering leaves, little birds moved from one branch to the next. Beau would know all their names and migratory patterns. Cash just thought of them as pretty summer birds.

Finally, he said, "Whatever the Hendersons are trying to pull, I'm here to help you. And I mean help, not blow up like I did back there. You are the best person for this job."

Mylie nodded. Nothing he said was untrue and she knew it. She brushed back a strand of hair, raising her luminous blue eyes to his face.

"Is that what you would have said about me three months ago?" she asked.

He shook his head, willing to admit his part in her persecution. "Three months ago I was floundering, trying to hold on to my family's land. We made mistakes starting up this business and I knew it. I was desperate."

"You were desperate, and I was judgmental. We were both at fault."

A little smile played across her lips. He looked up, heat rising to his face as he admitted, "I did have some fun with those arguments."

"Me, too. It was nice to have a worthy adversary."

Cash lifted a low-hanging branch that was blocking the path and indicated Mylie should go ahead. "Is that how you think of me?"

Her smile broadened. It put to mind another question: Did she think about him?

Cash reached out to touch a quivering aspen leaf, keeping his eyes on it as he said, "Three months ago I didn't know you at all."

She nodded, the clouds returning to her expression. "That's where the problem lies. The people I work with directly—the fire chief, the police department, public works—all take me for who I am. They know I don't love extra meetings, and for the most part the city employees don't love extra meetings, either. But for most folks in Ripple Creek, all they know is my reputation. And my reputation changes depending on who's talking."

The temperature dipped as they neared the creek. A breeze sent the aspen leaves quivering. Cash's heart echoed the excitement.

"Okay then, let's get talking."

Mylie glanced at him, questioning.

"Let's change the narrative. My siblings and I experienced a similar situation. Some people—" he held his palm out to her "—who shall remain nameless, used to have pretty set opinions of our family. We just kept showing up, being our nice, normal selves."

"Normal?" Mylie asked.

Cash laughed. "Or something like that. This pageant is a great place to show off how relatable you are. And once it's over, come hang out with us. We have guests at our events from all over the area. You can stop by and do the hand-shaking, baby-kissing thing you're so good at."

Mylie shook her head, but she didn't say no.

They emerged from the path at the banks of Ripple Creek. This spot was a little east of Beau's favorite camping spot. It was less dramatically beautiful, but Cash had always preferred it.

Sunshine reflected off the water, a hazy glow permeating the trees lining the creek. Mylie walked across the pebbles and crouched down, dipping her fingers into the water as though drawn to it. Cash wanted to leave the conversation behind them, to just enjoy this perfect spot with Mylie. But in order to help her, there was one more thing he needed to know.

"I gotta ask, though, why do you want to be mayor of Ripple Creek? That just sounds like one headache after the next."

She looked up at him as if surprised that he'd asked. Then her lovely smile broke out. "To understand that, you need to know about what brought me to Ripple Creek in the first place."

MYLIE WAS TEMPTED to suggest a fair trade. She'd tell him about her attachment to Ripple Creek, and in return he had to explain how he was still single.

And maybe provide a few thoughts on what might convince him to be not single. Just out of curiosity.

Asking for a friend.

Cash joined her at the edge of the creek. He glanced down at their feet, then at the water playfully running its course. He seemed to hesitate, then asked, "Wanna take your boots off? Do a little wading?"

It was exactly what she wanted. He'd read her

mind before she'd even been conscious of the thought. "I've never been one to turn down a good wade."

He grinned, keeping his gaze forward as he said, "Nope, you didn't strike me as a woman to pass up the chance."

Mylie sat down on the pebble beach to pull off her boots. Cash dropped down next to her. His feet, like hers, were pale, as though it had been a decade since either of them had enjoyed a carefree, barefoot summer day. He lined up his boots next to hers, then stood and offered her a hand.

"Now, tell me why you're in city politics. I want to know about the day you woke up and thought, I'm going to run for mayor!"

"Okay." Mylie took his hand and let him pull her to her feet. "It's pretty simple. I love Ripple Creek. It is my favorite place on earth. And, yes, I have been to Siena, Italy."

Cash laughed. "I hear it's nice there."

"It's stunning, and delicious." Mylie steadied herself by placing a hand on his arm. The pebbles were warm and smooth under her bare feet.

"I've been fortunate enough to see some incredible places." She headed for the water. "Ripple Creek, though, is home. Oooh! Cold!" Mylie jumped out of the creek, skittering back to the banks.

"You gotta take it slow." Cash stepped up to the creek, placing just his toes in the current. Mylie stood next to him, dipping her big toe back in.

"Ripple Creek is home, but you didn't grow up here, did you?" he asked.

"No, my family had a vacation home at Creekside Resort."

"Oh, cool. I've never been there. My dad scammed the contractor who built Creekside for somewhere in the neighborhood of twenty thousand dollars, so I never got the chance to check it out."

"Your dad." Mylie shook her head. "Seriously!"

"I know. Back to the story—your family used to come here." Cash stepped farther into the water.

Mylie inched up next to him. The rush of the cold water over her feet, and the pebbles and slippery rocks beneath her soles, brought her straight back to childhood. It was a feeling of peace and anticipation, and she'd found it nearly impossible to replicate as an adult.

Although she was definitely feeling it now.

"We came here for every vacation, and several long weekends each year. Growing up in Portland, my parents had high expectations for me and my brother. He's a doctor now, by the way. The youngest head of surgery at Mt. Olive Children's Hospital."

"I didn't know you had siblings," he said.

"Just one."

"You never talk about him."

"Are we judging each other on how frequently we talk about our siblings?" she asked.

He shook his head, chuckling. "Naw, go ahead.

Your parents had high expectations. You and your brother are high achievers."

Mylie exhaled. Mayor of Ripple Creek was not what her parents considered a high achievement.

"As a kid I was busy. There was always some assignment to be done to perfection, some activity I was supposed to be getting better at. But when we came here, to Ripple Creek, I could just be. You know? I was a kid. In the winter I played in the snow all day long, until Mom would call me in. In the summers I would spend all my time in the creek, letting my imagination run wild. I don't think I will ever experience anything as pleasurable as those long days by the creek."

Cash watched her, a smile playing across his lips. She could imagine that as she splashed on the banks of this creek farther upstream, he might have been wading in it here, same days, same times, same water running over their toes.

"You're welcome to come out and play in the creek at any time." He leaned down and picked up a flat rock.

She laughed.

"I mean it. The offer stands. If you have a rough day at work, you don't even need to call. Just come on out and skip a few rocks." He placed the stone in her hand. "You're always welcome."

"Thank you."

Mylie pulled her arm back, the movement deeply ingrained as she flipped her wrist, and the rock skipped twice across the surface.

Cash picked a rock and imitated the motion, getting four skips.

"So you liked Ripple Creek because you could be yourself here."

"Yes. As a kid, I used to dream that my parents would tell us we were moving here. That we'd come for the weekend and we'd never leave. But that wasn't my family. We'd pile back in the car on Sunday afternoon, homework on my lap in the back seat, and barrel down the highway, back to the grind of life. I did all the things, got into an exclusive college, then a competitive law school. My parents wanted me to go into politics."

"Umm?" Cash tilted his head to one side.

"What?" she asked.

"Gotta be honest, that sounds like a weird wish for parents to have for their child."

"I don't know. I was interested in law, I always ran for leadership positions. I like thinking about policy, and being part of making this world a better place."

"Your parents must be thrilled. Mayor, that's a huge accomplishment."

"Not exactly. I graduated, and Mom took me to meet with an expert to discuss political avenues. While they were contacting friends in DC, I applied for a job at a law firm in Ripple Creek. The minute I moved into my little apartment, just down the street from Karen's bakery, I knew I was home." A summer breeze kicked up, pushing her hair into her face. Mylie tucked a loose strand behind her ear.

"My parents were…not stoked. They kept referring to my time in Ripple Creek as my 'gap year,' even after I'd been here for several years."

"I have a little experience with parents not being real supportive." Cash bent down to scoop up two rocks, and handed her one. "What happened next? You live here, your family's not happy, Bruce Holiday is tearing through the county making plenty of work for lawyers."

Cash sent his rock scuttling across the surface. Three skips.

"I settled in, made friends." She pulled her arm back then whipped it forward, releasing the rock. It skimmed the surface of the creek once, twice, then submerged on the third hit. "After a while it became apparent that if Ripple Creek was going to keep its charm, I needed to step up and get involved. I ran for city council. I did a good job, and was encouraged to run for mayor. I want Ripple Creek to be a great place to live. Really live, you know? Not just battle through life, or barely hang on. I want good housing, opportunities for people to get outside and connect with their community. I'm happy to welcome tourists, but I want the focus on being an affordable, livable community."

"It's a great vision."

She nodded, scooching farther into the water. The cold felt so good; there was no better medicine in the world than stepping into a creek in summertime.

"And what about you?" he asked.

"What about me?"

Cash picked up a rock and set it in her palm. "Are you really living here?"

Mylie closed her fingers around the sun-warmed rock. She shook her head.

"No. I'm right back in the same pattern I grew up in. I work all the time. And if I run out of work to do, I make more work for myself. I keep saying that I'm doing all this so people can enjoy Ripple Creek, but I'm not taking the time to enjoy my life. Eight-year-old Mylie would be pretty bummed to see how completely I've blown my chance here."

Cash was silent for a moment. Then he nodded. "Alright then. Sounds like you need to start blocking out some creek time."

Mylie laughed.

"I'm serious. We'll start small, but by the end of summer I expect to see you out here three times a week, minimum." Cash released another rock, skipping an impressive five skips across the water.

A gust of wind kicked up through the trees, pushing Mylie's hair into her face. The water swirling around her feet no longer felt cold. She was possessed with the urge to splash in deeper, make boats out of leaves and try to catch a young rainbow trout with her hands. She felt, for the first time in a long time, like playing.

"You know if I start coming out here regularly, my rock skipping will eventually surpass yours."

He put his hands on his hips. "Those are some

big words, Saunders. You wanna take this to the lake?"

She laughed, the sound echoing up the creek bed. She didn't know where things were going with Cash, or if she could keep herself together when they got there, but her inner eight-year-old was all in on creek visits and rock-skipping competitions.

"Hello?" a voice called out from the aspens. "Cash?"

Elliana, in her trademark cotton dress and tennis shoes, emerged from the path.

"There you are!" Elliana cried. "I've been looking all over for you. I'm sorry to be weird and panicky, but can you do some emergency brunch prep?"

Cash glanced up at the sun. "It's gotta be five o'clock. Is that a little late for brunch?"

"Oh, sorry. The DuBoff bridal party asked if they could come out to do another walk-through of the property tomorrow. So I suggested brunch and they were like 'brunch!' But I hadn't exactly planned it so—"

Elliana paused abruptly, looking from Cash to Mylie and back again, then at the water splashing around their ankles. "Am I interrupting something?"

Mylie shook her head. "No."

No soul-baring, rock-skipping connections being made around here.

"Of course not." Cash shrugged. "What could you be interrupting?"

"An argument?" Elliana guessed.

That was fair.

"No, we were just…" Cash trailed off as he pointed to their boots in the bank and held up a flat rock. They were two full-grown adults wading in a creek. That's all there was to say on that topic.

"I'm having some political troubles," Mylie admitted. "Cash was listening as I talked it out."

"Political troubles?" Elliana's huge eyes widened further. "I'm so sorry. Can I help?"

The Holiday family could help. Every person willing to shut down the gossip and talk up her good points mattered. But asking for, and accepting help, had never been her strong suit.

"Thank you. But right now, I'd love to just not talk about it for a minute. You know?"

"I absolutely know." Elliana said. "Sometimes you just don't want to give energy to negativity."

"That's it."

Elliana tilted her head to one side. "But, would you have any interest in giving energy to brunch?"

Mylie laughed. There were a hundred things she could be doing back in her office—not to mention the prep work she still needed to put in for Ripple Creek Trivia Night. But there was only one answer to this question. "Yes. I'd love to."

"You would?" Cash asked.

"If…you want my help."

"Yes. I'd love…that. Your help." Cash shook his head, then turned to Elliana. "What were you thinking to serve?"

"I was thinking you'd know."

Cash chuckled as he stepped out of the water, then offered Mylie a steadying hand. "Okay, give me a few minutes. I'll run through the garden and see what we've got. Mylie, are you okay helping Elliana get set up in the kitchen and I'll meet you both there?"

Mylie joined Cash on the bank, then took one last look at the creek. By now, Brick and Alice would be back at their home in Banks Run, scheming to get her kicked out of office. She could head back to town, bury herself in the work that was always waiting and try to be a better mayor in the hopes that it would protect her against future attacks.

But like those long, delightful weekends in Ripple Creek as a child, she was ready to focus on the here and now. She glanced up at the cowboy: auburn hair, errant smile, honest invitation. The here and now was looking good.

"Absolutely. Let's do it."

WAS CASH SWAGGERING as he set up the assembly line in the kitchen? Possibly. Was he doing a little subtle bragging about his tomato crop? One could say that.

But Mylie's laughter and easy chatter with his family soaked up any uneasiness he might feel. She was enthusiastic as he set baskets of potatoes, fresh greens, tomatoes and other produce on the island, and happy to join in scrubbing veggies at the sink. Cash pulled up some old-school Brooks and Dunn on his phone. The cheerful conversation and music made the task feel like a party, rather than party prep. By the time they had the assembly line on the island set up, Cash had learned two important things about Mylie:

She didn't know how to cook.

She was really fun to have in the kitchen.

"Okay, this is an assembly for a lemon-berry French-toast casserole. We'll prepare two pans of this tonight, and I'll bake it in the morning." Cash gestured to a row of ingredients. "On the other side we have smoked salmon, potato and herb strata. As you two prep the overnight dishes, I'll wrap the asparagus in prosciutto and make the hollandaise sauce. All we'll need to do tomorrow morning is roast asparagus, bake the dishes and whip up a simple caprese salad."

"Where do you want me?" Mylie asked.

"You take the French-toast casserole," Elliana said. "I'll start on the strata."

The three of them bopped around to the music, assembling their respective dishes.

"Now, I know your secrets," Mylie said. "When I was here for Pam's bridal shower, I wondered how you were cooking and hosting at the same time."

"It's a system, not a secret." Cash said.

"Cash is a master at prepping events ahead of time," Elliana said as she arranged potato slices at the bottom of a casserole dish.

"Is this how you prepared for the Mobleys' anniversary, as well?"

Cash shook his head. "For something that big, we catered the meal, but the caterer agreed to use as much of our produce as possible."

"And to think I spent all that time glaring at you, assuming you were breaking some type of food-prep code."

"Speaking of—" Cash glanced around, wondering if he should be feeling guilty. "How are we doing?"

It was, of course, at that moment that Tia swept into the room, two greyhounds tangled up at her feet. Cash was able to see the situation from Mylie's point of view.

Dogs in a commercial kitchen.

Even if those things were more like two coffee-shop hipsters than dogs.

"Hi, Tia," Mylie said. Cash braced himself for her to scold his sister out of the kitchen. "It was fun to hang out with Alfonzo today."

"He adores you!" Tia said, not a speck of remorse over the incident.

"It's mutual," Mylie assured her.

"What are we doing?" Tia asked, scanning the tables. "Can I help?"

"You can wash your hands," Cash snapped.

"Umm, Cash?" Tia tilted her head at him. "I'm literally an adult. I know how to wash my hands."

"Then do it."

Elliana drew in a breath. She didn't love it when they bickered. Cash didn't want to bicker, either, but he also didn't want the Holiday Family Code Violation Show to break out in the kitchen.

"Could those—" Cash swallowed hard, then addressed the creatures "—dogs maybe go elsewhere?"

Before he'd even finished the sentence the greyhounds had plopped down on their cushy dog bed in front of the dishwasher.

"Where would they go?" Tia asked.

"Anywhere but in the kitchen—"

At that moment, the back door slammed open.

"Hey, fam! What's up?" Beau came striding into the kitchen, immediately dropping his hand into the bowl of raspberries and popping one into his mouth.

"Don't eat out of the bowl." Cash pushed his hand away. "That's for guests."

"What am I supposed to eat out of then?"

"Could you wait for dinner?" Cash asked.

"Sure." Beau paused for barely a nanosecond, then asked, "What's for dinner?"

Cash groaned. "Please excuse my brother, he's not always like this."

"He *is* always like this," Elliana said. "I wouldn't have him any other way."

"And the smooching begins," Cash said, as, indeed, the smooching did begin. "I'm trying to run a kitchen here."

"Okay, *Chef*," Tia said, mocking the title. It didn't help that Mylie giggled. Tia turned to her and said,

"Were you aware that our brother can get a little bossy from time to time?"

"People!" Cash banged the back of a pot with a wooden spoon. "We have the mayor in the kitchen. I love you guys—"

"We love you, too," Tia, Beau and Elliana responded.

"But could we not break any more health codes for a minute?"

"You want to wait until Mylie leaves?" Tia asked.

At that, Mylie burst into laughter. Cash groaned. He knew their practices pushed the limits of what was allowed for a commercial kitchen. He understood why it was important to toe the line. But did it all have to come crashing down around the lemonberry French-toast casserole?

"I'm not actually sure there's a problem either way," Mylie said. "Are the DuBoffs paying for brunch?"

"We are hoping they will be paying an enormous fee for the wedding," Elliana responded. "But they haven't paid anything yet."

"So brunch is free?"

"In a sense. Access to the site, meetings with me, general care and kindness are all part of our ethic—unreasonable hospitality."

"That's Elliana's magic." Cash wiped his hands on a kitchen towel as he came to stand next to Mylie. "She's not just hosting an event, she's creating a sense of belonging for the guests. These

DuBoffs are going to feel like Holiday Ranch is their second home by the time the wedding is over."

"I felt that when I was at Pam's shower, like it was easy to have fun. We celebrated Pam on her terms." Mylie's expression grew reflective. "You *planned* everything to make us feel comfortable?"

Elliana tucked her hair behind her ear and nodded.

"That party was fabulous. I'll be honest, I showed up ready to criticize."

"I'll be honest," Beau said. "We noticed."

Cash stiffened at Beau's criticism, but Mylie just grinned.

"I wasn't willing to admit it at the time, but that was hands down the best party I'd ever been to. It was so lovely, I had trouble finding fault with it. I finally had to land on a noise ordinance."

The room erupted into laughter. Cash remembered seeing Mylie's car from the barn, then running out to meet her before Elliana could smooth over the situation, his heart speeding up at the thought of another good argument.

"That's impressive," Mylie said to Elliana.

"That's my wife," Beau said, slipping an arm around her waist. "These DuBoffs are going to have a great time at their son's wedding before it even begins."

"If they book us," Elliana said.

"They will." Beau reached for a piece of prosciutto. Cash slapped his fingers away. Beau interpreted that as an invitation to wrestle and launched himself at Cash.

"Hey now," Cash grumbled. "We're trying to run a business."

But Mylie just smiled. "If the DuBoffs aren't paying for brunch, you aren't beholden to the health code. I'm not saying the code is a bad idea, but since they aren't customers yet, we can overlook the dogs and tabby cat in the kitchen."

Cash warmed as Mylie found a loophole to make everything okay. Then he frowned.

"What tabby cat?"

"In the box." Mylie pointed to the open shelving by a built-in desk.

Everyone except Tia, who got real busy peeling a carrot, turned to stare at the cat.

"How long has that cat been there?" Cash asked.

"How long…today?" Tia asked.

Cash exhaled as he dropped lids onto casserole dishes and put them in the fridge.

"Is this cat new?" Elliana asked.

"Well. No," Tia said innocently. "She's a senior cat. She's not new at all."

"New to this family," Beau clarified.

Cash noticed Mylie make an apologetic face at Tia.

His sister just shrugged and grinned back at her as she addressed her siblings. "Okay, the real question is how can you all live here, and you haven't even noticed a sweet new friend, but Mylie can see the cat the moment she walks in?"

"It *is* in a box," Mylie said.

"And speaking of Mylie," Tia continued, "can we extend a little hospitality toward her? It's like six thirty and she's been either on stage or in the kitchen since two. Can we feed this woman some dinner?"

Cash hadn't realized how hungry he was until Tia mentioned it. Most days he was on top of meal planning, but this day had gotten away from him. The room was a mess of breakfast and Cash wasn't sure where to start.

"I'm on it," Beau said. "Just give me fifteen minutes to get a fire going."

He opened the fridge and grabbed a package of venison sausages. Tia jumped in on the theme, grabbing buns and condiments.

"Ooh!" Elliana's eyes lit up. "And marshmallows?"

Beau was already pulling one of many bags of marshmallows from the cabinet, grinning at his new wife. "It wouldn't be a complete meal without marshmallows."

"How is venison sausage and marshmallows a complete meal?" Cash asked, but Beau was already out the door.

Elliana, Tia and two dogs followed, leaving Cash and Mylie alone in the kitchen.

Mylie grinned at him from across the island. Cash held her gaze.

"Are we good in here?" she asked.

"As far as the DuBoff brunch goes, I think

we're good." He held up a hand for a high five. She slapped her palm against his, lingering for just a moment.

"Dinner, on the other hand, needs more than sausage and marshmallows roasted over the fire."

"Agreed," Mylie said.

"Want to help me put together a salad?"

"I am completely ready to follow instructions."

The dinner turned out to be more well-rounded than Cash had worried. As he and Mylie made a salad, Tia returned to the kitchen to grab German potato salad from the fridge, and a bag of fancy corn chips left over from a party. It was still light out, but the day had cooled by the time Mylie and Cash left the kitchen to join his siblings. Crickets chirped in the evening air. Elliana had set up chairs for everyone, and they gathered around the firepit by the lake, roasting sausages on sticks.

"This is just like your engagement party, right?" Mylie asked, examining her sausage, before turning it to roast the other side. "Those pictures were gorgeous, even if everyone was surprised to hear you'd gotten engaged so quickly."

All conversation around the firepit came to an abrupt stop.

Then Tia tilted her head and said, "Umm?"

"Tia," Beau warned.

Cash kept his eyes on Mylie as she studied each of them.

"I'm just saying—" Tia leaned down and fed

a piece of sausage to one of the dogs at her feet "—she's really smart."

Mylie's eyes flickered from one family member to the next, as though she already knew what they weren't telling her. Could they trust her with the secret?

"Okay, about that particular party—" Elliana said.

"Which is my second favorite party on record," Beau interrupted. He took Elliana's hand. "My favorite party was our wedding."

Elliana patted Beau's arm as she continued, "We weren't exactly engaged at that point."

A slow smile spread across Mylie's face, like she'd found a particularly satisfying puzzle piece. "I wondered. Like, I remember seeing the pictures online, and thinking that happened awfully quickly. Then at Pam's bridal shower, Beau was always staring at Elliana when she wasn't looking, which I thought was odd. Not that he was staring at her, but that he felt the need to hide it. Over time there were a lot of little clues, but the kicker was when you switched out the rings at the prom."

"You saw that?" Elliana asked.

Beau crossed his arms and leaned back in his chair. "I thought I was being supersmooth."

"You were. I was just paying attention."

"I told you she was smart," Tia said, like she was the first person to ever notice how brilliant Mylie Saunders was. Hello, the woman had a law degree. "You could be a detective."

Mylie grinned at Tia. "I'm a regular Hank O'Brien."

Cash leaned toward her. "Mylie, I hate to ask this of you, but would you keep this a secret? It was an honest mistake, but the consequences could be pretty harmful."

"I'm loving these consequences," Beau said.

Mylie gazed at Cash, as though she was almost afraid to be included in the family secret. But she nodded, communicating all he needed to know with her pretty blue eyes. Their secrets were safe with her. A glimmer of a smile crossed her lips, then she turned to Elliana and Beau.

"You two are obviously in love, and very happily married. If some people in Ripple Creek don't fully understand the timeline, I'm not sure it's hurting anyone."

"Thank you," Elliana said. "But so you know, we didn't intend for anyone to think our engagement was real. It was supposed to be a fake engagement party, just for the pictures. A few folks got a little confused—"

"And Gramma Birdie started posting on social media," Beau added.

"Then people thought we were actually engaged and we didn't want to be accused of lying."

Mylie held up both hands. "I don't need to know. You got engaged, you had a party, you got married. All good." She paused, her gaze running across the land. "The real secret is who wrote those Hank O'Brien mystery novels. Because the more time I spend out here, the less convinced I am that it's a coincidence."

Tia's head sprang up. She asked, almost shyly, "Are—are you a Hank O'Brien fan?"

"Of course. Isn't everybody?"

Tia shrugged. "I don't know. I mean, I am. We are. How many of the books have you read?"

"All of them," Mylie said. "I love that author, whoever it is."

Tia nodded, taking her eyes off the fire to scan their ranch. She let out a happy sigh. For the first time in a long time, Tia seemed to really relax.

Cash sat back in his chair, watching Mylie and Tia bond over books they loved. Overhead, stars winked out, making the gathering by the firepit feel like their own private corner of a vast and miraculous universe.

A corner where Mylie fit perfectly.

CHAPTER NINE

MYLIE HOPPED OFF her stool and headed straight for Cash the moment he walked in the door at Ripple Creek Public House. Best to just tell him what she'd done and be done with it.

Of course, heading straight toward anyone was difficult in this particular establishment. Public House was packed. An assortment of small restaurants were located in what was once a stately Episcopal church. When upkeep on the historic brick-and-stone building became too much for an aging congregation, a generous donor built a modern structure on the edge of town. While the Episcopalians gathered peacefully in their new church, Ripple Creek erupted into a heated debate about what to do with the old one. Some people wanted it torn down, others wanted it preserved, but with what funding? As a city councilor at the time, Mylie stepped outside of the debate and looked to other communities to see how they dealt with similar situations. Ripple Creek couldn't be the only place with a beautiful, old, needy building in want of a second life. There had to be any number of business plans that could take flight in the old church.

In the end, the winning proposal came from a group of entrepreneurial-minded food-truck owners. This shouldn't have been a surprise. Folks who could imagine a kitchen on wheels would have no trouble seeing the dining opportunities in a former sanctuary. The pastor's office was retrofitted with industrial appliances. Sunday-school rooms were rented out for private events. A courtyard that had once encouraged contemplative thought was now filled with café tables. Most of the action took place in the former sanctuary, where tall tables dominated the center and cozy booths lined the walls, like pews turned to face each other. Light spilled in through stained-glass windows, reminding everyone that fellowship could be found wherever people gathered together, and tiny miracles came in many forms. Some even happened over fish tacos with friends.

It was going to take one of those tiny miracles now to keep Cash from starting out trivia night in a foul mood.

"You have to promise not to be mad at me," Mylie said.

"That's a heck of a conversation opener." Cash pulled off his hat and tapped the brim against his hand, grinning at her.

"I wanted to catch you before everything gets rolling."

Cash surveyed the crowded space. "Are we over there?" He pointed to the table where Mylie had draped her cardigan over two stools next to each other.

Not that they had to sit together for trivia night. But, you know…partners.

"Yes, and before we go over, I want to explain something."

"What's up?" Cash reached past her and hung his hat on one of the pegs on the wall, next to all the other cowboy hats from all the other ranchers in the area. How did they remember which hat was theirs? Cash generally opted for a tawny brown Stetson, but so did plenty of the other men around here. Did they ever mess up and wear someone else's hat home? Or did ranchers have some internal radar that allowed them to hone in on their particular hat, like the way salmon can return to their birthplace?

He grinned at her, and she couldn't remember what it was she was supposed to be explaining. His eyes flickered to her outfit. Mylie had opted for a tank top that read I <3 Ripple Creek, Oregon, and a pair of nicely worn-in, but certainly not frayed or ripped, jeans. She wore her hair down, sunglasses multitasking as a headband at the moment.

"You don't want me to be mad?" he reminded her.

"Right. Okay, do you remember how you got into it with Brick and Alice on my behalf?"

Cash bristled. "What'd they do?"

"They didn't do anything." Mylie bit her bottom lip. "But I might have had a little scuffle on your behalf." Cash furrowed his brow. Mylie plowed on.

"I asked Piper to explain why you didn't win work-attire modeling."

Cash groaned.

"You were robbed!" Mylie reminded him.

"It's not that big of a deal."

"It is a big deal if scoring isn't consistent."

"I'm still in the lead pack," he said. "Which is you, me and, somehow, an elderly librarian."

"Former librarian," Mylie reminded him.

"Myron is definitely a crowd favorite," Cash said. "And he's got to have Ripple Creek trivia down cold. Which is why I asked Piper about the scoring and she said—"

"Uh-oh," Cash muttered, his eye catching on something over Mylie's shoulder. "It looks like she's on her way to say it herself."

Mylie looked up to see the well-dressed matchmaker heading over. "I'm sorry." Mylie pressed her fingertips to her lips, then said, "I tried to be really nice and not implicate you in my concerns."

"It's okay," Cash said.

One look at Piper's pinched expression suggested otherwise. "Yeah, I don't know that it *is* okay."

Piper swept up in front of them. "I hear you have some questions about my holistic scoring system."

Cash raised both hands, declaring his innocence. "I'm fine."

Piper leaned in and spoke quietly. "Are you suggesting I have created a scoring system to keep all contestants within ten points of each other at all times?"

She raised her eyebrows and looked pointedly at each of them before continuing.

"Are you *suggesting* that in a competition where people put themselves out there, get vulnerable in what is arguably the most vulnerable space, the quest to find love, that I make sure everyone has a win?"

Mylie pressed her lips together as Piper's words became clear. The matchmakers didn't want anyone to feel bad by coming in last.

Piper continued, "Are you suggesting, that *I'm* suggesting, that once in a while we all need a win?"

"This seems very fair," Cash said diplomatically.

"Totally fair," Mylie agreed. "And very nice, but—"

"But how are you going to work this flexible, yet humane, scoring system and still win?" Piper asked.

Her words managed to make Mylie, and from the looks of him, Cash, feel pretty small. They were here to raise money for childhood literacy initiatives, and for some people to find love. Love and literacy were definitely more important than winning.

But still…

Winning.

Cash opened his mouth to speak, then exhaled. This had to be killing him. He was interested in the money, absolutely. But if they booked the DuBoff wedding, it sounded like that wasn't going to be a huge problem. The guy just wanted to win. And so did she.

"I think we're just curious," Mylie said. "Are we

actually competing? Is there going to be a real winner?"

"Of course, there's going to be a real winner." Piper's dimpled smile, a little more devious than Clara's, broke out. "It will be the person who wins."

With that, Piper swept away, heading for a raised dais that had once served as the pulpit. There, she helped her sister set up a microphone, keeping an eye on Cash and Mylie.

"We're doomed," Mylie said.

"I'm not sure we're doomed. Yes, Piper and Clara are keeping the scores close, but currently you're in first place and I'm in second. If we can keep ourselves in the top two spots, one of us will have to win."

Mylie gazed at Cash. Was it her, or did the definition of winning seem to be shifting?

"But are we gonna stay in the top two spots, now that I've tipped our hand? They know we both want to win."

"That may have been obvious from the start," he said.

"Good point." Mylie crossed her arms and glanced at the dais.

"Now, we know they've got an eye on our behavior," he said.

"Like two superperky Santas."

Cash laughed. "Should we try to curb our competitive intensity just a bit? Be more emotionally intelligent and poised?"

"Am I not poised when I'm competing?"

"I still don't fully understand what that word means. But we do know this—the winner of trivia night is the person who answers the most questions. That's a pretty simple scoring system. I know a lot of the local lore, and can handle geography questions. You're up on everything happening in Ripple Creek at present." He paused, raising his eyebrows as though offering a dare. "What do you say we work together for the win?"

"I've been told I could stand to practice collaborating."

Mylie held out her hand. Cash shook it.

"Agreed."

She held on to his hand a beat longer than completely necessary. Then two beats longer. Which meant it was high time she let go.

"Coming through!" She was saved by a server holding a plate of onion rings who was trying to get between them.

Cash watched the server deposit the plate in front of Daisy and Caleb. "You have any interest in collaborating on a plate of onion rings?"

"Absolutely! I'll hop in line at Deep Fried Dreams."

"And I can grab us a couple of beers. IPA okay?"

"That's my trivia night go-to!"

"Let's do it." Cash held his fist out, and Mylie bumped back with her own.

Mylie managed to keep her feet from skipping on the way to her favorite guilty-pleasure food stall, but her heart was definitely bopping along. She jumped in the back of the long line. Over at Creekbed Brews,

Cash leaned back as he studied the night's offerings on the chalkboard, then pulled out his wallet.

"Is he really what you're looking for in a protector?"

Mylie spun around to find Alice, standing a little too close in line behind her.

"I don't need a protector." She didn't. But it sure was nice to have an indignant friend by her side. "Cash and the Holiday siblings are friends."

"I'd be careful about your choice of friends. Not six months ago that family wasn't welcome in town. Probably not your best bet for political allies."

Mylie pulled in a breath. "We are a small town, Alice. I'm not worried about political allies. I'm concerned about doing my job."

"If I were you, I'd be concerned about *keeping* my job," Alice said, stepping out of line and heading back to her husband.

Six excellent comebacks came to mind the moment Alice was out of earshot, as was the way with all excellent comebacks. Whatever. It didn't matter. Mylie was not going to let the conversation get her down.

Onion rings, IPA and trivia with the rival who was fast becoming her favorite person to work with—that was the menu for tonight. A couple of long lines later and Mylie and Cash were seated next to one another, digging into a heaping plate of hot and crispy onion rings. Cash gave a slight nod to where Alice and Brick were talking to another couple, looking Mylie's way. "You have any trouble from those two today?"

She looped her finger through another onion ring. "No more than normal."

Brick handed a flyer to the couple, and he and Alice moved to speak with another patron.

"Welcome, Ripple Creek!" Clara said over the PA system. "This is our fourth of six events in the Mountain Country Most Eligible Pageant. Our contestants remain neck and neck for the win."

"Or are yoked together," Cash mumbled.

Mylie gave him a nudge in the ribs. Cash winked at her, then shifted so his arm was resting against hers.

"Tonight our singles will compete in a battle of wits. The rules are simple. Each contestant has a buzzer. If you think you know an answer, press the buzzer. In the case of a wrong answer, the contestant will be docked half a point."

"Oof," Mylie mumbled.

"We'll be fine," Cash said. "Between the two of us, I bet we know it all. We just need to alternate who answers."

"Are we ready to start?" Piper asked the crowd.

As a cheer went up around the room, Mylie felt an unexpected shiver of apprehension. This—whatever it was with Cash—was moving so quickly. Last night, tucked up in a lawn chair on their property roasting marshmallows, the Holidays had treated her like one of the family. Family wasn't a concept she'd ever been real comfortable with, for all she admired Cash's sibling relationships.

Was she ready?

"Question number one. When was Ripple Creek founded?"

Well, for an easy question like that, obviously.

Mylie slammed her hand down on her buzzer and jumped off her stool. "Founded in 1893, incorporated in 1949."

"That is correct! The first point goes to our mayor."

Mylie responded to Cash's offered fist bump, then said, "The next question is yours."

"Name one of the highest peaks in Deschutes County."

Cash pressed on his buzzer before Mylie could whisper *South Sister.*

"South Sister," Cash said confidently.

"One point for Cash Holiday!" Clara said as Cash and Mylie whooped, exchanging a high five. "Oh, it's nice to see contestants celebrating a win."

Mylie and Cash alternated answers, occasionally giving one up to another contestant, but widened their lead as the questions stacked up.

What year did the Ripple Creek softball team win state? 2015.

What famous boy band once trashed a room at the Creekside Inn? GuyzXtra.

"Wow!" Piper said as Cash snagged a point for volcanic tuff and basalt making up the majority of Smith Rock State Park. "A couple of you really know your Ripple Creek trivia!"

Cash grinned at Mylie. She allowed herself to bask in his smile, bumping her shoulder against his. He bumped back.

Somewhere during all the smiling and shoulder bumping, Clara and Piper started muttering to one another and shuffling index cards. The muttering intensified.

Cash nodded at the two of them. "Should we be worried about this?"

"Given their penchant for pivoting? Absolutely."

"Let's see if they can answer this one," Clara said. "How big is Ripple Creek?"

"How big, like how many people?" Mylie asked Cash. "Or how many square miles?"

Cash furrowed his brow. "Is she talking about the creek or the town?"

As Mylie and Cash debated the nature of the question, a buzzer sounded. They looked up to see Myron straightening the cuffs of his cardigan before he answered.

"Myron, do you have an answer for us?"

"Ripple Creek is bigger than Redmond, smaller than Bend and has more heart than any other town in Oregon."

"You are correct!" Piper cried.

Cash just managed to stifle a groan as Clara said, "Okay, next question. Who applied for a fly fishing license in 2022?"

"What kind of question is that?" Mylie asked.

Bobbie gave her buzzer a gentle tap. "I did."

"That is correct! How was the fishing?"

"It was great," Bobbie said.

"Excellent! Another point for Bobbie."

Cash turned to Mylie, a look of annoyed panic on his face. She caught his hand before he could make any kind of rude gesture in the direction of the podium.

“Poise,” she muttered under her breath.

“Okay, the next one is tricky,” Clara said. “Listen carefully. If a train left Ripple Creek at nine p.m., traveling west at forty miles an hour, then a passenger train left Ripple Creek at ten p.m., also heading west, but at sixty miles per hour, at what time will the second train catch up with the first?”

Mylie widened her eyes at Cash as he pulled out a napkin to start in on the math. Before he even picked up a pen, Caleb slapped his hand down on his buzzer for the first time all evening.

“Midnight.”

“That is correct!”

“Wow! He’s really good at math,” Piper said. “Let’s try another one. I’ll just freestyle this one. If four…no, five people were traveling in three separate cars on Highway 126 at seventy-five miles per hour—”

On and on the questions went. Some random, some niche and many subjective. No one else was even a little peeved. The other contestants were just laughing and having fun as they debated questions without clear answers and Caleb answered increasingly complex math problems.

What color best described the community? Yellow, apparently.

Where is the best place to watch the sun set in Ripple Creek? The Public House Bell Tower, according to Rafael.

Local businesses got shout-outs with questions like: Who just purchased, and plans to reopen, the iconic Ripple Creek Flower Shop? Charley Lansing.

Which are better, Karen Johnson's scones or her croissants? Both.

On and on they went. Cash and Mylie finally relaxed into the silliness. She forgot about winning, which was easy to do when hanging out with a gorgeous man, eating onion rings and laughing as they battled their way through an unhinged trivia game. How was it that the man who had inspired some of the biggest arguments of her life was now responsible for making her laugh so hard her chest hurt?

No, everything was going great, until Piper asked, "What is the innovative new site, located just outside of town, responsible for drawing new families to Ripple Creek?"

Brick and Alice sat up, preening as the matchmakers called attention to the Banks Run housing development. It would have been the perfect opportunity for Mylie to publicly recognize her opponents in a positive light. But something about the silliness of the evening and Cash's smile made her choose otherwise.

Maybe the onion rings had gone to her head? But Mylie reacted, slapping her hand down on her buzzer.

"Mylie's at it again!" Piper said. "What have you got?"

"An innovative new business just outside of town, bringing new people in, is the Holiday Ranch Events Center."

"Oh, my God!" Piper said. "You're totally right!"

"I keep forgetting it's new," Clara said.

"But, yes, well done. Holiday Ranch is fantastic. That counts."

Mylie should *not* have glanced across the room to check the Hendersons' reaction. She could have added a shout-out for Banks Run. Instead, she just smiled back as Alice and Brick glowered at her.

"Okay, final question," Piper said. "And this one has one concrete, correct answer."

"Finally," Cash muttered.

Clara took the question card from Piper's hand and studied it. "Actually, it might have two answers."

"I can see that," Piper said, then she looked up and smiled brightly. "Who is the mysterious author of the Hank O'Brien mystery novels?"

The contestants went silent. Across the room, Tia sat in a booth with Beau and Elliana. She pretended to be busy on her phone, but Mylie could see the color drain from her cheeks.

Mylie slammed her hand down on her buzzer. Then she stood up for good measure.

"We have an answer from Mylie! Who is the elusive author of the Hank O'Brien mysteries?"

Mylie kept her eyes firmly on Clara and Piper, and didn't risk a glance at Tia as she said, "No one knows. The author has chosen to remain anonymous, and that's all anyone can say for sure."

"Correct!" Clara cried out.

"We just hoped if we asked, someone would tell us," Piper amended.

"Literally so curious!"

"Well, folks, that's all we have for today. An excellent showing from all our contestants," Piper said, which was flat-out not true. "We will tally the scores and post the winners on our website."

Mylie opened her mouth to suggest that it couldn't take that long to tally the scores since only two of the eight contestants had answered more than four questions each. But that had the possibility of touching off another round of freestyle math problems and that really wasn't something she wanted to witness again.

"We'll see you Friday at the Fourth of July parade," Clara called out, waving at the crowd. "The grand finale and community dance is on Saturday night at Holiday Ranch."

Onlookers applauded, then throughout the hall people finished off beverages, rose from their chairs and headed out.

Cash remained on his stool, gazing at Mylie. "Just two more events to go."

Mylie nodded. Two more events to figure out what these feelings were, and if she was ready to take the risk and see where they might go. To do that, she needed to learn a little more about this man she was falling for.

TRIVIA NIGHT WAS OVER, but Cash didn't want to leave, not just yet. He bought time as Tia came over to congratulate them and chatted with Mylie.

But eventually, he'd have to man up and start

flirting. That was just hard to do when you were looking up from the bottom twentieth percentile of skills in that arena.

"You, uh, up for another round?" Cash pointed at their empty plate of onion rings.

Very smooth.

"Yes. Let's celebrate what may or may not be our victory."

"On it." He stood up and scanned the space. People were clearing out. "You want to grab a booth?"

Mylie blinked, as though a little surprised by the suggestion that they move to a more private spot to continue their consumption of fried foods. It was all he had. "Sure. I'll go find one."

Mylie picked up her sweater and headed to a booth as Cash jogged over to Deep Fried Dreams. He ordered fried pickles as well as onion rings, just to round things out a bit.

No one could deny the romance in a plate of fried pickles.

He slid into the booth to find Mylie no longer surprised by what was starting to feel like a date. She leaned forward, folding her arms across the table.

"I have a few questions."

Okay, maybe date/interrogation.

Cash rested an arm along the back of the booth. This was reasonable. He was ready to talk about his dad. It would help her put all their arguments into context. He took a sip of his beer, ready to explain everything.

"How is it you're single?"

Cash choked. The liquid shifted pipes and headed for his lungs like a toddler into a candy aisle. Cash placed a fist over his mouth to cough, but the swallow of beer was already halfway down his trachea.

"Sorry," Mylie said. But she really didn't look sorry. She looked curious.

Cash cleared his throat, managing to say, "Well…"

Mylie nodded, eyes still on him. Cash cleared his throat more thoroughly.

"I could ask you the same thing."

"But I asked you first," she said.

Cash set down his beer and leaned forward in his seat. "You promise to respond in kind?"

She shrugged in agreement.

"Okay. I guess I just never really…" He trailed off.

What was he going to say? That he hadn't tried, or hadn't ever been in love? He'd been very much in love at one point. Willing to do anything for Luna. He studied Mylie for a moment, then took another sip of his beer. What he'd been planning on telling Mylie about his father and what she wanted to know were very much intertwined.

"It all starts with my dad."

She nodded. "I'd love to know more about him. I only really saw one side of him, and I'm sure that's not all there was to his story—"

Cash shook his head. "There was only one side of Dad. If you mistrusted and disliked my father, you knew the real Bruce Holiday. But he was still my dad." Cash picked up an onion ring. "You won't be surprised to hear that I pretty much raised Beau and Tia. Our mom cut out early, and Dad wasn't much of a parent. I protected my siblings from the worst of our parents and tried to be the stability they needed."

"That's incredible. I can't imagine a kid with that kind of responsibility."

"There are kids all over the world with that kind of responsibility, and more. Parents check out all the time. I'm lucky it was just narcissism in this case, not drugs or extreme poverty."

"Well, you did a great job. Tia and Beau are excellent humans."

"They are. I'm proud of them. I would do anything for my siblings."

"That's admirable."

Cash gave a dry laugh. "It might be admirable, but I'm not sure a lot of women would find it attractive."

Mylie wrinkled her nose and turned her head to one side, like a cute, almost *umm*.

"I was never a free agent, you know? When I was young, I couldn't go out because I needed to be home to help my siblings. As I got older, I wasn't at liberty to leave for college. But more than that, Beau and Tia just came first. Raising my siblings was my job. They'd already had two parents opt out of the responsibility, and I wasn't going to abandon them again."

"No, of course, you wouldn't." Mylie looked concerned. Or more than concerned, she looked like she understood him.

"You—you think that's okay?"

"I think it's beautiful."

Cash nodded. "That's, uh, that's not what my fiancée thought."

Mylie leaned back in her seat. "Fiancée?"

"Yep." Cash nodded, studying his beer. He hadn't talked about Luna in years. Come to think of it, he hadn't ever really talked about her to anyone. Dad didn't care, and Cash hadn't wanted Beau or Elliana to know the full truth of what happened.

Mylie raised her brow, inviting more information.

"It's a sad story," he warned.

"I'd like to hear it."

Cash gazed at her. A few weeks ago, they'd have been locked in an argument if they found themselves in the same booth at Public House. Now, he was ready to tell her about a past he could barely stand to think about.

Mylie reached across the table and placed her hand on his. "For the record, she really missed out."

Cash stared down at her hand covering his. He'd always liked her hands. They were small, with nicely shaped nails covered in clear polish. She wore a simple gold initial ring on the fourth finger of her right hand that sometimes caught his eye when she gestured to emphasize her words in an argument. Her hands were like her: capable, pretty, always in movement.

Then, sadly, she removed her hand to snag a fried pickle. Cash pulled in a breath.

"I met Luna at the Bend campus of Oregon State University. She was pretty, and I was young. I fell hard."

He didn't care for her anymore, but mention of her name reminded him of the hopeless intensity of those feelings. It was as though he was addicted to the roller coaster of emotion she inspired, even when they weren't getting along. He'd mistaken a carnival ride of a relationship for love.

"I was still living at home, and running the cattle operation. Tia was fourteen. Beau was seventeen and a handful, so I didn't have much of a college experience. I think, looking back, maybe I was in a hurry. I'd been dad and mom to my siblings for so long. I thought if I got married, I'd have a partner in all this. I'd do it right, show my dad a man could have a good relationship with one woman, and stay together."

"That sounds very—"

"Twenty-year-old. Classic move for a guy with an almost-formed frontal lobe."

Mylie smiled.

"I brought her home to meet the family. She was very sweet with Tia, nice to Beau. Dad tried to flirt with her, and she ignored him. I thought 'This is it! I'm in love!' So I saved up every penny I could and went out and bought the smallest possible diamond."

Mylie laughed. The way he had felt about Luna

was so different from his feelings for Mylie. With Luna, everything was intense, tinged with a sense of panic. He thought his love was strong enough to make up for the red flags waving all around her.

Mylie, he respected deeply. He thought she was gorgeous and he had a great time being around her. He felt more capable, calmer and happier in her presence. She made him feel both free and secure at the same time. What did you call that feeling?

"So you got engaged?"

Cash nodded. "I brought her to the ranch, cooked her dinner, then took her out on the tractor and proposed in the moonlight."

"That is incredibly sweet," Mylie said.

Cash nodded. "I thought so. Luna knew the proposal was coming. She'd dressed up and looked ready, perched on the tractor seat as I climbed down to propose from the side step."

Mylie leaned forward. "I can just see twenty-year-old Cash doing this."

"Well, the story doesn't have a happy ending, so don't get too excited. The trouble started when she saw the ring. I could see it in her eyes—she was disappointed. It hadn't occurred to me that Luna thought we were rich. By that time, we were decidedly not rich. There's no way I would have bought a ring on credit, not with all the trouble my Dad got into. It sounds silly now, but I had expected her to be thrilled that I made a sensible choice with the ring."

"She wasn't?"

Cash shook his head. "She didn't say anything, but Luna was pretty good at conveying her disappointment in me without words. But she said yes, we kissed in the moonlight, then headed home to share the good news."

"How did your siblings take it?"

"Tia started crying."

"Oh, no."

"There was a lot of crying when she was fourteen. Beau was old enough to be polite, but you could see he didn't think it was a good idea. The whole evening was not going as planned."

"What did you do?"

"I glared at my siblings, made everyone drink sparkling cider and act like they were happy. I guess I should be glad Dad wasn't home to get in on the action. Then I took Luna back to her apartment and she was asking all these questions about the ring, wondering where I got it and what the return policy was, and why I'd chosen gold over platinum. By the time I got back to the ranch I was exhausted, and—" He shook his head.

Mylie finished the sentence for him. "Disappointed?"

"Very." Cash ran a hand over his face, remembering the evening, to this day wishing he'd handled things differently.

"What happened?" Mylie asked

"When I came into the house, Tia and Beau were waiting for me in the kitchen. I thought they were going to apologize, but instead we got into a huge argument. Looking back, I can see they were trying to protect me, but at the time—"

"At the time you were doing everything to support everyone else, and for once you wanted something just for you."

Cash's head jerked up at the insightful comment. "Yeah. That's exactly it. I mean, Beau and Tia were correct—Luna wasn't the right woman for me. But after years of caring for everyone else, I wanted someone to care for me." The words left his lips, a truth he hadn't realized until he heard himself voice it.

He had been so desperate to find someone who could care for him. He'd kept his head up, his heart on lockdown because he had no other choice. If he could be everything for Beau and Tia, they would never experience the confusion and loneliness that defined his life. In retrospect, he could see that Luna wouldn't have had the capacity to care for him. She would have been just another wounded soul he'd signed on to support. But at the time, she felt like the one indulgence in a life defined by work and responsibility.

"Did you break up with her after that?"

Cash shook his head. "Nope. I didn't have to. She called the next day to—in her words—clarify my responsibility to Tia and Beau. I was honest. I thought I'd always been honest. I told her their health and happiness was my primary responsibility. I could tell she was angry, so I suggested we talk about it the next day. I promised to come into town and take her out to dinner, which I really couldn't afford after the ring, but I wanted to do something right. Twenty minutes before I left the house to pick her up, she called again. She asked what would happen with Beau and Tia when I had children of my own. I said I thought that was a long way off. She was silent. We sat on the line, not speaking for what seemed like forever. Then she said I needed to choose between her and my family."

Mylie leaned across the table, wrapping both hands around his. The memory didn't hurt anymore, but the sense of unfairness was raw.

"That was never a choice," Mylie said.

"No." He shook his head. "I love my siblings."

Mylie smiled, moisture gathering in her eyes. "I know. It's one of the things I admire about you."

Cash didn't dare look at her, for fear he would start gushing about all the things he admired about her. Or cry.

He shook his head. "In a way she was right. Should a woman be expected to commit to a man who is raising his siblings? It's probably hard enough to put up with me, let alone my family, and all Tia's rescues."

"Everyone has commitments. I would suggest commitments are a sign of emotional maturity. People are responsible for their parents, children, friends. The fact that you care for your siblings suggests you are capable of selfless love. Whenever you do have children, you'll be an excellent father. No, she was dead wrong. Luna missed out."

He gazed at her. All this time he'd worried that she, too, would walk away when she realized how much a part of his life Beau and Tia were. It didn't occur to him that she'd always known. And here she was, eating fried pickles, not even on the verge of running away.

Cash readjusted his hands, turning his palms upward to meet hers. "Sorry the story didn't have a happy ending."

She tilted her head, questioning his words. Cash laughed. "You can say it."

"What?"

"*Umm.* I can see it in your eyes."

Mylie laughed. "Okay, *umm*? I think maybe that is a happy ending. Young Cash Holiday dodging a bullet? I'm ready to cheer for that."

Cash gave a nod as he felt the heat rise to his face. She still had his hands in hers, was still gazing at him.

"Now, what about you?"

"What about me 'what'?" she asked.

"Why are you single?"

"Because I have put zero effort into not being single."

"That's it?"

"That's it. There's literally no story there."

Okay, that called for the full *umm* experience. He couldn't believe that she was single because of a lack of work ethic.

"When I was in college and law school, there were plenty of guys. I never met *the one*, but I had fun trying to find him. Then I moved here." She raised her palms, as though that explained everything. He got the sense there was something vital she was leaving out of the conversation.

"You can't date in Ripple Creek?"

"The only single guy my age kept refusing to file a business permit. What am I supposed to do with that?"

Cash stared at her for a moment, wondering about this single guy who was missing out on a chance with Mylie because he couldn't get his paperwork done. She smiled.

Oh, wait. She was talking about him.

Cash cleared his throat, feeling the heat rise up his neck. "Maybe that guy will get it together."

She held his gaze and her front teeth sank into her bottom lip. "That'd be cool."

Cash didn't let out the whoosh of breath he'd been holding, because that would be a dead giveaway.

Mylie studied the table, then said, "I have another question for you."

By this point he was tempted to just lay his heart on the line. It had to be easier than Mylie slowly chipping away at him.

I like you.

I want to be around you.

You are the coolest woman I've ever met and I

really do think you could benefit by skipping rocks with me on a regular basis.

She looked up at him and asked, "Do you really not know what's going on with Tia?"

Something about the way she said it made Cash wonder if *she* knew. But that wasn't possible. If Tia hadn't opened up to her own family, she certainly wouldn't tell Mylie.

"I don't. I know it's got to seem strange, but that's the way Tia operates."

"I'm not judging, I'm just curious. Why won't she tell you?"

Cash nodded. "She will. She's just not ready."

"You're awfully patient with her."

"That works best with Tia. We were all punished for our father's actions by the community. Beau's response was to come out swinging. Tia's was to turn inward. She's private to the extreme. She's secretive, but not because she's doing anything wrong. Unless you consider bringing home ten alpacas and not telling anyone wrong."

Mylie laughed. "You'll get no complaints about the alpacas from me."

"I think she was just exhausted by the judgment, you know? It's hard to get anything out of her—favorite type of music, what she wants for dinner. She pretends to float through life, easy, breezy. But the truth is she's afraid to open herself up for criticism."

"I hear that," Mylie said, eyes darting to where Alice and Brick had long vacated their seats.

"When she says she needs time, she needs time. She'll tell me eventually. I could have given her an ultimatum—tell me what's up or I won't agree to use money from the business, but then she wouldn't have taken the money. She's stubborn that way."

Mylie studied her nearly empty glass, turning it slightly. "Family trait?"

Cash chuckled. "I guess so."

His gaze connected with hers. He hadn't asked anyone out in a long time. Mylie was stubborn, argumentative and she liked to be in charge; they had so much in common.

He leaned across the table. "You got plans for tomorrow night?"

She wrinkled her nose. "Town-hall meeting at four, but I'm free after."

"Is that gonna go okay?"

"It's nothing I can't handle."

"I know, but could you use a cheering section?"

She laughed. "I could always use a cheering section."

"Okay, I'll try to make it. Afterward, if you want to, we could practice?"

"That will give me something to look forward to."

Cash leaned forward and wrapped his hands around hers. "Mylie Saunders, I think the two of us have a lot to look forward to."

CHAPTER TEN

WHAT WAS IT she'd said about the town-hall meeting? *Nothing I can't handle?*

Mylie lifted her chin, determined not to let it quiver as she stared out at the crowd. This entire meeting had been set up to make it impossible for her to handle anything.

A woman Mylie had never seen before, wearing an aggressively embroidered sweatshirt, stood at the microphone, facing the city officials. Behind her was a long line of other people Mylie had never seen before, and she had a pretty good guess as to who had encouraged them to come to the meeting.

"I would like to see more collaboration with our city leadership," the woman said. "More listening. More presence from our mayor."

It would've been hard for this woman to "see" Mylie collaborate, listen, or be present since she'd literally never been to a single city-council meeting or work session.

Alice nodded vigorously. "Hear! Hear!"

The regulars at the town-hall meeting listened with curiosity. They were generally here to complain about parking on Main, or criticize the speed at which out-of-towners took the curve coming into town. It hadn't occurred to them that their mayor wasn't collaborating correctly.

"Ripple Creek is a special place," the woman said, placing a hand over her heart. "I just think we deserve the best—"

"I'm sorry," Mylie said, interrupting the woman. "But can I ask—"

"I don't want you to *ask*, I want you to *listen*."

Brick, seated in the front row, nodded solemnly. Mylie swallowed her anger. It didn't go down well. The regulars were confused. The newcomers were relentless.

Mylie scanned the community center. She had a few allies in the room. Myron, along with his corgi, had already joined the line of people wanting to speak, giving her a thumbs-up in support. Cash's Gramma Birdie was in the back row. She'd listened for a bit, then snapped a picture and got busy on her phone. A few other generally supportive folks scowled when someone insulted Mylie's leadership, but Alice and Brick had planned this too well. While Mylie was running around trying to get crowned most eligible, the Hendersons were laying the groundwork to get rid of her.

Mylie's stomach tightened. She had gone too far with Alice and Brick, underestimating them due to their lack of intelligence and creativity. They were serious about this recall. What they lacked in nuance they more than made up for in drive.

Best-case scenario, Mylie would have to apologize for being a leader, and allow Alice to call the shots for the rest of her term. Worst case, there would be a messy recall process. It would be one of those salacious small-town dramas the news media lapped up like melted ice cream. Mylie could see her picture juxtaposed with a glamor shot of Brick and Alice on some national news syndicate. Over the static in her mind, she could already hear morning-radio hosts poke fun at her as listeners drove to work.

Her parents would not be impressed.

"Mylie, I know it hurts to hear this," Alice said sweetly into the microphone. "I just want to say that I really like you, as a person."

Lies.

"But you're young. You're single. You should be out having fun. Like you are, spending all your time in the Most Eligible Pageant."

"It's a fundraiser—"

"We don't want to keep you from finding a boyfriend."

"A *fundraiser*," Mylie said, a little too forcefully.

Alice smiled, knowing she'd pushed Mylie into snapping at her. "At present, you need to listen to what people are saying about you. We all can benefit from honest feedback."

Mylie would love to give Alice a little feedback.

The woman at the microphone droned on. Some of what she said was even true. Mylie wasn't good at collaborating. She did make changes in documents without consulting a work group, particularly if those changes included correcting spelling and grammatical mistakes.

Mylie counted the people in line to speak. Eleven folks she'd never seen before waited, all holding similar-looking flyers that she could assume listed her faults. Then there was Myron, with a cheerful smile, holding nothing more than a cardigan and Rocky's leash. He was followed by four other women holding flyers, then Principal Mary Ellen Torres, who was here to talk about changing the traffic pattern in front of the middle school.

There would be no vote at a town-hall meeting. Mylie wasn't going to lose her job today. But anything she said or did would certainly be weighed in the balance. She just had to sit here and try to look pleasant while community members insulted her for hours.

Cash hadn't made it to the meeting, leaving her equal parts disappointed and relieved. Maybe it was for the best that he wasn't here. They didn't need a repeat of the last time.

The doors at the back of the hall opened. Mylie, and everyone else sitting at the long table on the dais, looked up.

What fresh horrors have entered the room this time?

It wasn't a horror, or at least Mylie didn't think so. Jean, one of Cash's cousins and a regular at the pickleball court, slipped inside. She had a lot of opinions and a mean serve, but Jean had never had an interest in civic government before. Mylie watched as she exchanged a look with Gramma Birdie, then got in line to speak.

Huh.

Sweatshirt Lady droned on, occasionally glancing at her flyer. Alice nodded along with her as other city-council members started to look uncomfortable, eyes darting from Alice to Brick to Mylie.

A few minutes later, the door opened again. This time it was Liz, another Holiday cousin, and all four of her kids. The kids headed straight for Gramma Birdie, while Liz got in line behind her sister. Brick frowned at Alice from his seat in the front row. She shrugged, as though this wasn't her fault.

"To conclude, my biggest concern about our young mayor is that she hasn't yet learned to use those listening ears—"

Listening ears? Who in Sam Hill used the term *listening ears* for someone over the age of nine?

Better question, who under the age of ninety used the term *Sam Hill* when thinking disparaging thoughts toward someone else?

The door opened again. Comically, Alice gawked, straining to look past her handpicked lineup to see who was joining them.

It was Cash, holding a plate, accompanied by his siblings.

"Oh, no! Are we interrupting?" Tia said loudly. "Mylie, we brought you dinner. I didn't know this was a whole thing." Tia strode to the front of the room, and turned to Brick. "Can we stay?"

"Sorry." Beau raised a hand in apology at the

crowd, his charming smile winning over all the regulars, and a good portion of the newcomers, too. "We thought this was just one of those work-session meetings. Our mayor works so hard she forgets to take breaks."

Cash locked eyes with Mylie. "We'll be quick."

The gorgeous, charming family completely disrupted the vibe. Elliana got busy complimenting the woman who had been speaking on her sweatshirt, then asked how long she'd lived in town and complimented her choice to be a snowbird. She asked about the flyer she was holding and complimented her for taking an interest in local government. Beau was joking with Chris Watson, the fire chief, while Cash made his way through the crowd with the plate, heading straight for her.

"If the mayor would bang her gavel, we could get back to the meeting," Alice said primly into her microphone.

Cash scooped up the gavel before Mylie had the chance to consider the request. Then he set the plate in front of her. It smelled heavenly. Mylie was tempted to take a peek beneath the tinfoil.

"Just dropping off dinner," Cash said. He smiled at the city councilors. "This woman works nonstop, between her duties as mayor and volunteering, not to mention her bid to win the Most Eligible Pageant, which is raising money for a great cause."

"Did Mayor Saunders tell you about Work for Warriors?" Beau asked Chris loudly. "Because there were several guys from the National Guard on the wildfire crew last summer who might be interested in work around here. Mylie, you've got that program running, right? The one where we help veterans find work that pays a living wage?"

A few of the people who had been standing in line made their exit. Others looked at their flyers as though they were reevaluating. In the back row, Cash's Gramma Birdie was now taking pictures of Cash serving Mylie her dinner.

Gramma Birdie might be a lot more savvy about social media than she let on.

"Is this where we talk about things?" Tia cut in line, and tapped a finger against the live mic. "Sorry," she said to the woman who was championing collaboration moments before. "I'll just take a sec. Um, what are we talking about?"

Alice, who had turned a robust shade of red, stared down her nose at Tia. "We were discussing the mayor's efficacy, and if you want to speak you're going to need to—"

"Oh, we're talking about Mylie?" Tia's face lit up as she looked at the crowd. "Isn't she great? I honestly can't think of anyone who does more for our community. She shows up to everything."

Alice scoffed. "I'm not sure she shows up for everything—"

"Do you all know about Club 75, her initiative to help our senior citizens connect with wildlife-preservation efforts?"

The crowd, a good third of whom would be served by said club, perked up.

"The city's going to have a club for us old people?" Myron asked.

"Sounds amazing, right? I'm working with her on the handshake. And the best part, the most exciting thing?" Tia's dazzling smile broke out. "Mylie said I could bring Alfonzo to the meetings!"

The crowd stared at her blankly.

"Alfonzo," Tia said. "The alpaca."

And that's when the meeting officially went off the rails. Alice grabbed the gavel from Cash, but her banging did no good. The people she'd recruited might not know Mylie, but they knew the Holiday family from attending events at their ranch. They knew Alfonzo because of his visits to the school and the library, and his general penchant for riding around in the back of Tia's jeep. They were here because they'd been swayed by Brick and Alice's rhetoric. It made sense that they were just as easily swayed by new evidence of Mylie's true character.

Mylie gazed at Cash, then finally peeked at the plate he'd prepared for her. Lemon-berry French-toast casserole, potato salmon strata, prosciutto-wrapped asparagus: Cash had brought her his favorite meal, leftovers. Nothing could be better.

"Thank you," Mylie said.

Cash lowered his voice. "I didn't want to come in and pick another fight this time."

"No, you picked a party by the looks of it. This is way more fun."

Fun for her, anyway. Alice, who was complaining to another city-council member about protocol, could be heard above the general hubbub.

"But we're not out of the weeds yet."

"Nope." Cash crouched in front of the table so he was eye level with Mylie. "Weeds are a sign that you've got good soil. We've just got to stay on top of them, and focus on what you want to grow."

"That's a nice piece of advice, Mr. Holiday."

She looked into his eyes. Were these feelings for Cash something she wanted to grow? Because they were going gangbusters either way.

"You ready to get out of here? Go practice for our final performance?"

Mylie glanced over to where Alice was seething. Brick glowered in the front row.

"Not quite. I need to address this head-on. Alice and Brick were embarrassed today, and that's dangerous."

Cash looked at Alice, then swung his head to look at Brick. Mylie could already see what he was thinking.

"I've got this," she reminded him.

"I know. I just haven't had a good argument since you and I stopped fighting. Seems like a waste of talent if you ask me."

Mylie laughed. He held out his fist and she bumped it back, then sauntered to the back of the hall. Audience members were packing up, eager to get home and tell the story of an unhinged community-listening session. Cash gave Gramma Birdie a hug, then held the door for his family. Just before slipping out he glanced back and gave Mylie a brilliant smile.

Incorrigible.

As they exited, she pulled in a deep breath, then picked up her plate.

"Alice, Brick, do you have a minute?"

"No," Alice snapped. "We have—"

"The meeting ended early," Mylie reminded them as her heart thundered in her chest. "We all have time. Let's head back to my office and talk."

THE OVERHEAD LIGHTS in the barn were way too bright.

Cash headed to the switch plate and turned on the fairy lights, then switched off the compact fluorescents.

Too romantic? He and Mylie were definitely headed out of the friend zone, but he didn't want to get pulled over for speeding.

He scanned the barn. Delicate bouquets of snapdragons and sweet peas were interspersed with the larger daisy arrangements. Evening light and cool air floated in through the open doors at either end of the space, and the fairy lights sparkled overhead.

Definitely too romantic.

He jogged back to the switches to get a little compact fluorescent in on the action.

"Hello?"

Too late.

"Hey! You made it." Cash dropped his hand from the light switch. It didn't matter. Mylie kicked everything over the top where romantic feelings were concerned. No amount of lighting made a drop of difference at this point.

"How did the conversation with Brick and Alice go?"

"It didn't." Mylie pulled off her blazer, revealing one of the simple knee-length dresses she wore. So cute. "They were hoping to attack me for not maintaining order, but the rest of the council shut that down. They've called for a closed-door meeting to discuss the recall. They're not thrilled with Brick and Alice right now."

"That's good, then."

Mylie shrugged. "It's a small town. We've all got to learn to get along. The Hendersons aren't going anywhere."

Cash took Mylie's hands in his. "I'm not going anywhere, either. You need help, or brunch leftovers, just call me."

She smiled as she readjusted her hands in his. "Thank you. You guys saved the day."

"I meant to be there earlier, but I had to finish mowing hay if we're gonna bail it next week. By the time I was showered and ready to go, Gramma Birdie started posting about what was going on. We had to come up with a strategy."

"I love your Gramma Birdie."

Cash had to blink back the emotion her words sparked. Her acceptance, and even appreciation, of his family meant so much. Maybe this was the time to ask her out? No, that should happen at the end of the date… Evening, not date. This was just a rehearsal.

A rehearsal where they would slow-dance in this rustic barn with romantic lighting, after he'd made a big public declaration of his admiration for Mylie.

"Do you still want to use your tractor for the parade?" Mylie asked, releasing his hands to wave like Miss America.

"Absolutely. Unless you want Beau to hook us up with something from the fire department?"

"Ooh! The firemobile?"

"I think they call it a fire engine."

"Not if we're talking about a Richard Scarry Busytown book."

Cash laughed. "Naw, let's take a slow drive in my sweet rig." He had plans for decorating the old Case International with blue streamers and bright white daisies.

Mylie's gaze connected with his, a question in her eyes.

"What?"

Mylie shrugged. "The tractor doesn't have, like, bad memories?"

"Tractors don't have memories. It's a machine."

She laughed.

Cash frowned as he thought about it. "I mean, it does manage to cut out when I've only got an hour or so of work left. That machine can bring the drama when there's one last row to go."

"You know what I mean." Mylie glanced away, as if she was shy to bring it up. "About the proposal."

Luna was the last thing on his mind right now. He truly felt indifferent. It didn't hurt, he just didn't have the desire to prove her wrong, or to show her his life had turned out okay. He just felt relieved they weren't together anymore.

"That tractor and I have been through so much, a botched proposal hardly registers at this point." He dipped his head to look into her eyes. "We'll make some new memories."

Good ones this time, memories worth replaying in his head for years to come.

Mylie's slow smile emerged. "I like that plan."

The telltale low grumbling of an unhappy alpaca sounded outside the barn, followed by Tia's voice. "I'm not any happier about it than you are, but believe me you're not going to want to be around once they start setting off explosives."

Mylie raised her brow in question.

"I think they're called fireworks, not explosives!" Cash called to his sister.

"Same thing," Tia grumbled. She and the small herd of alpacas paused by the open door. "Mylie, can we ask the Fourth of July planning committee not to set off anything really loud? Like, I get that we have to host the fireworks by the lake so we don't burn up the arboretum, but we should keep the noise down. It's super-upsetting to the fish."

"Fireworks upset fish?" Mylie asked.

Tia stared at Mylie. "Umm? Yeah. Huge, earth-shaking booms. Why would they not be upset?"

"I didn't know fish got upset."

Tia launched into a monologue about fish feelings as Mylie nodded along and asked questions. Mylie's connection with Tia had been one of the most unexpected gifts of the last week. The two of them were on their way to being good friends.

After the parade, Cash would ask Tia to sit down and discuss her legal issue with him. Maybe they could solve it without handing ten thousand dollars over to a lawyer. Mylie could win the pageant, fund Club 75—

Wait, was he seriously thinking about throwing the pageant and letting Mylie win?

He had it *bad* for this woman.

"What?" Tia asked abruptly, looking directly at him.

"What do you mean 'what'?"

"Okay, I love you, Cash—"

"I love you, too."

"But you are plotting something right now."

Cash held up both his hands. "No plotting. Just thinking about fish and their opinions on fireworks."

"Explosives," Tia corrected him. Then she looked from Mylie, to Cash, then back again. Her face, which had been pale and worried for three weeks now, brightened a bit. "I should let you two practice."

"Thanks again for today," Mylie said, then leaned past Tia to scratch Alfonzo's neck. "You and the promise of Alfonzo at Club 75 saved the day."

"That was all Cash's idea." Tia grinned, giving

one alpaca a tug, and another a little push until they all started off in the same direction. "I'll see you at the parade."

Cash watched as Mylie waved goodbye, then came back into the barn.

"So… Saturday night?" Mylie asked. "And you're going to wear that suit?"

Cash nodded. Mylie wrinkled her nose and let out a huff. "How is it fair that you have a custom Armani suit?"

"I didn't say it was fair," he teased her. "But I have it, so I'm gonna wear it."

"Who even owns a suit like that?"

"Bruce Holiday."

"Ah, right. That tracks."

"Yeah. My dad had the suit made for himself. A complete waste of money."

"Not in the family budget?"

"Not even close. But the story gets better. In Dad's will, which was a mess, he specifically left the suit to Beau. The guy didn't fill out the important parts, like naming an executor, or providing important financial information. But he did manage to write a detailed paragraph about the suit, saying his younger son wore it better than I did, and it wouldn't hurt Beau to change out of jeans for once. It was a dig against Beau's style, and my looks. It also assumes either of us care about external signals of status, which we don't."

"That's— I don't even have a word for it. That's horrible."

"It's a pretty good illustration of his relationship with us." He put a hand on the small of her back, leading her toward the stage. "What about you? Did you find a dress?"

Because he needed to be prepared. If Mylie was going to look any more beautiful than normal, he wanted that information upfront so he could be ready.

She shook her head. "The dress situation is really bad."

"I bet it looks great."

Mylie was beautiful in everything. The dress could be made out of plywood and she'd look adorable.

She shrugged. "No, it's just this dull dress I bought for an awards ceremony. I won the award."

"That's cool."

"I guess. It's just, all of my clothes are somehow related to work, you know? I've never picked something out because I thought it was going to be fun to wear, or just plain pretty."

"You look pretty no matter what you wear."

She held his gaze, then grinned at him. "You're just trying to get me to wear a dull, old dress so you can win."

Cash laughed. He wasn't quite ready to tell her he felt like he'd already won. A blue sash didn't have anything on the chance of being with Mylie.

"What are we dancing to?" she asked. "Have you got the playlist?"

Cash pulled up the list of suggested song titles

on his phone. Mylie came to stand next to him, her finger bumping against his as they both scrolled through the songs. "You think they're really gonna let us pick our song this time? Or will there be another last-minute shift to Ed Sheeran?"

"Maybe we should pick an Ed Sheeran song, just in case."

Cash brushed his thumb against the screen, song titles rolling past. Something caught his eye.

"Wait." Mylie ran her index finger over the screen, then left it to rest on the very song he'd been struck by: "It Had to Be You."

"Well, now. That's got a certain potential," he admitted.

She grinned up at him. "Let's give it a try."

Cash clicked on the song, a blast of big-band music filling the old barn.

"That's dramatic," she noted dryly.

"We'll have to do a big entrance," he said.

"Okay, Mr. Pageant King."

"I like that title, 'Pageant King.'"

"Well, you are the one dead-set on winning," she reminded him.

Cash took Mylie's hand and spun her onto the stage. "Maybe."

They practiced for over an hour. Dancing, watching videos of other people dancing to this song. They made up silly moves, incorporated them into a routine, then abandoned them. It was so fun and sweet. Mylie's laugh rang out, and Cash suspected eight-year-old Mylie would be very happy to know what a blast she was having right now.

As the light outside faded, their steps slowed. They went from flashy ballroom moves to light embrace, moving closer together as the air cooled. Cash cradled Mylie in his arms, closing his eyes as they swayed to the music.

Once again, they came to the end of the song. This time, Mylie didn't step away. In the silence, he wrapped his arms more tightly around her, and pressed his lips to the top of her head.

"You dance like that on Saturday night, and I don't think you can lose," he whispered.

"You dance like that on Saturday night, and I don't think I can claim to be eligible anymore."

Cash's heart caught in his throat. Color flooded Mylie's cheeks. Then she reached up and placed a hand on his cheek, unleashing words that had been piling up inside him for months.

"I don't think I've been eligible since the day I met you, Mylie Saunders. You're too smart, too stubborn, too beautiful not to fall for." He held her gaze, and finally asked, "Mylie, would you like to go out with me? I'm thinking Sunday morning, July sixth."

Her laugh rang out, filling the barn. "I'm free that morning."

He nodded, feeling the heat rise to his face. "Alright then." He spun her under his arm, then caught both her hands in hers. "Brunch?"

"Perfect."

She was perfect. He could make this work. Mylie knew who he was, understood and even respected his relationship with his siblings. In the next couple of days, he would solve Tia's problem, Saturday he'd watch Mylie win the pageant, and by Sunday morning he hoped to be in a relationship with this incredible woman.

"GOOD NIGHT," MYLIE SAID, offering Cash one last wave from where she stood at her car.

"Good night." Cash's deep voice settled directly in her heart.

He waved; she waved.

Neither of them moved.

This goodbye had been going on for nearly as long as their practice session. It really was time to get in the car.

"Okay, seriously. I'm out!"

Cash laughed. "Me, too. See you soon."

Mylie was tempted to say "not soon enough," but managed to stop herself and get in the dang car. She did, in fact, have to go to work tomorrow and there would be a big Alice-and-Brick infused mess on her desk by 8:00 a.m.

Cash offered one last wave from the kitchen door, then headed into the house.

Mylie sat behind the wheel and pulled in a deep breath. Then she started the ignition.

The moon was high, illuminating all of Holiday Ranch as she exited the circular driveway. Over a period of six months, through a series of arguments with Cash, she'd seen its transformation. Buildings were treated to a fresh coat of paint. Crushed white gravel dressed up muddy pathways. The front drive had been repaved.

At the time, Mylie had wondered where they'd gotten the money to do the renovations. More than once she'd asked Cash if he was on the verge of losing the land, or did he have money to renovate? She'd assumed there'd been some money in the will slated for care of the ranch, but after the conversation today it didn't sound like there'd been much of a will at all.

Mylie paused at the edge of the split-rail fence before taking the long winding drive off the property. She scanned the central yard. Light spilled out of a little bungalow, and through an open window, Elliana and Beau's laughter drifted into the night. The massive family home was dark, with the exception of a light on in the kitchen. What leftovers was he getting into right now?

As she passed the rolling front lawn, a second guesthouse caught her attention. The first level was dark, but warm yellow light winked out of an upper window. A figure paced across the room. Tia.

On an impulse, Mylie put the car in Park. She hopped out of the car, cut across the rolling front lawn, moving quickly past the big house and into the central yard. In front of the guesthouse was a small structure. Mylie peeked inside and found a turtle curled up with a potbellied pig. This confirmed her suspicion. Mylie knocked on the door.

Silence, then a series of footsteps. After a moment, the door flew open.

Tia's wild hair was pulled up in a knot at the top of her head and held together with a pencil. Tendrils worked their way out in all directions. Two slender dogs paced at her ankles, and a sleepy cat was draped in her arms.

"Hi," Tia said, then added, "Mylie."

"Hi, Tia."

The cat gazed at Mylie through barely open eyes, clearly upset about the disappearance of a lap, but too exhausted to put up much of a fuss.

"Did you want to come in?" Tia asked. "I have, uh—" Tia gestured vaguely.

"I don't need anything," Mylie said. "I just wanted to say thank you for this afternoon at the town-hall meeting."

"You already did—"

"And I wanted to ask you a question."

Mylie let the sentence hang, giving Tia the chance to brush her off, or prepare a lie. Instead, Cash's sister inhaled a deep breath, then nodded.

Mylie smiled, and after a moment, Tia did, too.

"You're a fantastic writer," Mylie said.

Tia flushed, emotion flooding her face. She glanced down, struggling to respond, then finally said, "Thank you."

They stood at the door, moonlight the only illumination.

"How'd you figure it out?" Tia finally asked.

"Aside from the fact that you're a regular Hank O'Brien."

"Hard to say at this point. There were a lot of little things that stacked up, but the first and, honestly, most compelling piece of evidence, was Hank's dog, Stevie. That dog is so well written. So…*dog*."

"Thank you!" Tia said. "I'm really proud of Stevie."

"You should be incredibly proud of all of it," Mylie said. "That's what didn't make sense to me. Why would you—?"

"Keep it a secret?" Tia asked.

Mylie nodded. "I can absolutely understand having a pen name, but you didn't tell your brothers?"

Tia studied the flooring for a moment. "I think you should come inside and we should drink tea." She stepped back and held the door open. "I'm pretty sure there's tea involved in any sort of big reveal."

Mylie followed Tia into the guesthouse. The furniture on the first floor was draped with sheets to protect it. Patches of dog, cat and who knew what other kinds of fur suggested this was a good call. Mylie followed Tia up the stairs, and into a second-floor bedroom. After the ghostly feel of the rest of the house, this room was a riot of color and mess: papers, notepads, boxes of books, pictures, corkboard with images and notes pinned to it. The dogs immediately sprang onto the bed. Tia set down the cat on a wingback chair by the window. A kettle and three boxes of tea were set up on an old sideboard.

"Do you like Bengal Spice?" Tia asked.

"I'm not sure," Mylie admitted. "It sounds good."

"It is." Tia flipped the lever on the kettle, and pulled mugs out of the cabinet. Mylie remained silent as Tia prepared the tea. There was plenty she could say, and more that she could ask, but she needed to give Tia a chance to talk.

Cash had said patience always worked with his sister, but patience wasn't Mylie's strong suit.

Finally, Tia held out a steaming mug of tea, a sweet, spicy scent rising from the top.

"I was so excited when I got the first book offer," Tia said.

"I bet."

"I wanted to tell Cash, but he, well— Has he ever mentioned a fiancée to you?"

Mylie nodded, feeling the jab of jealousy that the mention of Luna brought. "He told me about it."

"Really?"

"Yep."

"Wow." Tia shook her head, more auburn hair falling from the topknot. "He must really like you."

Mylie blushed.

"I mean, I like you, too. We all do. It's superfun to watch Cash falling in love with you."

"I don't know that he's—"

"I do. He doesn't meet many women who are as smart and competitive as he is. Or any woman as cool as you." Tia waved a hand, as though Cash falling for Mylie was good, but old news. "Anyway, I wanted to tell him, but right around that time Luna got married to someone else. Cash found out about it, and he was heartbroken, or ego broken, or whatever you call it when someone who isn't good enough for you in the first place marries someone else. He wouldn't have been able to fully appreciate what a huge deal this was for me. He didn't know I'd been writing, so he didn't know how many rejections I'd gotten, which was well into the hundreds. I didn't want to share my big news, only to have him shrug about it."

"I totally get that."

"Beau was away fighting fires. And I certainly wasn't going to tell Dad, because he'd have—I don't even know—tried to sell the movie rights and gotten me blacklisted from every publisher in the country? Dad knowing would have been a *disaster*."

Mylie shook her head. "I can't imagine having Bruce Holiday as a father."

Tia shrugged. "That's just the way it is for us. Bad parents, best possible siblings."

"That's a good way to look at it."

"That's the way it is, no special lens required." Tia took a sip of her tea, and the steam rising from the cup inspired a few more strands of hair to make a break for it. "Anyway, I just kept it quiet. I gave Cash the first book when it came out, and he was like 'Oh, a mystery novel. Thanks.'" Tia studied

Mylie over the edge of her teacup. "But a couple of weeks later, I saw him reading it."

The spark in her eyes spoke volumes.

"And he loved it?" Mylie guessed.

"He told me it was the best mystery he'd ever read."

The warmth in Tia's voice took Mylie's breath away. "That must have felt—"

"Incredible. You can't even imagine. That anyone has read my books is incredible and that my brother loved it, all on his own, without knowing I'd written it?" Tears appeared at the rims of Tia's eyes. "I was thrilled. I'm grateful for the first contract, and for every subsequent contract. I can't even believe how the books have taken off, but I don't think anything can compare to that moment." Tia paused, then glanced up at Mylie. "Keeping this secret has caused some problems, though."

"I know you're in some legal trouble." Mylie perched on the sill by the open window. "I'd like to help."

A mix of emotions stormed across Tia's face. "There's a guy."

"Okay."

"He's claiming he wrote my books, and that I stole the manuscripts off his computer. It's not uncommon. It's almost like a sign of success, when someone tries to sue you for plagiarism. The problem is, because I've been so secretive, literally no one knows. I don't have witnesses, or anything. I don't even have an agent to fight this battle for me.

I just want it to go away, but the guy's lawyer says they won't settle for less than two hundred thousand dollars, which is significantly more than I've made."

"Who is representing you?" Mylie asked.

"Um. Jordan Ritter?" Tia gestured toward town, in the direction of a mediocre family lawyer. "I guess. I signed a retainer, but we haven't even met yet. He hasn't returned my calls, and it's so expensive. Our family business is doing better, but we should be reinvesting that money, not throwing it out the window to fix my mistake."

"Stop. This isn't your mistake. There is nothing wrong with keeping something private."

"But if I'd been upfront—"

"You had your reasons for keeping this secret. Have you talked to Ritter at all?"

"No. I went to the office after he didn't call me back, but he wasn't in."

"Okay, that's actually a good thing. This isn't Jordan's bailiwick."

"What's a bailiwick? Is that a law thing?"

"No, it's a…it's just an old word. Never mind. I have some friends from law school who specialize in intellectual property who could lend advice." Mylie thought through what she was about to say, then offered, "If you'd like, I'll take your case, pro bono."

"I couldn't let you—"

"You can pay me back another way," she said.

"Maybe I'll have an engagement party someday and you all can host it."

Tia's eyes widened. "Maybe you'll have an engagement party with my *brother*!"

Oof! Not at all what she meant. Maybe what she hoped, but not what she meant.

"You're getting way ahead of things."

Tia pressed her lips together, but Mylie could see her imagination working overtime. Truth be told, Mylie's imagination had been putting in a few extra hours on its own.

But that wasn't what they were here to discuss.

"I'll make a couple of calls in the morning. If you're okay, let's terminate your agreement with Ritter, and get the retainer back. I'll start with a cease-and-desist for the person making the false claim, as well as report his behavior to the administration of his social-media services. We'll make a couple of bold moves, and assess from there. Have you told your publisher?"

"Should I have?"

Mylie nodded. "Yes. And if they don't know, that's even better news. It means this guy doesn't have enough to go after a company, so he's targeting you."

Tia swallowed, eyes wide. "You think that will work?"

"You worry about writing." Mylie gestured to the room. "You left us with a cliffhanger in your last book. From what you've told me, this could be a fairly simple fix."

Unexpectedly, Tia's lower lip began to wobble.

She started to speak, but tears coursed down her cheeks. Mylie was reminded of Cash telling her that Tia used to cry a lot. “Mylie, thank you—”

Mylie held out her arms and Tia stepped into a hug.

“It’s my pleasure,” Mylie said. “Since I can’t fight with your brother anymore, I need a battle.”

Tia sputtered out a laugh. “Thank you for that, too. For seeing my brother for the awesome person he is. I haven’t seen him this happy in a long, long time.”

Mylie hadn’t been this happy in a long, long time, either. Possibly ever. It was as though Cash had helped bring back the joy and idyllic pleasure she’d always associated with Ripple Creek.

After the exchange of numbers, and some information on Tia’s publisher, Mylie finally headed out. She took long strides across the property. The kitchen light was on in the main house. Should she stop in and tell Cash? Tia hadn’t authorized her to share her secret. And Cash always said patience worked in the end with Tia. She had told Mylie; that would probably make it easier to share the information with her brothers.

Whom Tia shared her secrets with was her business. Cash had the strongest possible relationship with his siblings. Mylie didn’t need to interfere with any of it.

The only one of Cash’s relationships she needed to be concerned with was the one that involved her.

CHAPTER ELEVEN

MYLIE TOOK ANOTHER look out the window of her second-story apartment, scanning for Cash's tractor. He'd be driving slow enough that when he made the turn into town, she'd head over to the city park and arrive just in time to meet up with him and the rest of the parade entrants.

So, yes, she'd officially become the woman whose heart sped up at the thought of her man on an old work vehicle that couldn't hit the speed limit.

She hadn't seen Cash since their evening in the barn, not that she would have had time. Thursday had been a full-on hurricane of work. In between her regular duties and a closed-door city-council meeting where Alice had been formally reprimanded, Mylie contacted old friends from law school. Turns out a situation like Tia's wasn't uncommon, or difficult to handle. Mylie filed a cease-and-desist, and sent the man's lawyer a strongly worded letter. Her workday ended with a lovely conversation with a representative from Tia's publisher, who was all in on protecting their beloved author. Their legal team was appreciative of Mylie's work, but happy to take it from there. Just before eight o'clock, she popped in and out of a few little boutiques in town and bought a new dress for the parade. Something fun and cheerful, something no one would be tempted to wear to a meeting.

It had been a great day, even if it felt like twelve days combined into one. And today was going to be even better. The parade was the second-to-last event. Two days until their first date.

Mylie glanced out the window again. Three blocks down Main, on the edge of town, a red tractor decorated with white flowers and blue streamers waving off the back, puttered into town. The driver pulled off a Stetson and waved to her.

Mylie's heart jumped. She jumped with it and ran down the stairs. People were already gathering on the sidewalks along Main Street. Mylie wove through the crowd, heart hopping as she headed to the park.

"You look nice," Karen Johnson said, coming out of the bakery.

"Oh?" Mylie looked down, like she couldn't remember what she was wearing.

That's right. A brand-new, blue-striped linen sundress with spaghetti straps tied in bows on the shoulders.

"Thanks. It has pockets."

"Gotta love a dress with pockets."

Mylie placed her hands in said pockets and kept walking toward the fairgrounds. She honed in on Cash immediately. He wore jeans, cowboy boots and a pearl snap shirt that strained at his biceps.

He grinned at her, a spark in his eyes as he scanned her dress.

"You look beautiful," he said, holding out a hand to help her onto the tractor.

"Thank you." How was he able to make stepping onto this piece of farm machinery feel like being helped into Cinderella's carriage? "This tractor is adorable."

"Looks better with you on it. I like your dress." Cash kept his eyes on her as he rounded the front of the tractor and slid into the seat next to her.

Mylie widened her eyes at him and whispered, "Shh! The matchmakers will hear you and we'll get kicked out of the pageant for not being single enough."

He held her gaze. "Two more days."

She grinned back. "Two more days."

Cash fired up the tractor, which took several complex maneuvers on his part, then they rumbled over to join the rest of the contestants. Rafael and Bobbie were in a golf cart decked out in red, white and blue. Daisy and Caleb were zipping around on a matching pair of scooters. Myron and Nesa had decided to promenade, and were dressed in their Sunday best, both wearing hats. Rocky the corgi joined them, with a little flag kerchief tied around his neck.

"The Ripple Creek Fourth of July parade," Cash said, shaking his head.

"It's a scene."

Everyone was welcome to register a float for this

parade. Everyone. There was no selection process, no rules. So long as you weren't rude or offensive, you could be part of the parade. Some years there were so many people in the parade, Mylie wondered if there'd be anyone on the sidelines to watch.

"I haven't been to one since I was a kid." He scanned the crowd. "Did you know my dad is one of only two people in Ripple Creek to ever get kicked out of the parade?"

"That's quite the claim to fame. What did he do?"

"Decorated the Buick with signs accusing a local electrician of negligence."

"That'll do it."

"Yup." Cash nodded good-naturedly. Mylie remained saddened by the occasional revelations like this, but the Holiday siblings really didn't dwell in the past. It was truly a lemons-and-lemonade situation for them.

"Looks like a good turnout," Cash said. "Who's your favorite so far?"

"Aside from us?"

"Obviously."

Mylie scanned the parade entries.

The entire staff of the Ripple Creek Credit Union were dressed as yellow Minions.

Three of the girls from Dance 'n' Do, wearing sparkly outfits, were practicing a dance that somehow included glue guns.

As always, the Van Dynes' two-tone, green-and-white 1977 Chevy Silverado pickup had color-coordinated 4H flags hung on either side of the bed, and was filled to overflowing with 4H kids.

The local insurance agent, riding in a single-shaft sulky pulled by a massive Clydesdale, was explaining homeowners' coverage to a group of young men about to complete the route on pogo sticks.

Cash's cousin Liz and two of her kids were there on a riding lawn mower. No decoration, no message, just the mower and the twins.

Completing the lineup was the entire fire department, and every firemobile they owned.

"I'm not sure I can pick just one," she admitted.

"Me, neither. Although that makes me happy." Cash pointed toward the front of the lineup to where Tia, looking relaxed and happy, was standing between Alfonzo the alpaca and Kevin the donkey. Mylie's gaze flickered from Tia to Cash. Something about his expression suggested Tia hadn't yet talked to him about her writing.

Which put her in a funny position. She didn't want to keep this secret from Cash. At the same time, she shouldn't be the one to share Tia's news. So what exactly did she do?

"You ready to smile and wave?" Cash asked.

Smile and wave it is.

Mylie pressed the fingers of her right hand together and angled her wrist back and forth. "So ready."

Cash gazed at her for a moment, then fired up the tractor again and roared off at five miles an hour to claim their place in line. They were right behind an old Jeepster full of veterans of foreign wars, and just in front of the Deschutes County mounted posse.

It was a pretty good spot, given that last year she'd been behind the Knitters for Nkindness club, and they kept dropping balls of yarn for the entire parade route. Mylie wasn't feeling particularly nkind after one and a half miles of tripping over balls of wool.

At the parade marshal's orders, after a long blast of a French horn, they took off. As he had in other events, Cash lit up as things got under way. He was a regular pageant king, waving, calling out to people he knew, throwing handfuls of candy at anyone under the age of twenty-five. Or anyone over the age of twenty-five.

"You're really having fun with this," she noted.

"Elliot, Katie, what's up?" he called out to a pair of teenagers. Their Carhartt pants and sawdust-sprinkled boots suggested the kids were part of Team Oregon Build. They waved back with enthusiasm, and collected candy like the kids they still were.

"This would not have happened a year ago," Cash reflected.

"You and me on a tractor together?"

"You and me on a tractor together, people lining the streets waving as a Holiday rolled past." He shook his head, gazing at her. "It's a whole new world."

Mylie dipped her head in acknowledgment as she admitted, "That it is."

Cash held eye contact, setting her heart racing. Emotions Mylie had kept on lockdown her entire adult life unfurled in her chest, like a spray of peacock feathers, bright and outrageous.

This was what love felt like: a bumpy ride on a flower-trimmed tractor with a man whose smile lit up her world. Who on earth could have predicted it would be Cash Holiday?

"Hold up there, youngster."

Cash managed to get his eyes off Mylie and back onto the parade route before he crashed into the Jeepster. A man who'd survived two wars gave them a stern look.

"Sorry, sir!" Cash said, holding up a hand.

"Thank you for your service," Mylie added.

Three floats ahead, Tia had collected a gaggle of children. While others threw candy, Tia just existed with her animals. Kids tagged along, gingerly petting the creatures and peppering Tia with questions.

Mylie pointed ahead. "I love how Tia lets each child take a turn helping her hold the reins."

"She does, but let's be honest, Alfonzo's reins are merely a formality. Alfonzo is here because he wants to be, not because anyone was making him."

Mylie laughed as Alfonzo graciously lowered his head to a child so she could pet his topknot.

"Kevin, on the other hand, is plotting a way out of his harness," Cash said. "That is one sneaky donkey."

Cash's banter was casual, but his eyes weren't on

the quadrupeds. It was his smiling, laughing sister who caught his attention.

Finally, he asked, "Does my sister look…?"

"Happy?" Mylie suggested.

"Yeah. She seems happy. Way more relaxed."

Mylie pressed her lips together and nodded.

Cash furrowed his brow. "You know something?"

Great question. She didn't have permission to share Tia's secret, but she also felt like Tia should have told Cash two days ago. Or several years ago.

"Why would you think I know something?"

"That sentence, for one." He turned on the narrow seat so he was facing her. "I know you, Mylie. What's going on?"

"Mayor Mylie!" A group of students from the Future Leaders of America called out to her. Mylie reached into the bag of candy and hurled Tootsie Rolls at the kids.

She could feel Cash getting tense. Part of her understood. He was worried, and she hadn't shared news with him that would have kept him from being concerned.

On the other hand, she didn't like being snapped at.

"If you know something, I'd appreciate it if you'd tell me. I've been worried sick." His words, again, were harsher than she felt was necessary. Of course, she didn't have the same relationship with her brother, so she didn't fully understand his concern.

She plastered on a smile as she kept waving. "I, uh, I was able to help Tia with her issue."

Cash stiffened, his shoulders setting in a swift movement she recognized from countless arguments. He cleared his throat, staring ahead at the parade. "You helped Tia without telling me what the problem was?"

"It was a spur-of-the-moment thing."

Mylie instantly recognized this as the wrong thing to say. Helping his siblings had never been spur-of-the-moment for Cash; it was a lifelong commitment.

But it didn't justify the hard stare he gave her.

Mylie pulled back her head. "Don't look at me like that."

"My sister's been suffering for weeks and you just solved the problem on the fly?"

Yes, actually. That's exactly how it went down.

"You don't sound too happy about it."

He studied his hands on the wheel, then nodded. "Sorry. Just kinda shocked here. Thank you." The words came out formally. "I appreciate your help."

Nothing about his posture or expression suggested he appreciated her help one bit. Mylie's heart slipped, as if the fluffy cloud of rainbows she'd been riding on had started to leak rain.

She'd been expecting—or at least had fantasized—that Tia would explain to Cash what a big help Mylie had been, causing Cash to be forever grateful and fall in love with her. This conversation seemed to be going in the opposite direction.

Mylie pulled in a breath. "It was not my intention to keep anything from you. I could have told you I spoke with Tia—"

"How long have you known?"

Mylie exhaled in frustration, just as they rolled past Piper and Clara. She immediately sat up straight and plastered on a grin, waving her cupped hand like a pro. Cash didn't follow suit.

She elbowed him. "They're watching. Elves on the Shelves and all."

"It doesn't matter if I win now. Since you've taken care of everything."

"It matters if *I* win."

"Right." He glanced at her disdainfully. "That's what this has all been about."

"Cash—" She turned to face him. "I can hear that you're upset, but I don't understand why. Tia had a problem. I was able to help."

"And you didn't think to ask for my input?" He looked into her eyes, hurt evident as he said, "I guess you have to do everything on your own, don't you?"

"Ouch."

Seriously. *Ouch.* She thought he might be upset with Tia for not telling him sooner, but upset at her for helping?

He shook his head, as though trying to shake off this mood. "I'm sorry. That was uncalled for."

"It was completely uncalled for." Mylie blinked hard as the situation hit home. His friendship *had* been conditional. She thought she could slide in with the open, loving Holiday family, but one misstep and Cash was pulling back.

"I'm just—" He looked up at the sky. His words were harsh as he said, "I don't know what to say here."

"How about 'thank you'?"

His jaw set in a hard line. Gratitude was the last thing on his mind. Two nights ago, she'd been spinning in his arms, falling in love. And now, he was huffing and grumbling because she'd helped his sister?

Mylie scoffed. "Are you actually mad at me right now?"

"No, I'm not mad. I'm—"

Cash didn't seem capable of finishing his sentence. Mylie stared straight ahead, filling in the words for him.

I'm not mad, I'm furious.

I'm unreasonable.

I'm breaking your heart.

Hurt WAS THE word he couldn't bring himself to say. He glanced at Tia again. There was a lightness in her step he hadn't seen in a long time. If that was due to Mylie, he was grateful.

But when you've been protecting someone since you were seven, and sacrificed everything for their well-being, it didn't feel great to have that person turn to someone she hardly knew for help.

It was even worse that Mylie couldn't understand that.

For the first time, Cash had felt like a woman truly saw him. Mylie understood his drive, his competitiveness, him. The sheer sense of relief of being with someone who got him, and liked him for all his quirks, was heady.

But she obviously didn't, not if she could keep something like this from him. He was used to Tia keeping secrets. That's who she was. And he knew, without doubt, that on her own time his sister would confide in him.

Anyone who understood him, or even respected him, would never have kept a secret from him about one of his siblings. It hurt so deeply he didn't know how to even start processing the loss.

This growing connection with Mylie, the bright and precious emotion, delight and comfort in the intensity of life, slipped. It was something he wanted so badly; someone to care for him. Someone to have his back while he fought on behalf of everyone else.

Mylie didn't have anyone's back but her own.

Cash tried again, digging deep for something reasonable to say. "Can you at least tell me what she said?"

Mylie crossed her arms.

Cash dropped his voice, not liking the tone of desperation as he said, "She's my family. I've been so worried."

Mylie turned to him, placing a hand on his arm. Involuntarily he leaned into her. He was worked up, it'd been a heckuva two weeks. Maybe he was overreacting.

Tia's troubles, trying to book the DuBoff wedding, the pageant.

Mylie.

Falling in love.

The final thought came to him unbidden, and scared him to the core. Cash shook out his shoulders, then lifted a hand from the wheel to wave at the crowd lining the street, turning away from Mylie.

"I wouldn't ask you to give up her confidence," he said through a faked smile, "but there may be more to the situation than she shared with you. Tia is secretive to a fault. I know you think you're doing the right thing in helping her—"

"I am doing the right thing."

"You don't know that. There could be more to the story."

"How would I not know that? Her troubles were legal. I'm a lawyer."

"I'm her brother."

Mylie's expression hardened. "I've represented any number of people I wasn't related to. It's all turned out pretty well."

Three floats ahead of them, Tia's laugh rang out. Did any of this really matter if she was okay? He didn't have to be the one to help her. In fact, it would be nice to have some backup. But not backup from someone who didn't think it was an issue to keep him in the dark about his sister. Mylie knew how much family meant to him.

"Just seems like this might have been a nice moment for a little collaboration," he muttered under his breath. "You use those legal skills, share them with someone who actually knows Tia."

"So all this would have been okay if I'd gone to Beau? If I'd chosen to tell Beau and ask his advice?"

"Beau just got married."

"So?"

"So let's give the guy a few days off to enjoy his life."

"Cash, you're being unreasonable."

"When you've raised two siblings since you were old enough to change a diaper, you can tell me how this works. I have to take care of them."

"You *had* to take care of them. Beau and Tia are adults now. Capable, functioning humans. You don't always have to come crashing in to save everyone."

"You didn't seem to mind my help at the town-hall meeting."

"I might not have needed your help at the town-hall meeting if you hadn't stirred things up with Brick and Alice in the first place."

The words hit so hard he could barely breathe. She didn't want his help. She didn't appreciate that his altercation with the Hendersons had been a reaction, born out of concern for her.

She didn't want *him*. And it all circled back to the same thing: his responsibility to Beau and Tia.

He looked straight ahead. "My family means everything to me."

"So you've mentioned," she said dryly.

"You have a problem with that?"

"Of course, I don't. It just seems like Beau and Tia are doing fine and maybe aren't the full-time job they once were."

"You don't get it."

"I don't. No argument there."

He gazed at her. So beautiful and capable. That's who she was. But she worked alone.

It just confirmed what he'd always known. Outsiders weren't to be trusted. And he wasn't fit for a relationship so long as he had Beau and Tia to look after.

He shook his head. "I can't move forward in this if I don't trust you."

"Why wouldn't you trust me?"

"Because you know my family means everything to me. You know how worried I've been, and you can't take thirty seconds to send me a text and tell me Tia's gonna be okay? Why wouldn't you do that?"

The putter of the engine and the roar of the crowd seemed to grow louder, almost as though issuing a warning. Cash didn't heed it.

Mylie closed her eyes. "I didn't tell you because I've been too busy doing the work to help your sister to even think about it. It wasn't until I saw you today that it occurred to me you might be upset since I hadn't said anything. It *never* occurred to me that you wouldn't appreciate the help."

"I do appreciate it."

She ignored him, continuing to stare forward.

Cash tried again. "Maybe you need to think about working with other people before you jump right in to solve a problem."

The blood drained from her face. She shook her head slowly and Cash knew he'd gone too far. But like the argument with the Hendersons, he was fired up.

"You're the one waiting for someone else to do the work and fall into your life. It takes two to—" He didn't want to say tango. He'd never tangoed, but felt like if Mylie got creative, she actually could tango on her own. "You just don't want to have to compromise with other people."

"I've been working very hard to collaborate. You know that."

"By funding Club 75 on your own, then forcing everyone to go along with the idea? That's not collaboration, it's just a plot to get what you want."

Mylie turned on him, the flash of anger in her eyes familiar. "You think you *collaborate* with your family? You just boss them around and then you're surprised when Tia doesn't want to share information with you."

Her words didn't just cross a line, they leaped over it, landing them in no man's land.

Cash gripped the wheel with both hands, keeping his eyes firmly on the Jeepster as he said, "You can keep my family out of this."

"Isn't that what we're fighting about? I had the audacity to help a Holiday without getting written permission first? Maybe she didn't tell you because she knew what your reaction was going to be."

"What kind of trouble is she in?" he snapped.

Mylie glared at him, then looked over at Tia. He could almost read her thoughts as she gave up on him, on Tia, and the whole family.

"Ask her."

The parade looped past the community center, heading back to the park. Mylie crossed her arms, face grim as they finished out the parade route.

He wanted to say something, to roll back the argument, but what was there to say? This was about his family—this was sacred. All around them joyful citizens waved and laughed, cheering on Ripple Creek's own. He and Mylie sat side by side, silent as the parade ended back at the park.

He'd barely come to a stop when Mylie hopped off the tractor, getting her foot stuck in one of the blue streamers. She kicked, tearing the streamer loose. Her face was set like she was about to cry.

Cash rubbed a hand over his brow. "Let's talk tonight—"

"Not interested."

"Mylie, come on. When you come out to the ranch—"

"Why would I be at Holiday Ranch this evening?"

"It's the Fourth of July," he reminded her.

"Yeah, I think I'm gonna skip out on fireworks. Thanks."

Mylie turned away. Cash hopped off the tractor and ran around to her side.

"Look, Mylie—"

She shook her head. "I'm not going to 'look.' I'm not going to try to see this from your point of view. I helped Tia, and I don't regret it. She made a small problem much bigger than it was by not telling anyone. I just saved your family a significant chunk of money, and your sister from a world of heartache. Your response is to tell me I don't have what it takes to be in a relationship? Cool."

"I didn't say that."

"But you meant it, Cash."

Did he mean it? More to the point, was it true? He'd done the heavy lifting for a relationship with Luna, he didn't need to repeat the same mistake again. Mylie had been clear; any man needed to fit himself into her life without effort on her part.

Mylie pushed past him, then stopped and spun back around, gorgeous and furious. He waited, like some bolt of lightning was going to split the sky and resolve their issues. But the sky overhead was a clear blue; the only storm brewing was in Mylie's eyes.

She glanced at Tia, who was laughing as she chased Kevin into the horse trailer.

"You want to know what kind of trouble Tia was in?" She cocked her head and glared at him. "It's a *mystery*."

CHAPTER TWELVE

CASH HAD NEVER thought of it as a long drive from the city limits to Holiday Ranch, but when you're heartbroken, with a top speed of fifteen miles an hour, it's a real slog.

As he drove home, he couldn't shake the image of Mylie, hurt and angry, with a blue streamer stuck to her sandal. The look she gave him was clear: *This is over.* Why had he lost it on her? She'd poked a tiny hole in his self-image and he had a full meltdown. He was as bad as Brick and Alice, threatening to recall her when she didn't reinforce their sense of their own importance.

A car, tearing up the drive between Bend and Ripple Creek, leaned on his horn behind Cash. He didn't even have the energy to get indignant about his right to drive a farm vehicle in a farming community.

His world felt heavy, like it had the day Mom first put Tia in his arms. His sister was two days old, swaddled up tight in a blanket, big eyes staring at him. He was so afraid he was going to drop her, even though he was sitting in the center of the big sofa, both arms and his full body intent on holding on to the precious seven pounds of a human. Even then, on her second day on earth, Cash could see Tia's potential. Even then, he knew it was going to be his job to help her realize it.

"You take good care of your sister," Mom had said, handing him a bottle. "She's your responsibility."

Mom left the room. And Cash, by the age of seven, knew Mom might be back in five minutes, or the next morning. He'd already taken on the chore of getting Beau up in the morning and making sure he ate something before he was dropped off at preschool. Now he had this little one to look after.

He'd lost it on Mylie because at heart he was still a scared seven-year-old, with an impossible burden he was so afraid of dropping. He didn't know who he was if he wasn't Beau and Tia's protector.

In an ideal world, Mylie would have told him about Tia straight away. That didn't mean she should have. But she could have acknowledged his concern.

Still, he was fully responsible for letting the argument spin out of control. Disappointment seeped through him, settling deep. Heartbreak, he realized, wasn't a bruised ego or indignant anger. It was a bleak emptiness.

He was heartbroken over Mylie, and he was gutted that after everything he'd done for his sister, she didn't tell him about her writing. Cash didn't have to ask. The minute Mylie had told him the trouble was a mystery, the whole situation became clear. It was almost like he'd known from the moment Tia handed him the first book for his birthday. But in the years to follow, he'd been too busy protecting his sister to realize she was thriving in an endeavor he couldn't begin to help her with.

Clouds bussed over the sun, casting shadows as Cash pulled off the highway, onto the family property. He passed the lake, the acreage he'd replanted in cutting flowers, puttered over the little stone bridge and into the circular drive.

There, waiting at the split-rail fence, was Tia.

Tia, two greyhounds, four of the peacocks, Alfonzo the alpaca and a three-legged turtle.

Cash cut the engine, then pulled off his hat and studied the rim.

He felt, rather than saw, Tia take a step forward.

"Okay, I love you, Cash—"

He didn't answer right away. Tia waited until Cash was able to make himself do the right thing.

"I love you, too."

"But you cannot be mad at Mylie about this."

"I'll be mad at whoever I want to."

"Umm? Actually, no."

Cash looked up. "What?"

"No." Tia nodded, as though the word resonated with her. He was reminded of her at three years old declaring that she would no longer be consuming broccoli. "I forbid you to let my weird neurosis around secrecy interfere with your relationship with Mylie."

"Mylie doesn't matter in this situation." Even as the words came out of his mouth, he heard the lie.

Mylie mattered to him, but like everything else he wanted, he was going to have to give her up for his family.

"How can you say that? Also, get off the tractor. I need to talk to you and it's hard when you look like you're about to start harvesting wheat on an inspirational World War One propaganda poster."

Cash glared at Tia, but he got off the tractor. The flower-decorated piece of machinery was ridiculous. He'd been up early, trying to guess which blooms Mylie would like best, trying to keep with the red, white and blue theme.

Tia pulled in a deep breath as Cash neared her. She ran one hand over Alfonzo's topknot, then scratched beneath the red and blue ribbons tied around his ears.

"You needed an audience?" he asked.

"I needed support," she said.

"I haven't been supportive enough, since you were born?" he asked. "I have protected you, and Beau—"

Tia held out a hand, but it was the look she gave him that stopped his words.

"I'm going to start at the beginning. I know you're mad—"

"I'm not mad, I'm hurt." Saying the word out loud this time seemed to create a hole in his chest, darkness rushing into the void. His vision swam, and it took him a moment to realize it was his tears making it hard to see. He was hurt that Tia had kept this from him, hurt that Mylie, like everyone else on earth, didn't consider his feelings before she acted.

Tia's boots crunched across the gravel, then she wrapped him in a hug. Cash started crying harder. It was as though all the tears he hadn't let himself shed for the last thirty years of caring for his siblings had just been building up.

"I should have told you," Tia said. "That's on me. I wanted to tell you, and I came so close."

Cash pulled back to look at Tia, wiping his eyes on his sleeve.

"Why didn't you?"

She swallowed, then nodded. "Um. I have a lot of excuses in my head. But, I guess I just didn't feel like I could deal with the rejection of you not liking my books."

He stared at her. "How could you possibly think—I mean that's just—"

Tia's chin wobbled. She was secretive because she was exhausted by being the object of other people's judgment. She didn't share her opinions on anything for fear of criticism. Of course, she would be afraid that people might not like her books. Cash backed off the offensive for a moment and told her the truth.

"Tia, you're my favorite author."

Now, it was Tia's turn to burst into tears. That didn't sit well with the menagerie, and all the animals responded to her emotion, crowding around to comfort her.

Finally, she drew in a deep breath and gave a shaky laugh. "That, uh, that means a lot to me."

"But you know I love those books. I told you after the first one."

She nodded, a smile crossing her face. "You said it was the best mystery you ever read."

"It was. So why didn't you—"

"Because then I was afraid you wouldn't like the second one."

She was so sincere, and the statement was so ridiculous, Cash reacted by chuckling. "People love your books, if you haven't noticed. You are exceptionally—I don't know the word for it. Do you call writers talented, or hardworking, or creative, or what? You're good. You have to know that, right?"

Tia shook her head. "It's not that simple. It takes a lot of mental tenacity to keep writing through the voices in your head."

"Okay. I'm sure it's complicated. I wouldn't know. But why would you think I wouldn't support everything you do?"

She held his eye for a moment, then said, "Sometimes your support comes out more like a fence than a bridge, you know?"

Cash wasn't one for metaphors, but he got what she meant. He opened his mouth to defend his way of protecting her and Beau, but Tia interrupted him.

"Let me explain a couple of things. First off, it took a long time to get a book published. I've been racking up rejections since my sophomore year in college. I was thrilled when this book got accepted.

In the beginning, it wasn't much money at all. My first advance was three thousand dollars, which—" she turned dramatically and gestured to the split-rail fence "—paid for the wood we had to buy to fix the fence."

Cash nodded, remembering how Tia had come to him with the money shortly after a conversation about how desperately it needed repair.

"It looks great."

"Thank you." She gave a firm nod. "Then the book just kind of took off. I don't know why or how but it struck a chord with people."

"Because it's a great book," he said. "The characters are so relatable. I love the grumpy old police chief..." He trailed off. She grinned at him guiltily.

"You did *not*."

"Just a little bit."

Cash crossed his arms and made a noise that was almost *pshaw*, but he couldn't quite hide his smile. If a character had to be based on him, at least it was the best one.

"Let me finish," she said. "I'm here to apologize. I should have told you and Beau about the books. It was wrong to keep a secret like this from my family when I love you more than anything. I keep secrets because I'm insecure and don't want to face criticism. That's my issue."

Cash nodded. This wasn't a problem he could solve for her. He was going to have to be okay with that.

"Your issue is that you're hiding behind your responsibilities."

"Whoa, whoa, whoa." Cash stepped back. "We're not here to talk about me. And I'm not hiding behind anything."

"If you're not hiding then why aren't you off with Mylie, acting like you have to practice or something?"

"Because she didn't tell me she'd helped you out."

"So it would have been better if she hadn't helped me at all?"

"No... I mean. Obviously not, but—"

"You've been falling in love with her since the first day she showed up and asked about our business permit. I'll never forget it. You two were out there arguing for, like, an hour, then you came into the kitchen with a big grin on your face. You'd met your match."

Cash swallowed as images from that day came floating back: Mylie climbing out of her car and pushing a pair of sunglasses up on her head, her snort of derision as he said they didn't have the money to file a permit, her selective use of words like *hitherto* and *higgly-piggly.*

"Luna was never right for you," Tia continued. "She wasn't a match for you in any way. I'm sorry if she used your commitment to our family as an excuse to leave you, but I'm not sorry she left. You can't use our family as an excuse not to move forward with Mylie. Ever since opening our event center, we have had a steady stream of nice, single women on the property, and you haven't noticed one of them. All you can see is Mylie. And zero people are fooled by her frequent excuses to stop by and argue with you. You both need to do us all a favor and quit pretending like you haven't met the love of your life."

Cash stared at his sister. His brilliant, precious baby sister. She'd gone from a pair of huge eyes swaddled in a blanket to an imaginative teenager, to a veterinarian, and now a writer. Her potential expanded in all directions, and her message was loud and clear: She was ready for bridges, not fences.

Maybe it was time Tia went from being his responsibility to being a friend.

"You're right."

"Yes!" Tia threw a fist in the air, startling the turtle. "He admits it!"

"But I really blew it with Mylie today."

"I noticed. Everyone noticed." Tia wrinkled her nose. "Kinda got awkward there once we passed Eighth Street."

Cash let out a breath. He'd been helping his siblings, smoothing the way for them his whole life long. Maybe part of their new relationship could include her helping him.

"You wanna help me write an apology?"

Tia's eyes brightened. She clapped her hands together. "Better yet, let's do a grand gesture!"

Cash tilted his head to one side. "Grand gesture. That has a nice ring to it."

Tia looped an arm through his. "We have until

tomorrow evening to plan. I'm thinking alpaca involvement, yes?"

"No."

"Donkey?"

"Absolutely not." Cash wrapped an arm around his sister and messed up her already wild hair. "You want help getting these guys to the other side of the property before the fireworks start?"

"Yes. We can talk about which rescue animals will be the most helpful in winning Mylie's heart along the way."

MYLIE SPREAD HER SMALL, red-checked blanket out in the empty city park and plopped down on it. From the crest of the low hill, she could see the fireworks exploding over Holiday Ranch, five miles out of town.

She could see them, but she couldn't hear them. Hopefully, the fish were happy. Or if not happy, at least not completely horrified.

A burst of red and gold showered the sky. Mylie watched until the last drops of light had faded. Then she sighed, reached into her bag and pulled out a sandwich.

She tried to take a bite, but the ache in her throat intensified. Tears threatened again, but she was not going to cry. She was going to sit here and watch the fireworks like the mayor she was.

Mylie forced down a bite of her sandwich. Then she lifted the top slice of bread to remind herself of what she'd put on it. Mustard, lettuce, cheese and potato chips. An overwhelming urge for venison sausage and roasted marshmallows pulsed through her.

But, no. She and Cash, hanging out with the Holidays, and considering party leftovers a food group wasn't going to happen. These feelings for Cash that had swept over her from out of left field were just that—feelings. They weren't a job, or a commitment. And apparently they weren't even reciprocated.

They were just feelings. She could get over them.

Another rocket soared into the sky, bursting into a shower of sparks that faded in the night. That's exactly what her relationship with Cash had been. An exciting, outrageous moment in time that wasn't coming back.

"I wondered if I might find you here."

Mylie startled, dropping her sandwich.

"I didn't mean to scare you." Myron sat down next to her. Rocky immediately began to investigate the sandwich.

No big loss.

"You didn't scare me. I just wasn't expecting anyone," she said. "Shouldn't you be out at Holiday Ranch?"

"Rocky's not a big fan of fireworks. Then I saw you out here and thought maybe we three could avoid the crowd together."

Mylie nodded. He pitied her, and stayed behind so she didn't have to watch the fireworks alone.

Totally awesome.

Mylie looped her arms over her knees. Another

rocket launched, this one into a series of explosions in red, white and blue.

"That's pretty," Myron said.

"Sure is."

Myron gave his corgi a scratch as he asked, "Did Cash ever tell you how his dad used to drop the three of them off at the library?"

Mylie shook her head, throat tightening at hearing his name.

"I guess he must have been twelve by then. Tia was maybe six, Beau would have been in the third or fourth grade. Cash had a time of it with them. Tia only wanted books about animals, and she didn't care for the simple ones in the children's section. Meanwhile, Beau's running wild in the stacks and won't look at a book to save his life. Somehow Cash would manage to keep the two of them occupied and mostly out of trouble. Some days Bruce dropped them off for a few hours, sometimes they'd be there until closing. The staff would do what we could to help, but Cash didn't want to draw attention to the situation. I'll never forget the look of determination on his face. He'd say 'Beau, you have ten minutes to pick out a book, then we're all gonna sit down and read until snack time.'" Myron furrowed his brow as he imitated young Cash. "It was never fair, how much responsibility was heaped on that boy." He gave Mylie a long look. "Gotta be pretty hard to work your way into a new mindset after all those years."

"I know." Mylie nodded. She also knew how Cash reacted when his emotions were strong.

"It's pretty common to have a spat every now and then, particularly when you really want something to work out."

Mylie threw back her head and groaned. "Did anyone not hear us arguing?"

"You both were pretty animated. And I had a few friends in the Jeepster."

"Of course, you did." Mylie gave a dry laugh. "Thank you, Myron, for checking in on me and for hanging out with the sad, lonely mayor on the Fourth of July."

"Oh, I didn't figure you were sad. I thought steaming mad was more likely."

"I'm that, too." Mylie looked up at the sky. "But I'm mad at me. Cash was right. I act without asking anyone for their opinion. I always think I'm right, that I know what to do."

"You *are* right most of the time, if it's any consolation."

Mylie warmed at his words. "It is a consolation. A small one."

Mylie had known exactly how worried Cash was about his sister. She could have asked Tia in the moment to go with her and talk to Cash and Beau. Instead, she was so wrapped up in her own cleverness, so pleased with her plan, she didn't stop to think how it would affect others.

Cash had been right. She hadn't put work into finding a partner because the compromise inherent in being with someone seemed impossibly difficult, and the fear of not living up to yet another person's standards felt exhausting.

"You know what to do when you mess up?" Myron asked.

"Sulk alone in the city park with a terrible sandwich?"

Myron laughed. "You may think I'm just here to get you and Cash back together, because if you're dating, I have a better chance at winning tomorrow."

"I would never think that of you."

A gleam in Myron's eye suggested she'd been underestimating his competitive nature all along.

"Truth is, I like the two of you together. Two strong people, with some big ideas for this little town. A lot of good could come of it. I just hate to see it ruined by a run-of-the-mill squabble."

Mylie let the words sink in. For her, arguments always ended in winning or losing. It's why she'd been so hesitant to tell her family about her plans to stay in Ripple Creek. That would lead to a huge argument, one her parents would be angry if they didn't win. None of them knew how to talk something out. It was possible that two people could argue, and see the other's side, and both…what was the word? Compromise?

Myron was right. A lot of good could come from her and Cash being together. But he was also underestimating the amount of damage they'd both done in one short tractor ride. "I'm not sure I'd call our squabble run-of-the-mill."

"I'm sure it was an excellent squabble," Myron said.

"It was. A fine, quality squabble, if you ask me."

"I wouldn't expect anything less." He scratched Rocky's ears, and the dog shifted half his long body onto Myron's lap. "And I also expect you can muster up a fine, quality apology to go with it, and so can he."

"I don't even know where to begin."

"Then maybe it's time to ask for some help. I hear he's got some siblings he's pretty close with. That might be the place to start."

Mylie pulled out her phone, then she set it back down, only half-joking as she asked, "Seriously? Ask for help and apologize? What do you think I am, some kind of superwoman?"

Myron chuckled. "Nope. But your emotional intelligence has made you hard to keep up with in this pageant."

Mylie picked her phone back up. She hesitated for a second before dropping her thumb down on the contact. It rang twice. Tia answered in a whisper.

"Hello?"

"Tia? This is Mylie," she said, also whispering, for no reason at all.

"Hi, Mylie! I'm so glad you're you. I mean that it's you, on the phone. I'm sorry I'm talking so quietly but I'm trying to make the animals think I'm calm."

"Are you calm?" Mylie braced herself for Tia's anger. She hadn't come right out and told Cash Tia was a writer, but she'd been clear enough saying the problem was a mystery.

"Ish. As much as I can be with explosives going off on the property. How are you?"

Surprised, Mylie pulled her phone back and looked at it. Before she could answer, Tia asked, "Are you better than Cash? Because he was crying."

"Crying?"

"Bordering on blubbering. He was so upset about the way he spoke to you, then about the loss of his identity. Then some more about you."

Dang.

"Also, to circumvent your question, it's okay. When I told you about the whole, umm—" Tia's *umm* had a new intonation, suggesting *highly successful, secret author thing* "—I understood that word would get out." She drew in a breath. "I can handle the word being out. Among family, anyway. I really, really, a billion times over, appreciate your help."

Another spray of light burst in the sky.

"I'm glad I could be helpful. That's why I'm calling." Mylie pulled in a deep breath. "Would you and Elliana be able to help me with something?"

"Yes! And I hope it's about what you're going to wear tomorrow, because we've already got some ideas."

Mylie laughed. "It was mostly about how to talk to Cash, but a dress would be great. I don't have a formal gown."

"Elliana rescues dresses from sales racks like they're kittens. We've got you covered. Get here early, about an hour before the pageant starts?"

"Okay."

A muffled shushing came over the phone, sounding like Tia comforting someone, or some animal. Then Tia said, "Okay! I'm excited. And again, thank you, Mylie. You're the best."

"I don't know…"

"Kevin, knock it off! I mean it…" Tia's voice trailed off.

"See you tomorrow," Mylie said loudly.

The scuffle with Kevin continued, with a faint "'Bye, Mylie!" thrown in.

Mylie hung up the phone and glanced at Myron.

"That's a brave first step," he said.

Mylie nodded, then swallowed. The second brave step, talking this out with Cash, was going to be a little harder. But it could wait until tomorrow.

She set her phone on the blanket where it immediately buzzed. The name *Cash Holiday* appeared on her screen.

Mylie scooped up her phone, clicking on the text before she could worry about what it might say.

A picture. No words, no accusation or apology. Just an image of the sky lit up with a spray of fireworks, like someone had released handfuls of confetti against the velvety black night. One beautiful moment in time.

She studied the image, then looked up as the

gentle pop of an intentionally quiet firework filled the sky.

Mylie snapped a picture and sent it back to Cash.

Bubbles popped up like he was texting, disappeared. Finally, a thumbs-up appeared on the image.

Classic.

Moments later her phone buzzed again, another shot of the fireworks. She stamped a like on it. A few explosions later, she sent him another picture.

Back and forth, they messaged images of the mesmerizing bursts of light and color, Cash on the ranch, Mylie in the city park. It made her think of how they might have been standing in the creek at the same time as children, water flowing over her toes before it wound downstream and covered little Cash Holiday's bare feet.

Two exhausted, overburdened children finding a moment of peace wading on the pebble shore of Ripple Creek.

There was every indication that they could be the cool, constant water for one another. It was going to take both of them some time to trust and get used to the idea. But they'd grown up tough. They could move past this squabble, and all the others inevitably waiting for them downstream. They could be the brilliant moments of joy and peace for each other, forever.

CHAPTER THIRTEEN

MYLIE PARKED HER car at Holiday Ranch then checked her phone. After a flurry of messages from Cash the night before, today had been silent.

If she knew him, the silence meant he was scheming, preparing for their next meeting the way he used to prepare for their arguments. All she could do at this point was hope it was good scheming. But somehow, arriving here on his turf after a fight felt like an invasion of his privacy. She was early for the pageant, but late to meet Tia and Elliana.

Mylie blew out a breath and opened the car door. Had Cash seen her approach? Would he come flying out the kitchen door to argue with her like in the old days? She needed to stay the course, say what she needed to say and not back down until they'd both apologized.

The back door of the main house flew open, hitting the cedar-shingle siding. But it wasn't a glowering Cash who stormed out.

It was Elliana. She didn't storm. Rather, she sprang down the steps with a Julie Andrews-appreciating-Austrian-hills type of vibe, and she was…*singing*?

"DuBoff! DuBoff! Boff-boff-DuBoff!"

The elegant, refined event planner bopped around as she sang. If you could call the sounds coming out of her mouth singing.

"Hello?" Mylie pushed her sunglasses up on her head as she approached the central yard.

"Boffity-boff, the fence they are o-o-off!" Elliana did something that might have been a dance move, or a way to fend off an aggressive animal in the wild. "Gonna bo-o-o-ok after a good long look!"

Mylie had arrived feeling this might be an invasion of Cash's privacy, but now had far more serious concerns about Elliana's privacy. There was no way she wanted anyone to witness this…whatever you called this conglomeration of movement and noise.

"We booked a wedding! A great big weh-eh-ehding—" Elliana turned and pointed both index fingers straight at Mylie. Then she repeated her refrain of "DuBoff, DuBoff, boff-boff-DuBoff!"

Okay. Elliana knew she wasn't alone, and still she sang.

A peacock advanced and fanned his tail feathers threateningly. It had no effect. The singing and dancing continued, along with a stream of joy.

Maybe it was an event-planner thing?

"Mylie!" Beau came jogging out of the main house, good vibes radiating from him as well. "I take it you heard the good news?"

"I heard it," Mylie said, eyeing Elliana. "I'm not sure I understand it, but I definitely heard it."

Elliana stopped singing and wrapped her arms around Beau.

"We just booked *the* wedding. The only son of the DuBoffs of DuBoff Industries."

"Congratulations," Mylie said. "That's…a really big deal?"

"The biggest, most massive deal of all deals," Elliana said, her shoulders shimmying once more. Beau danced with her, twirling her under one arm as she picked up the song. "DuBoff son gettin' ma-a-arried! We're gonna plan a party, serve some be-e-er-ries—"

"That's fantastic," Mylie said.

Tia, either interested in, or concerned about, the singing, came striding across the yard, two greyhounds tangled at her feet, hair flying in all directions. She stopped when she saw Mylie.

"Oh, my gosh, finally!" Tia ran over to her, and grabbed her hand. "I'm so glad you're here."

"I have to be?" Mylie made the statement into a question, because did she really have to be? Would the world stop spinning if she skipped out on this one event?

Well, yes, actually. There were two matchmakers who seemed more than capable of stopping the world from spinning if she didn't show up.

"Elliana!" Tia called, then pointed at Mylie. "She's here."

"Oh!" Elliana's eyes widened. "Right! Sorry, I was just a little—"

"Overwhelmed with glee," Tia said, finishing for

her. "We're all superexcited about the DuBoffs. I want to remind you that a month and a half ago you were superexcited about the Most Eligible Pageant, and it's happening." She inclined her head toward Mylie. "It's project time."

Very little question as to whom the "project" was.

"You guys, I'm fine. I just need to talk to Cash—"

"Oh, you'll definitely be talking to Cash. But he's getting ready." Elliana looked at Beau, who nodded. "And you need to, as well. Let's go!"

"You guys good?" Beau asked.

"Yep. See you in—" Elliana checked her watch "—fifty-six minutes."

"Elliana will be officially late in fifty-six minutes," Beau noted.

"Completely on brand." Elliana grabbed Mylie's elbow, ushering her in the direction of the guesthouse. She dropped her voice, but was still very kind as she said, "I want to be clear on one thing. You don't have to allow yourself to get made over. We just heard you were complaining about your dress and pulled out a few other options for you."

Mylie stopped walking in the middle of the central yard, staring first at Elliana, then at Tia.

"Why are you so nice to me? I was awful to Cash as you were getting this business running. We just had a huge argument."

Tia and Elliana exchanged a confused look.

"You're not awful, you're powerful," Elliana said. "Which is exactly what Cash needs."

"Plus, you mopped up Tia's legal troubles in a day, for free. Hello?"

"Also, we're just naturally really nice." Tia looped an arm through Mylie's. "It's literally not hard for us at all."

Mylie laughed, pulling them each a bit closer as they crossed the central yard and entered the guesthouse. The downstairs had been taken over by floral prints, silky fabrics and sequins.

"Oh, wow. It's like a boutique ran away and has been hiding out on your property."

"I like fancy dresses," Elliana admitted. "So what speaks to you?"

Mylie was quiet for a moment, lifting the gauzy fabric of one dress, then running her hand down the smooth silk of another.

"This," Mylie finally said, gesturing to the two of them, the dresses, the room. "Holiday Ranch, this family. The way you all work together. The way you're always pulling for each other, no matter what. I can't even imagine what that's like. Or rather, when I do imagine it, it scares me to death. I don't know how to do any of this, but I want it all so badly."

Mylie dropped her arms. Elliana and Tia were staring at her.

"Overshare?" Mylie asked.

Tia shook her head fiercely, then walked up to Mylie and wrapped her arms around her. "Not even close."

Elliana joined in the hug, saying, "There's no such thing. I'm literally minutes away from describing my lunch to anyone who passes by at any given moment."

Mylie laughed, relaxing into the group hug. "In that case, what am I going to say to Cash?"

"Oh, you really do not need to worry about Cash," Tia said. "He's very interested in collaborating with you. On everything. He'll make this up to you."

"We do need to get you dressed, though. That Armani suit has a personality of its own. I'm not kidding. Unless you make a big splash, he could walk away with the crown."

"But don't you want him to win?" Mylie asked.

Tia shook her head. "Nope."

"But I thought you signed him up so he could win the five thousand dollars..." Mylie trailed off. They didn't need the money anymore, not since Mylie took Tia's case. Not since they'd booked the big DuBoff wedding.

"No. I never even thought about him winning." Elliana bit her lip and gave a guilty shrug. "I signed him up because he's such a great catch. I wanted him to meet someone."

"But then Beau saw that you were signed up, and he was all 'He doesn't need to meet someone, he just needs to realize he's in love with Mylie.'"

"So, yeah." Tia nodded, her hair emphasizing the action. "It was a setup."

Mylie stared at Tia, then Elliana.

"You all are devious."

"But you like Cash, right?"

"It's a little more than like at this point."

"So pick out a dress and let's finish this!"

"YOU LOOK SHARP," Beau said. "You gotta admit it feels good to prove our old man wrong."

Cash studied his reflection in the mirror. He was showered up, the suit fit and his good boots gleamed in the late-afternoon light.

"But you're gonna lose any chance of winning if you don't wipe that look off your face."

"What look?"

Beau mugged a mournful, goofy expression that had no relation to Cash's face. The emotions shifting through Cash were complex and unfamiliar. He needed help, not mockery. So he responded to his brother with a quick punch on the arm.

"Ouch!" Beau placed a hand over his bicep.

Cash smiled.

But rather than take the next logical step and initiate a wrestling match, Beau met his brother's gaze in the mirror. "What are you thinking about?"

"I don't know." Cash smoothed down the lapels of the Armani suit. "Everything's…pivoting. I'm trying to catch up and not mess up this time."

"You'll do great tonight. You've got your plan for the dance, Piper and Clara know what's coming. Just be honest with Mylie when you walk up to the mic. She's gonna love it."

Cash readjusted his tie and finally admitted what he was feeling. "It's more than Mylie. I'm struggling to figure out how all this is going to work with you and Tia. Who am I if I'm not the head of this family, taking care of everyone?"

"You're our *brother*."

"I know, but look at you." Cash gestured to Beau. "You're happy, you're married, you're back on the Ripple Creek Fire Department."

Beau tilted his head to one side. "Umm? Is that a bad thing?"

"No, of course not," Cash said. "I want you and Tia to thrive. It's all I've ever wanted. But I've been worried about you for so long, I don't know how to turn it off."

"Gotta tell you, man—the street runs two ways."

Cash furrowed his brow.

"While you've been worried about me and Tia, we've worried about you. I get that it's not the same. You had your childhood hijacked by us, so we won't ever fully understand."

"I don't think of it as hijacked."

"You should. There's no excuse for our parents turning you into our care provider. I get mad when I think about how unfair it was to you, and how Tia and I didn't realize how our difficult behavior affected you."

"You were—" Cash cut Beau off before he could even get started on an *umm*. "You were a handful. You both were. But I didn't resent you or the responsibility. I'd do it again in a heartbeat."

Beau rested a hand on Cash's shoulder.

"Maybe you can do it again, with your own kids

and a partner to share the experience. And under much better circumstances."

Beau's words tugged at a dream Cash had long abandoned. A family he was grown-up enough to handle. Parenting that was more than a few moments of fleeting relief in an overwhelming ocean of stress. He wanted the joy of watching kids grow up and take on the world from a place of stability. A wife and partner in the endeavor, someone who cared as much for him as he did for her. Someone headstrong and capable, who didn't back down when it came to doing the right things.

Someone with luminous blue eyes and a penchant for using last century's slang.

Cash reached out and pulled Beau into a hug. "I love you, man."

"I love you, too. Let's go get it. You can let Mylie win if you want to, but don't tell me you're not gonna bring it on the runway."

Cash took one last look in the mirror and adjusted his cuffs. He looked good. He was nervous. There was a lot he needed to say to Mylie, and it was all going to have to be spur-of-the-moment, and in front of an audience. But if he had to go off the cuff, they couldn't get much nicer than the ones on this suit.

Cash and Beau headed down the wide double staircase, then out the massive front door into the sunshine. The other contestants were already gathered next to the barn. They looked great. Maia, the Holiday Ranch house photographer, was snapping pictures of the contestants. Caleb wore a retro white blazer and slacks, Daisy matching with him in her sparkly white cocktail dress. Rafael wore a tuxedo with gold lamé trim along the collar. Bobbie looked striking in an off-the-shoulder dress in a bright print. Nesa was elegant, her white hair pulled up to show off the flowing lines of a sweeping yellow gown. Myron's suit looked like it had been purchased in the late 1950s, but had been well cared for and worn with pride in the decades since.

They looked great, and were great people. Cash was glad he'd gotten to know this team over the course of the pageant. But there was one conspicuous absence.

"Why is she always late?" Cash grumbled.

"I'm sure she'll get here," Myron said.

"And Clara and Piper have you going last, anyway," Nesa said.

"Okay, crew, gather up!" Clara called. "We have one last event! Formal-wear modeling, dancing and an interview—"

Piper interrupted her. "You all look amazing, by the way!"

"Amazing!"

"I mean it," Piper continued. "This time, everyone will have the same interview question, and you'll answer for yourself. 'What did you learn by being in this pageant?'"

"Yay!"

Cash nodded, even if he wasn't fully listening. Mylie's penchant for being late was going to drive him nuts. Would it get better or worse as she aged? And was she going to let him stick around long enough to find out?

"Then you'll all come back on stage and we'll announce the winner!"

"After which we expect you'll all want to stay for the dance."

"Then more fireworks!" Clara clapped her hands. "Except, apparently, they're quiet fireworks?"

"Something about the fish," Piper said.

Clara checked her clipboard. "As of right now, the scores are incredibly close, so anyone could win."

The other contestants had to know that wasn't true, but they all nodded joyfully, anyway.

"Currently, Mylie is in first place," Clara said.

"Mylie's not here," Cash grumbled.

"Cash is in second, and will remain there so long as he has poise."

Cash did not yell "what even is poise?" because he was pretty sure that whatever poise was, yelling wasn't it.

"And Myron is close behind in third. That said, it's still anyone's game."

Piper pointed a finger at Rafael. "Provided they are still single. I heard about your date with Karen last night."

Rafael grinned good-naturedly. "I'm still single, but all bets are off after the dance." He glanced at Cash, then at the other contestants. "Hey, did you guys know there were a couple of awful people who tried to stage a recall of Mylie's mayorship? Karen was telling me all about it."

The other contestants expressed shock and confusion.

"Yeah. Karen said they could kiss their morning scones goodbye if they kept it up."

"That'll keep 'em in line," Myron said.

Cash nodded appreciatively. He might not be Mylie's only champion in this town, but he still aimed to be her favorite.

Clara and Piper hustled the contestants backstage, talking excitedly. Cash lingered, scanning the property one last time. He pulled out his phone and scrolled through the pictures of fireworks they'd exchanged the night before.

Eventually he gave in and texted Mylie.

Where you at?

Bubbles popped up, then disappeared as he stared at the screen. Finally, the text he'd been waiting for swooped in.

Incorrigible.

Cash laughed. Then he stamped a like on the text and slipped his phone into his pocket.

He grinned, muttering, "I'll show you incorrigible."

CHAPTER FOURTEEN

IT TOOK MYLIE'S eyes a moment to adjust as she stepped into the barn from the bright sunshine. The Holidays had kicked up the decor a notch in preparation for the after-party.

Nesa was on stage, the song "Walking on Sunshine" a perfect accompaniment to her flowing yellow dress. Her white hair was pulled up, showing off a vintage necklace and drop earrings. Nesa was having a blast in the spotlight, and everyone could feel it.

The audience was dressed up, too, ready for the dance afterward. Mylie recognized a number of people who'd been at the meet and greet. Clara and Piper must have invited their clients. The atmosphere crackled with anticipation, as singles in the audience, and on stage, wondered who they might meet tonight. Add in most of the population of Ripple Creek, and this was gonna be a party.

Mylie glanced down at her own dress, a strapless red organza gown with a flowing skirt. Elliana had styled her hair in soft waves and expertly applied her makeup. Mylie looked like herself, if she was stylish, relaxed and fun-loving. It was a good look and one she intended to cultivate.

She skirted the audience, heading along the row of renovated stables toward the backstage area. Feeling eyes on her, she glanced at the seating. Alice sat on the aisle, as though ready to bolt as soon as she'd shown her face for long enough to get credit for coming. Next to her, Brick looked bored. He gave Mylie a sulky glance, then pulled out his phone.

For the first time Mylie didn't feel scared, or angry. She felt sad. Brick and Alice were unhappy people. They were threatened enough by her that they'd laid substantial groundwork for a recall. Mylie had no choice but to learn to work with them. She was going to have to take a deep breath on Monday morning, walk into her office and sit in a committee meeting with Alice. Then she'd need to do it the next day, and the next day. Even when she stopped being mayor, this was a close-knit community. The Hendersons were always going to be here.

In the competitive home Mylie grew up in, there was always the sense that you were moving through. Relationships didn't matter because you were on your way to somewhere bigger and better. You used people, they used you and everyone was okay with being out for themselves.

But she was looking forward to a lifetime in Ripple Creek. Shutting out Brick and Alice, or going on the offensive weren't sustainable. Winning the crown tonight, then publicly donating the prize money to her pet project, as worthy as the project was, wasn't going to build any bridges.

Mylie gestured for Alice to come speak to her. Alice looked over her shoulder, as though Mylie might be trying to get someone else out of their seat. Mylie rolled her eyes, pointed straight at Alice, then crooked her finger. Alice stood, smoothed her coral jumpsuit and walked over. At the very last minute, she remembered to fake a smile, but didn't try very hard. It was more of an obligatory showing of teeth.

"I might not see you after the program, but I wanted to check in with you about Club 75."

Alice pulled back her head in shock. She opened her mouth, closed it, then looked around in case someone was listening.

Mylie continued, "You've mentioned some concerns."

"There *are* people who have concerns," Alice said, distancing herself from the hordes of unknown folks who weren't in favor of programming for seniors.

"Let's sit down and talk about it then." Mylie swallowed, and forced herself to continue. "You have a lot of experience getting community-engagement programs rolling in this town. If you have time this week, I'd like to pick your brain about ways in which we can tweak this program so it can get the community backing it needs."

Alice clearly didn't know what to do with her face. Shock, concern, anger, even a little embarrassment all got in the mix. She looked like a first-year theater student practicing facial expressions.

"I'll send you an email, and we can set up a meeting," Mylie said.

Alice turned to her husband, as though he might know what to do with all this, but he was engrossed in a game on his phone.

"We're going to be working together in this town for a long time," Mylie said. "Let's figure out how to do it well."

Alice opened her mouth, various sounds coming out as though questioning where Mylie ever got the idea they hadn't been working well together.

Mylie gave her head a quick shake. "I mean it, Alice. I'm not going anywhere, and I hope you're not, either. This is our town."

"Thank you, Nesa!" Piper's voice came over the speakers. "Truly the epitome of elegance. Can we get another round of applause?"

Mylie watched Nesa walk up to the microphone, where she talked about what this pageant experience meant for her. That's when she saw Cash looking on from the wings. He looked *good*. She'd said what she had to say to Alice, now it was time for an entirely different conversation.

When she turned back to Alice, she had her phone out, calendar app up. "Two o'clock on Wednesday?"

Mylie had no idea what she had going on at that time, but she'd shuffle her calendar to make this work. "Perfect."

Then she took off for the backstage area, the

skirt of the gown fluttering around her ankles. She felt Cash's eyes on her as she wove through the other contestants. Arriving by his side, she took a moment before risking a look at his face.

But when she did, *wow.*

Cash's dark hazel eyes met hers before traveling appreciatively to her dress. He cleared his throat, then said quietly, "You look beautiful."

"Thank you." Mylie dipped her head, accepting the compliment. "You look fabulous."

Cash cracked a grin. "You like this?"

"I like it. Contrary to popular opinion, I think you wear it better than Beau."

"Don't let him hear you say that."

Mylie laughed. "There are a number of things I need to say to you that Beau probably doesn't need to hear."

"Same." Cash ran a hand down her arm, then laced his fingers through hers. After a moment he said, "You ready for this?"

Yes.

She really was ready. Mylie had always known deep down that the patterns of her own family didn't have to be her patterns. She loved a lot of things unconditionally, the community of Ripple Creek for starters. All around her was evidence of people expressing love without reason, and in front of her was a man she'd come to love beyond reason. She could fall, and still be a fallible human.

Cash dipped his head to look directly into her eyes. "We're up next."

Oh, okay. He was talking about the pageant.

"Yep. Ready for that, too."

He turned her hand in her, smiling as he said, "You'll enter the stage first, after you show off that—" he paused, taking in her ensemble once more "—incredible dress. We'll have our dance, then the interview. We'll exit the stage together."

"Got it."

He pulled in a deep breath. "After that, I was hoping you'd take a walk with me. I've got a lot to apologize for, and to explain."

"Me, too," she admitted.

"You don't have a thing to be sorry—"

"Fine. I won't be sorry, but I am *not* having an argument like that again. We need to hash out some ground rules."

The corners of his mouth twitched up. "You always have loved your rules and regulations."

"That's me." She grinned at him. "Like it or leave it."

He leaned down, placing his lips next to her ear as he said, "I like it."

Cash didn't step back, but lingered there, his cheek next to hers, their fingers intertwined. Winning anything entitled "most eligible" felt suspect at best by this point. Piper's voice came rolling through the speakers. "Up next we have Ripple Creek's brilliant mayor, Mylie Saunders, followed by her cowboy, Cash Holiday."

He grinned. "I like the sound of that."

Mylie liked the sound of it, too. She liked the

spark in Cash's eyes, the feel of her hand in his. There was a lot to like right now.

A more insistent voice came through the speakers: "Mylie Saunders!"

Mylie spun around and marched on stage. The lighting in the barn was more dramatic this evening, and she truly felt like a beauty queen, sweeping onto the stage in her red gown. The audience, joyful and enthusiastic, applauded as she channeled her inner pageant girl. The only way she could have felt more confident was if the interview section included a geography quiz.

"Mylie, you look fabulous," Clara said. "You are fabulous."

"Can we hear it once more for the most stylish mayor in Oregon!"

The crowd applauded, then burst into full-on cheers as Cash walked on stage. She couldn't blame them. He'd obviously been practicing, cruising across the stage with the confidence of a first-round NFL draft pick, looking amazing.

He was going to win this pageant, no question. If she was the one tallying up points, she'd just toss aside the clipboard and sticky notes at this point and enjoy the show.

"Thank you, Cash!" Clara said.

"I foresee another career option for you if you ever decide to quit ranching," Piper quipped.

Cash shuddered dramatically and stood next to Mylie, placing his hand at the small of her back. She grinned up at him as they waited for the music.

He winked, then whispered in her ear, "Don't be surprised."

She kept a smile plastered on as she whispered back, "How am I supposed to not be surprised with that opener?"

"I might have switched a few things up."

"Switched things up?" she whispered. "You are—"

"Incorrigible?"

Cash took her hands in his as music swept through the speakers. It was definitely *not* a big-band rendition of "It Had to Be You."

It took Mylie a moment to place the song. She laughed when she realized it was Brooks and Dunn again, this time "Brand New Man."

Cash pulled her close, then spun her under his arm, then into a promenade. Like their practice sessions, dancing with Cash was playful and fun. Everything else seemed to evaporate. They could be dancing in the barn alone for all she was concerned. The sweet words of the song, Cash's strong arms and his steady gaze were everything.

This was where she wanted to be.

As the song continued there was less dancing, more slow hugging. Mylie was snuggled deep against his chest by the time the music ended. Applause sounded all around them, and she wondered briefly if they'd been listening to an in-concert version.

Nope. The applause was coming from the community of Ripple Creek, who'd just witnessed the most romantic moment of her life.

"Aww! That was so sweet," Clara said over the speakers.

"Now, are you ready for your interviews?" Piper asked.

Cash didn't let go of Mylie's hand as they stepped up to the microphone. Okay, technically, she wasn't letting go of his hand, either.

"Mylie, what have you learned from being in this pageant?"

Mylie glanced up at Cash. Then she took a deep breath and addressed the audience.

"I've learned the importance of collaboration. Most of the time, I'm more comfortable working on my own. But through this experience I've learned that working with others, leaning into their strengths as you lend yours, we can achieve so much more. I'm grateful to everyone involved in this pageant, but in particular to the Holiday family. Beau, Tia, Elliana—" she paused and turned to Cash "—Cash, you are an inspiration. I'm so grateful you all call Ripple Creek your home, and that I can call you my friends."

The audience burst into applause. Piper nodded seriously as Clara moved around sticky notes.

Then Piper asked the question, "Cash, what did you learn from being in the Mountain Country Most Eligible Pageant?"

Cash glanced down briefly, then turned his gaze on Mylie.

"I learned that I'm no longer eligible."

A gasp rose from the audience. Or was that her?

Cash continued, "I've never really been eligible. Before this pageant I had my heart locked down, unable to see what was right in front of me—the most beautiful, brilliant woman. I respected Mylie from the first time she and I ever had a disagreement about zoning laws, but I fell in love with her when I stopped trying to be right all the time." He took both Mylie's hands in his. "Mylie Saunders, I am in love with you. I haven't been an eligible bachelor since the day you first showed up at Holiday Ranch. I feel like a brand-new man, but the truth is I probably still have all my same bad habits. All I can ask of you is to give me a chance."

If there was a reaction from the audience this time, Mylie couldn't hear it over the beating of her heart. She linked her fingers more firmly through his.

"I love you, too, Cash. I'm not remotely eligible and I really don't ever want to be again."

He placed a hand along her jaw and drew her into a kiss, warm and free. She wrapped her arms around his neck, pulling him closer. This moment was all she wanted. Kissing Cash felt like the only right thing.

A loud, whooping cheer sounded from backstage. It took Mylie a second to remember where she was, but her nervous system caught on fast, responding with a full-body blush. It was sweet that their competitors were cheering them on. She leaned back in Cash's arms to see Myron running on stage, followed by the rest of the crew.

"Did I hear that right?" Myron asked. "Are you both forfeiting?"

Mylie caught Cash's eye. *Forfeit* was such a strong word.

"'Cause if those two are canoodling, that can only mean one thing—"

"That we have the opportunity to be really happy?" Cash guessed.

Myron raised his arms, elbow patches and all, over his head. "I win!"

The iconic Miss America song started up, and confetti was released from the ceiling.

Piper took the microphone and announced, "Congratulations to Myron Banks, Ripple Creek's Most Eligible Bachelor!"

Myron placed his hands on both sides of his face, as though he was surprised. Cash draped an arm around Mylie. She snuggled into his chest as they watched Myron accept the crown and the sash, then wave at the crowd. Gramma Birdie wasn't the only octogenarian with her phone out snapping pictures.

"Thank you!" Myron addressed the crowd. "Thank you to Clara and Piper, and to my fellow contestants for making this all so fun. And to Cash and Mylie, for coming to their senses in time to let me win!"

Mylie could feel the rumble of Cash's deep laugh in his chest. That was something she could get used to. She wrapped her arms tighter around his waist and glanced into the audience. She was not expecting to see Piper and Clara grinning at her, shoulder-to-shoulder as they watched her and Cash "canoodle." They didn't look at all surprised. They looked like two women who were satisfied with the execution of their masterplan.

Was there anyone around here who *wasn't* trying to set them up?

"I wanted to win so I could attract a little attention to my single state," Myron continued. "It gets lonely, just me and Rocky." Rocky wagged the back half of his body, a large doggy grin suggesting he'd never been lonely a day in his life, but he wasn't going to contradict his human friend. "But as far as the prize money goes, I'll just donate it back to the literacy efforts we're raising money for."

Cash and Mylie cheered loudly, along with everyone else. Finding love and funding literacy; who would have thought?

Mylie wrapped both arms around Cash and breathed in his warm scent: irascible rancher with a hint of beeswax soap. He kissed the top of her head, then leaned down to whisper in her ear. "Would you be interested in heading out to the creek, maybe skipping a few rocks?"

Mylie grinned at him. "That's your plan for the after-party?"

"I've got a lot of plans, Mylie Saunders." He kissed the back of one of her hands, then the other. "And they all begin and end with you."

EPILOGUE

THE DUBOFF FAMILY knew how to party. Tia could appreciate that. Mrs. and Mr. DuBoff had made a pile of money, and were having a fabulous time spending it on their only son's wedding.

It was late August, and the DuBoffs were currently on day three of a four-day prewedding extravaganza at Holiday Ranch. The wedding itself wouldn't take place until December, but why wait to start the celebration?

Day one: Bridal Luncheon concurrent with Bachelor Fly-Fishing Expedition. Although could one really call what those guys were doing fishing? It was more of a groom and his buddies sitting on the banks of Ripple Creek talking about fishing as a life metaphor. Beau said it went really well.

Day two: wedding planning and family dinner. An elegant evening for forty-five, completely farm to table. For that one meal, everything really did come from Holiday Ranch. Except for the salt. It went so well the groom's mother asked for a tour of the garden so all their fancy friends could see actual tomatoes on the vine. Cash, of course, was more than happy to brag about his garden. Mylie was delighted to brag about Cash and his superior gardening abilities.

Day three, today, had been going on since sunup. Photoshoots of bridesmaids in matching robes and absorbent hair towels. Videography of the groom and his friends stalking around the ranch in their fancy man clothes and sunglasses. Cash and Mylie led—and won—a lawn-games tournament. Currently, they were in the throes of the engagement party, an epic event in the renovated barn highlighting the betrothed couple's mutual interest in classic films.

Basically, just a big excuse for the guys to dress up like they were in the Rat Pack, and women to indulge their Aubrey Hepburn dreams.

Tomorrow, day four, they'd prepare a big brunch and the whole lot of them would plan the bachelor and bachelorette parties. The ladies were headed to Nashville, Tennessee, the guys had vaguely golf-related plans in Scottsdale, Arizona.

After all of this, and getting her edits done on the latest Hank O'Brien mystery, Tia should have been exhausted. Instead, she felt exhilarated. The DuBoff family and friends were nonstop character watching for her, and there were some real characters here.

The bride and groom were on the dance floor with their friends. These sweethearts served the drama, but also appreciated each other and the abundance that made their drama-chasing dreams possible. Off to the side two aunties gossiped. Tia drifted past, not to catch the gossip, but to listen to their vocal patterns and word choice.

Okay, maybe catch a little gossip.

One side-eye later, Tia hustled over to the open barn door. She'd come clean to her siblings about one secret, but still held another close to her heart. Leaning against the weathered wood, Tia couldn't help but wonder again, what if he showed up one day? Walking across the yard like he used to, a smile for her, an affectionate pat for a dog before he took off with Beau on an adventure. It wasn't going to happen. Heath McIntosh had made it clear he never wanted to hear from a member of the Holiday family again.

As she stared out into the darkness, a figure materialized. Tia straightened. A man *was* walking toward her. Not Heath, but probably not a party guest, either. He was tall, his shoulders straight, chin angled down. At first glance, she thought it was Cash, but no. Her brother was still in the barn arguing with Mylie. Or kissing Mylie. One of the two. The stranger was classically handsome, but not what Tia would think of as attractive.

Admittedly, she had a very narrow view of attractive, based on a childhood crush from which she'd never really moved on. But this was a season of change, for the ranch, for her brothers and possibly for her, too. It was time. Past time.

That didn't make this particular guy any more attractive, but there was literally a barn full of men here tonight. Maybe she should start looking? Not that she would *ever* date someone who was into catch-and-release fishing. You want to be an omnivore? Be an omnivore and catch your supper out of the stream, but don't make a hobby out of terrorizing fish for fun.

"Hey there!" Tia stepped forward, waving.

"Hello." He greeted her with a smile. "I'm afraid I'm a little late. And underdressed." He looked past her into the barn. "The party's still going on?"

"It is." She tilted her head to one side, taking in his canvas duffel bag, cargo pants and T-shirt. "The more the merrier, I guess. Are you…?"

He gave one nod, like Beau did sometimes. "I'm reporting for duty."

Tia waited for more information.

He waited for her response.

She wracked her brain, thinking about recent family conversations, Mylie's latest projects, Eliana's plans…

Oh, wait.

"Are you the veteran?"

He pulled his head back. "I am *a* veteran—"

"You're here for a job?"

"I guess you could call it a job—?"

"Sorry. Hi." She held out a hand. "I'm thrilled you're here."

He shook her hand, still a little confused. That was okay—she was confused, too. But if the guy was a veteran, he had to be here through the Work for Warriors program. Holiday Ranch was in dire need of new employees, or any employees. Mylie had filed the paperwork for Holiday Ranch to be eligible to hire veterans at a substantial wage increase over what they, as a small business, could pay.

"Cash is gonna want to see you right away." Tia spun around and headed into the barn, then she spun back around. "Thank you for your service! And thank you for wanting to take a job here. We're literally desperate."

The man didn't seem to know how to react. He shook his head and chuckled. "I'm Waylon Cross."

"What a great name!"

Stealing that one for a character, for sure.

She strode into the barn and Waylon followed, scoping out the party in full swing.

"Is that a llama?" he asked.

"That's Alfonzo, an alpaca. He loves the photo booth. I'm Tia."

He started to respond, but she felt the need to clarify. "I also love the photo booth, but part of my job is to keep the party rolling."

Waylon exchanged a nod with one of the men in the wedding party. Tia skirted the tables surrounding the dance floor, scanning for her oldest brother. She found her second-oldest brother, instead.

"Beau, this is Waylon. He's a veteran."

Beau grinned and held out a hand. "Nice to meet you. I'm Beau and this is my wife, Elliana. She's responsible for all this." He gestured to the party.

Waylon nodded, but the furrow of his brow suggested he was still confused. "This is very…nice?"

"Thank you." Elliana smiled. "We are booked solid for the next eight months. I'm so grateful you're here to help."

"Do you need my help?" he asked.

"Desperately," Elliana said. "We have been non-stop around here since April."

"Okay?" Waylon tilted his head to one side. If Tia didn't know better, she'd say he was about to *umm*.

"Waylo-o-on!" Barrett DuBoff's bellow filled the room. The groom loped off the dance floor, tie askew, drink in his hand, heading straight for Waylon. "You made it, man!"

"I did."

"Take my shot." He handed the glass of amber liquid to Waylon. "Zack's got your suit in the bunk-house. Let's do this!" The groom raised both fists over his head, as though having fun at an engagement party was akin to taking the field at a homecoming football game.

Waylon raised the glass in a toast. "Be right with you."

Barrett whooped in approval, then turned to address Beau. "I'll take another when you get the chance." He clapped Beau on the shoulder with one hand, pointing to the bar with the other, then bounded onto the dance floor.

Waylon politely refocused on Elliana, who had frozen on the spot. Being inadvertently rude to a guest was her literal nightmare. "I'm *so* sorry—"

The newcomer chuckled. "It's fine."

Elliana's huge eyes got wider as she shook her head. "It's *not* fine."

"I'm happy to be here." He gave her a reassuring smile. "I do need a job. I've been full-time with the National Guard for ten years. Yesterday I signed my release. That's why I'm late to the party. I was raised outside of Outcrop. I have experience with horses and cattle, and could use the work while I figure out my next steps."

Beau and Elliana turned to one another. He raised his brow. She blinked. A world of communication ran between them.

"Cash?" Tia suggested.

"Yes. Let's go get Cash," Elliana said. "Then you should get changed and enjoy the party."

Waylon scanned the crowd, waving at a few people, nodding to others as the elegant party guests parted to make way for the former soldier. Tia wasn't one to categorize people into groups, but if someone had asked, she'd say Waylon was a much better fit with the Holiday family than the DuBoffs.

Cash and Mylie were not to be found among the guests. That probably meant they were hiding out in the former tack room, now serving as Cash's favorite place to arrange flowers for an event.

Tia walked ahead of the group, looking over her shoulder to chat with Waylon, explaining that while they were still a working ranch, they made a significant portion of their income hosting events.

He nodded along like he was listening, a bemused smile on his face. Maybe after they sorted things out with Cash she'd see if he wanted to go visit Kevin. A meeting with the donkey tended to wipe out any awkwardness. Or at least be more memorable than whatever awkward thing had happened previously.

"Cash will have a sense of what needs to happen with the ranching operation." Tia told him. "Our brother is the best. You'll love him." She strode up to the tack-room door and pulled it open.

At which point the whole family, and Waylon, stopped in the doorway. On the far side of the room, Cash was speaking earnestly to Mylie. The big smile on her face suggested she liked what he was saying. Tia was about to call out to them when Cash dropped to one knee. With a row of old saddles on one side, and a counter full of vases and sunflowers on the other, he pulled a ring out of his jacket pocket.

Mylie's hands flew to her lips. Her face lit up as Cash held a ring out to her.

Elliana slipped an arm around Tia's waist, Beau crowded into the family hug and at some point Tia realized she'd grabbed Waylon's arm as well, drawing him in as they watched the proposal.

Cash was serious as he spoke, his face breaking into a grin as Mylie joyfully accepted the ring. She said something to make him laugh and he whooped, picking her up and spinning her around, finally setting her on the counter next to the sunflowers. He placed a hand on her cheek and Mylie leaned forward for a kiss.

Tia felt a slight tug on her waist. Elliana was backing everyone up. Together, the four of them shuffled out of the doorway, then Beau reached over their heads and silently closed the door.

Very quietly, they all burst into celebration. Even Waylon, despite being a guest they were trying to hire in the middle of a party and not knowing the two people who'd just gotten engaged, joined in their silent cheers and hushed high fives.

Mylie was everything Tia wanted for her brother. This was so good.

It inspired her to place both her hands on Waylon's shoulders as she said, "Welcome to Holiday Ranch. You're gonna fit right in."

* * * * *